# The Road to Cromer Pier

## Martin Gore

*Dedication*

*The Road to Cromer Pier is dedicated to the people of Cromer in thanks for my much-loved childhood holidays, and to the people in theatres throughout the land who keep entertainment alive and relevant to thousands of people, yet seldom see much financial reward for their labours. All of the characters in the Road to Cromer Pier are fictional, but I suspect that the personality traits depicted are recognisable.*

*I must give my thanks to the real-life licence holders of Cromer Pier, Openwide Coastal Limited, and in particular Deb Lewis who so kindly assisted with the background research for this book. The battle for control of the theatre depicted in the book is entirely fictitious, and in reality, the only full season end-of-the-pier show left in the world goes from strength to strength, now in its 42nd year.*

*My thanks also go to James Bustar, a 2017 cast member, for agreeing to an interview between shows. The love that he has for the show, and the dedication and hard work people like him put in, are evident in the quality of the outcome.*

*I could have portrayed the show as an outdated dying breed, but that would be inaccurate. It is a commercial venture, and it works.*

*In talking to theatre management, it was clear that they know their customers, and treat them with respect. It was particularly touching to see cast members talking to the audience afterwards, signing autographs and posing for selfies with awe-struck children.*

*In many ways, knowing the reality of how slick and sophisticated an operation like the Cromer Pier Theatre is has made this book much more difficult to write as a readable human story of fiction. I can only hope that I've succeeded.*

*My thanks also go to my editor Alice Baynton, and to Margaret Berry and Celia Standen, who made valuable comments on the draft. Simon Hartshorne once again provided the graphics and the stunning cover.*

# 1.

## Winter 2008

The meeting had not gone well. But then, these sorts of meetings never did. The star blamed the agent and the agent blamed the record company. Frank Gilbert had been in the business long enough to know that, as the grey hairs in his receding hairline bore testament.

The girl sitting in front of him had been in tears at receiving the news, of course. It was a couple of years on and her star was waning. She'd not had a bad run, considering. The shelf life of talent show stars sometimes lasted no more than a few months.

But this girl could really sing. She had real talent, if somewhat raw. But the record company hadn't really moulded the raw material. Frank knew that only too well. He blamed himself for giving the company too much rein, but she was keen to sign, seeing the pound signs as they all did.

The London weather outside matched his mood; damp and drizzly with no chance of sunshine. The early darkness of a winter afternoon was setting in. He decided to leave early to beat the worst of the inevitable crush on the Underground.

His mood was downbeat but, for once, he had actually caught the early train home. He read the Evening Standard, which only heightened the gloom. It was as if the entire world was waiting for the next bombshell. Which bank would fail next? He thought of his artist as the train pulled out, heading north to the leafy Buckinghamshire suburbs where he lived. His artist was heading west. Back to Wales from whence she came, full of hope and ambition. Now, as she would doubtless see it, her dream was at an end.

He needed to find her something. He felt that he had let her down. There must be something, even in this market. But what skills did a singer like her have? In the evolving maelstrom, everyone was frightened. Nobody in their right mind would launch a new venture now.

He cast the paper aside with displeasure. Instead, he took out a copy of the list of the latest opportunities, prepared each Monday by his diligent PA. It was much thinner than usual. She also included clippings from press reports, as a way of keeping him up to date. There must be something, he thought, as he read each item.

He paused at the bottom of page three, where a clip caught his eye. He dismissed it initially. His star would say it was beneath her, still viewing the world through starry eyes, and these people didn't do big names. Stars were too expensive for them. But they had a shrewd eye for quality and talent, and ran their operation without a penny of Arts Council money.

But she would need to do something. She has expensive tastes, he reflected, remembering the designer outfit and shoes she was wearing that afternoon. Well he could only explore the possibility. It was his job after all. A season or two in an established show would consolidate her financially and give her back her confidence, which was never very robust under the glossy veneer people who became overnight stars were apt to develop.

Yes. He would send an email in the morning to explore the possibility. Trying to get her financial aspirations to match that of these people would be a considerable task, he knew. He'd had dealings with these people before. He thought that the father was a tough cookie. But the daughter? Well, she was something else.

\* \* \*

Les Westley walked past Cromer Parish Church, and down through the narrow street leading towards the seafront. It was blowing a gale and he was buffeted by the heavy rain seemingly coming horizontally towards him as he progressed.

The stormy weather was in-keeping with the news, which was getting worse by the day. The banking crisis had hit that autumn and it seemed to Les that the world was going completely mad. What savings he had now seemed to be in considerable jeopardy. In October, the government had bailed out the Bank of Scotland, amongst others. Northern Rock had seen a run on the bank and the FTSE had seen calamitous falls.

Amid this mayhem, it was business as usual for Les. He was heading down to Cromer Pier Theatre for a meeting with the proprietor, Janet Wells. It was likely to be a sombre affair. It had not been a good season.

The weather hadn't been great. Or was the financial crisis to blame? Or the quality of the show? He wasn't precisely sure. How could he be? What was apparent was that the accounts showed a loss. Ticket sales were significantly down. Even a comedian like Les knew a loss when he saw one and, as director, he was ultimately responsible.

But Les was an optimist by nature. What was one bad season out of the many he had directed? Janet would give him a few choice words, but then they'd get down to planning next season. All would be well in the end.

He reached the seafront and saw the pier being buffeted by big waves crashing against the shore. He really loved Cromer on days like this, when an irresistible force of nature did battle with the pier as it had for over a century.

Pulling his coat tightly around him, he headed for the pier box office. Fortunately, he wouldn't need to venture to the theatre itself. Stuck out into the North Sea, it was a fabulous tribute to Victorian engineering.

Instead, he had only to join Janet in her small room tucked away behind the box office at the front of the pier.

He pushed the door open and had to close it forcibly behind him. Betty, the Box Office Manager, smiled at his obvious discomfort.

'Good morning, Mr Westley, turned out nice again?'

Les had used the George Formby line quite often himself, so the irony wasn't lost on him.

'Good morning to you, Betty. I assume Mrs Wells is punctual as always?'

'On the dot, Mr Westley. Whereas you are reliably 15 minutes late, as always. Black coffee?'

'Thanks. Make it strong. I rather think that I'll need it. What mood is she in?'

Betty thought for a moment, sprinkling coffee into a genuine Pier Theatre mug.

'Rather like the weather, a deep depression with storms gathering in strength and augmented by occasional thunder and lightning.'

She smiled as she handed over the coffee. He grimaced.

'Bugger it. Here goes then. I'm going in.'

As he entered, Janet was on the telephone. She smiled thinly and motioned him to sit. He sipped his coffee as she rolled her eyes.

She mouthed 'Barry De Longue' and grimaced. Les laughed. An agent from hell our Mr De Longue, he thought. He sipped his coffee and leafed through the local paper. Another hotel had gone under.

Eventually she got the pushy Mr De Longue off the line, and smiled.

'Good morning, Leslie. Is it me or is the world about to end?'

'Well, looking at the news, you might think that, Janet. You've seen the latest? Another of our hotels bites the dust.'

He pushed the paper across to her.

'Yes. I saw it. It's all a bit scary. And our figures don't make good reading either. I don't think the bank will be overjoyed.'

'They'll be OK. You've been a customer for years. It's a one season blip.'

'Well I'd hope so but in this climate, who knows?'

'Christmas show bookings OK?'

'They've been better. Nobody wants to spend any money right now. The one night shows are being affected, too. Hotels are reporting a drop in weekend trade. It's time to batten down the hatches.'

Oh dear, thought Les. This didn't sound too good.

'I've cut the hours of the office staff, and let one of the cleaners go. It went down well in the current job climate as you can imagine but I need to get the costs down over the winter.'

Les looked across at Janet. She was a very calculating individual not given to precipitous action, so the fact she had acted so swiftly indicated that she had thought things through already. Let's get this over with, he decided.

'So how do you see things for next year?'

She paused. Les sensed the worst.

'Well that's what we need to discuss. This isn't going to be an easy conversation. I've been over the figures for last season in detail. I've taken a salary cut of five percent, and I'm asking for you to do likewise.'

Les paused mid-sip, and set his coffee cup down.

'Good grief. You don't beat about the bush, do you?'

Janet leaned forward, a look of concern on her face.

'I know it's a lot to ask, but if I can show some savings, it will make things easier with the bank. I'm asking all of the creatives on the team for the same sacrifice. I'm not going to ask anyone to do what I'm not prepared to.'

Les slumped back in his chair. The money didn't really

matter that much to him as a single bloke, and his other sources of income, mainly on the cruise ships, seemed sound, at least for now. He saw a look that he had not seen in Janet before. She seemed genuinely frightened. The storm on the pier outside would pass, but the greater financial storm the world was facing would take much longer to abate. There had already been bigger casualties than the Cromer Pier Theatre Company.

'You're overreacting, Janet. Things will blow over by the spring. There are too many fat cats with too much to lose.'

Janet had anticipated this reaction. She pushed the newspaper back across the table.

'That's what Jim Collins said to me last month, and now his hotel and livelihood are gone. Are you that confident? Really?'

He considered the position, and Janet sat back sipping her tea from her china mug. Her own special cup. She was content to let him think.

Les pondered. This was not the conversation he had expected. He quietly chided himself for not drawing all of the strands of the situation together as clearly she had. What planet were you on, old son?

He thought about playing for time. It would have been easy to stall her, but they would have to plan the show very carefully if they wanted to keep up the standard they had set on less money, and that would take time. He responded in a calm and measured voice, which still had more than a trace of his Birmingham accent.

'Well, you've certainly put me on the spot.'

He paused to reflect. Janet sat back in her chair sipping her tea, her face implacable. He broke the silence, as she clearly had no intention of doing so.

'Look, I think I can go with it, just as a one off. I see your predicament. But what does this do for the budget for the show? Are you seriously proposing to cut that by five percent, too?'

Janet shrugged, arms folded.

'Sadly, yes, I am. I'm going to need to demonstrate that I've eliminated the trading loss. The maths is easy to explain if you look at this spreadsheet.'

She pushed a sheet of figures across the table. He pushed it back. He'd never really liked numbers.

'No worries, Janet. I'll take your word for it. If it will do the trick then I'm in.'

Janet smiled, but her eyes looked tired. She hadn't had much sleep recently.

'I think it will. But even then the bank might counter that ticket sales could fall again next year. I really can't predict how this will play out.'

Les shook his head. Don't push your luck, Janet, he thought. He picked his words with care, sensing that he had capitulated a little too quickly.

'But we've always maintained that unless we offered a West End standard show, the brand would suffer. You, of all people, have said that season after season. It's why we're still here and the others aren't.'

'Yes. I know I did. And I haven't changed my opinion. But we dare not overcommit after this season. We need to consolidate through this, however long it lasts. If banks are going under, what does that say for the rest of us?'

Les nodded quietly, still adjusting to the harsh reality of the situation. He began to pick his way through the implications.

'So you're going to renew the second year headline acts and get them down five percent too? What about Karen?'

'Karen has agreed. She is family so she understands. But I fear you're going to have to sacrifice Ron and Mike altogether, great though they are. They will simply cost too much. That's your decision, of course.'

Now this was a shock. Les slumped back in his chair.

'My God, that will go down well. They expected another season at least before getting rotated out. That's what we usually do.'

'Yes. I know that's what we normally do. I'll break it to them if you like. I know they're friends of yours. It's only fair.'

She sipped her tea once more. He shrugged and finally smiled grimly.

She opened the old tin on the corner of her desk, an heirloom of her father's.

'Biscuit?'

She smiled, as if relieved that the difficult conversation was done. Negotiating with friends was always difficult, and Les counted both as a friend and a hired employee.

Les took a cookie and nibbled it. He shook his head, sensing that she'd mugged him.

'So, have you got any good news this morning? I'm thinking of taking a one-way walk down the pier.'

Janet laughed. Once Les started cracking jokes again, you knew he was on board, however reluctantly. She took out a letter and pushed it across the table.

'Well, it depends what you think of this lady.'

The letter was from Frank Gilbert Promotions, a London-based agent, boasting a few big names. The name of the artist being promoted surprised him. He dismissed it, pushing the paper back across the desk.

'You have to be joking, Janet. We don't have the money to shop at Harrods. Now more than ever.'

Janet smiled. She handed over a printed copy of the email she'd received earlier that morning.

'Take a look at that. Her star has passed its zenith. She's been dropped by the record company and has had a bit of dodgy publicity recently. Hit a reporter outside a nightclub apparently, if you believe the tabloids.'

Les read the email and looked up.

'Bloody hell, she'll do the season for that? She must be desperate.'

'Or maybe Frank knows the score.'

'Meaning?'

'Meaning that this is going to be a bloody awful market in which to be unemployed, and Frank knows it. He's perfectly capable of taking his luvvies down a peg or two. Three months of guaranteed work here looks attractive at the best of times.'

'And in this climate, the bird in the hand–'

'Exactly.'

'So, if I read you correctly, you are saying that I need to build a show around the money left over after we've hired her?

'Pretty much. Yes.'

'That's a pretty shitty job.'

'But someone has to do it. In this case, you and I.'

Janet shrugged and smiled. They'd been together too long for hidden agendas, and besides, Les had seen enough crises in his time in this business. He was not one to panic.

'So I guess we're going to have to go for up and comers then. Take a few risks on less experienced people?'

'That's what I was thinking. But our star is big box office this time. I think we'll get her fan base to come out for her. The mothers and daughters will know who she is and they're the ones who buy the family tickets. That should underpin the sales.'

'And, of course, you'll tell the bank that we've signed her?' Janet laughed.

'Oh, I hadn't thought of that.'

They both looked at each other. They were realists and experienced enough to think that they could spot talent and bring it through.

'But can our star do more than sing? I can't even recall seeing her in panto.'

Janet shook her head.

'I rather doubt that she has any stage experience whatsoever. She came through a talent show route, so she won't have had any stage school training at all. I suspect that's why Mr Gilbert has priced her so cheaply. She didn't broaden out her skills as she should have, so what has she to offer? Other than having a singing voice as good as anything I've heard this decade? At least she can do the crossover from classical to pop and show tunes.'

Les could only wince at the prospect.

'Joy. So we have to teach her to dance, too?'

'I'm sure Isobel will cope. She has to do it with most of the headliners every season.'

'But they normally rotate. This time, they'll all be new except Karen and myself…'

'That's about the size of it. Look, I've sifted these CVs thus far, and I'm getting loads of offers both from within the UK and the EU. I've even got a Polish magician from their state circus.'

Les took the pile of papers. There were many more than Janet usually gave him at that time of year. She read his mind.

'The market is scared. The entertainment sector is going to get a hammering. The Arts Council is going to be a soft target for budget cuts, and local authorities will want to keep essential services running so other theatres are going to need to wise up sharpish. The one big thing we have is our strong reputation for running a quality show and offering three months of employment in the worst recession of our lifetime.'

'So you'll play hardball with the agents?'

'Absolutely, and I'll start with Mr Gilbert. I'm not about to accept that offer for our star, even if she is a steal at that.'

'But you will get her? Despite what I've said, I think you should. In singing terms, she's a one-woman variety show. Anything from opera to rock.'

'If you want her, I'll get her. You have my word. Then I need you to create an audition shortlist. We'll hold auditions next month when you're back. I want to create a competition between the shortlisted acts and beat the agents down on price. One or two owe me. It's time to call in those favours.'

'You seem to be on a mission.'

'I am. I've been thinking this through since the season ended, and I've lost a lot of sleep over it, too. Now I'm sure in my mind what we need to do. I think that with your help we'll keep the wolf from our door.'

They talked over one or two of the acts, but neither of them knew or even recognised many. Janet had pre-sifted out those they could not afford or who were so left-field as to be ridiculous. This was not at all the usual calibre in terms of track record and experience. This worried Les. He was used to selecting from a high-class field who queued up to be in the show, such was its reputation.

It was not all about talent. The show ran night after night in season – with matinees, too. It required physical and mental resilience, which tended to come with experience. But experience costs more.

As he got up to leave, Janet also arose. She hugged him. She didn't often do that.

She was several inches taller than Les, a little taller than average. Les was short and had that tubby comedian look. Janet's hair was highlighted, disguising the onset of grey hair in a 50 plus female. He had no such problem, his hairline having receded completely some time ago. She'd put on a few pounds since her days in the show, but was still pretty slim. He'd put on more than a few pounds as his dinner jacket would testify. He looked into her now weary eyes.

She was close to tears.

'Thanks, Les. Look, I know it's tough… just… well, thanks.'

'We'll be OK, Janet.'

She smiled and pulled herself together.

'So, remind me, Mr Westley, where are we headed this time? Go on, make me jealous.'

'The Caribbean.'

'Jammy bastard. Enjoy.'

'I will. See you later, Janet.'

With that, he headed off back up to the promenade through the gale, which showed little sign of easing off. It was high tide and the waves were breaking spectacularly against the sea wall. Janet, on the other hand, had business at the theatre, and put on her long, black winter coat for the journey. It seemed appropriate that she felt the full force of the gale.

\*   \*   \*

In the quiet residents' lounge at the Seaview Hotel on the promenade, Lionel Pemrose sat quietly picking his way through the documents that had arrived that morning. They were Administrator's documents offering for sale the latest hotel in the town to go under.

Lionel knew the hotel trade intimately, having worked his way up from the bottom. He had been a pot-washer in a hotel near Ipswich at 14, and joined full-time at 16. He was a comprehensive kid made good. Having done every shitty job a hotel could throw at him, he had been promoted through the ranks to manager. He liked to think he could assess a hotel in a single visit. Was it clean? Had the rooms been updated or left to decay? What state was the bedding in? Did the staff have a rapport with the manager and, more importantly still, the customer? Could the chef actually cook? What happened on the chef's night off?

He looked below one of the windows and spotted an odd-looking patch of wallpaper. He knelt down and probed it with his fingers. Blown plaster. He checked the rest of the windows in the lounge. Only an isolated spot, he decided. He took out his diary and made a note.

From across the other side of the bar, Jim Tyler smiled. It was typical of Lionel. When Jim had joined Pemrose Leisure, Lionel told him to sweat the little stuff because, if you did that, the bigger stuff took care of itself. Tyler knew that Lionel paid both him and the staff well. In return for this, he expected everyone who worked for him to have the same eye for detail. He carried out inspections without notice, and expected his managers to do likewise. Tyler knew that Lionel had fired people who didn't follow his rules. He had no time for people who took their eye off the ball.

Tyler had seen both sides of this mercurial business-man. Lionel could be ruthless, vindictive, overbearing and a bully at times, and yet he managed to remember Tyler's wife's birthday and covered for him as he sent them away for a surprise weekend break. Tyler had given up trying to read this man.

Lionel even replied to each and every TripAdvisor review personally – an increasingly difficult task as the business grew. He not only had hotels now, of course. He also owned two amusement arcades and the pier. Well, part of it anyway.

As the rain lashed the windows, Lionel got up and looked out. The pier was being buffeted by the waves. He could see a lonely figure walking up towards the theatre. He knew who it was, even from this distance.

He poured himself a coffee and his steak sandwich duly arrived, courtesy of a trim waitress dressed in a tight, short skirt and the black uniform blouse bearing the gold Pemrose logo.

'Can I get you anything else, Mr Pemrose?' she asked, politely.

He thought momentarily.

'No thank you, Charlotte. That's fine.'

She smiled and turned away. Lionel couldn't resist checking her out as she left. If you only knew what you could do for me, he thought.

He returned to his papers as he ate. His belt buckle strained as he sat there, and he recognised that he'd put on weight once again. He immediately forced to the back of his mind the fact that stuffing the 800-calorie sandwich in front of him was unlikely to make him any thinner.

His telephone rang, featuring a Hammond organ playing 'I've Got a Lovely Bunch of Coconuts'. He checked the caller identity and chose to ignore it. It was Mr Gillespie of

Greaves Gillespie Insolvency. There were 24 hours left for expressions of interest in the bankrupt hotel and Lionel was in no hurry. In the current climate, there would be few buyers, so Gillespie would be getting nicely desperate as the deadline approached. Lionel's offer would be emailed five minutes before the deadline.

Lionel had spoken to his friends in the trade to make sure that they knew he was to be the only one in the field, and the bank were supportive of the proposal at the pittance Lionel was proposing to pay. Doubtless it would be well below Gillespie's expectation, but he would simply want to get rid as soon as he could and collect his fee. Business was brisk in insolvency. Lionel viewed such people with contempt.

He wouldn't take on the staff, of course. He would simply buy the building. Gillespie could have all of the human resources hassle. He would promote Tyler to oversee the refurbishment and run it for him. A hard case was Tyler. He was a man after his own heart. They would close the place immediately and get the contractors to gut it so as to be able to open in the spring. He would seek his wife's assistance in overseeing the new décor. She had a real eye for style. She said that Lionel was colour blind. Lionel couldn't be bothered to disagree after all these years.

He'd visited the dying hotel the day before yesterday and realised that his luck was in. According to his surveyor, there was nothing wrong with the fabric of the building, and most of the bathrooms were in good condition, so it was mainly a paint and furnishings job. At a time when builders were laying off trades on a daily basis, he would secure a rock-bottom price for the refurbishment, and impose heavy penalties for late completion.

Lionel had learned a long time ago that adversity could be a friend if you ran a sensible business when times were good. He had a strong track record with the banks and was seen as a man who got things done. In the current climate of opportunity, Lionel had positioned himself well to take full advantage of the maelstrom. As far as he was concerned, a recession could be good for business. People would still go on holiday, but would stay in Britain. And Pemrose Leisure Group would be there to cater for them, with a brand new hotel in a prime position to boot.

But looking out to sea, he was still dissatisfied. The one prize he wanted was not for sale. At least, not yet.

# 2.

## Winter Sun

Les stood on the deck in his dinner jacket. He'd flown out the day after his meeting with Janet Wells, thus leaving the winter behind, at least for three weeks. The Caribbean cruise he had joined attracted a broad range of mainly English speakers. The ship was much better appointed than some he had travelled on, and the clients were noticeably richer.

The champagne being served was clearly not a cheap variety, and most of the people standing in front of him were dressed very well and sported healthy-looking tans. He sipped his mineral water.

He was a comedian on this cruise, but also increasingly advised the cruise line on casting, and the ensemble were a pretty professional lot, unlike some that he had had the misfortune to have encountered in his younger days. He was particularly impressed with the Swedish tenor. He was a younger guy in his early 30s with a voice capable of a broad musical repertoire. Ideal for the Cromer Pier show but, from a brief conversation, it was apparent that the young man's financial aspirations were more Covent Garden than Cromer. Maybe next year, Les thought.

He had completed the afternoon show, and was now meeting passengers. Most asked similar questions, which he answered affably. Les was nothing if not easy to get to know, at least superficially. He'd learned his trade over many years and could switch on the charm in an instant.

He was just short of 50 and, although slightly overweight, he had become a distinguished and not entirely unattractive middle-aged man. Given his quick wit and easy smile, on a cruise with a number of divorced, widowed or, for whatever reason, allegedly single ladies, he was not short of female attention, especially as he was divorced himself.

On previous cruises, he had taken full advantage and bedded a number of the more affluent female passengers. But as he got older, he rather yearned for a more long-term relationship than a cruise ship fling, and in any event, this cruise line had very strong rules against fraternisation between staff and passengers.

As he got older, he liked the nicer things in life, of course. He liked the ship, the food and the company, so he was not about to break the rules. Only last night one of the passengers seemed to be flirting with him quite openly, so he was keeping a wide berth.

Upon seeing her approaching this afternoon, he greeted her with a polite peck on the cheek, then pulled out his phone, indicating to her that a call was coming in. It wasn't quite a lie. He moved to the far side of the deck and read a text that had come in. Quite when it was sent was unclear, presumably before he left England. He didn't look at his phone very often.

Telephones were for phone calls. One day, he might have to do this social media stuff, but he lacked any great inclination.

'LE all signed up for season. Looking forward to the auditions. See you soon. J'

Excellent, he thought. Good job, Janet. He looked out towards St Lucia, which was coming into view. This was paradise. But it wasn't home. With his career, you didn't really have a home. But the Cromer Pier Show did give you somewhere that you might call home for the three months of the English summer, and Les had bought himself a flat with a sea view, so he could offer digs to a couple of performers each summer, which helped with the bills.

He returned to the meet and greeters. He beamed broadly and dropped into a gag routine he'd developed, which went down well with the punters. He posed for selfies, signed autographs, and managed to keep away from his admirer.

He would exit the vessel at St Lucia, and then pick up another, then another. A couple of nights on each boat as a maximum. And as Simon and Garfunkel said, every stop is neatly planned for a comic with a receding hair band. Les would joke about his nomadic trips, but he would soon be homeward bound, as the song said. Then the search for the talent for next year's show would begin in earnest.

He had found one candidate in Cromer of all places. The night before he had left for the Caribbean, he had spotted that a local pub had an open mic night. He wouldn't usually have attended such an event, but he noticed that the headliner was a local girl called Amy Raven.

He recalled seeing Amy busking by the pier one afternoon last summer. She had a distinctive voice, clearly not coached, but with a warmth and resonance that seemed different. He had bought a CD from her for a fiver. It had eight songs – all covers. The production quality wasn't the best but she was clearly talented. She was too young and unprofessional for the show, he had concluded at the time. But after the conversation with Janet, the circumstances were different. It was now worth an hour or so of his time.

The venue for the open mic night had been rundown with paint peeling off the walls and a smell of stale tobacco mixed with Domestos from the gents' loo nearby. His glass had briefly stuck to the table, having been cleaned with a mucky cloth, if at all.

Some of the acts were passable semi-professionals who had plied their trade and just enjoyed performing with their mates. Others were first-timers, clearly terrified by the experience and hamstrung at the mercies of the in-house sound engineer. Doubtless Gerald, his Musical Director, would have been most scathing at the attempt of the individual concerned to produce a competent clarity of sound.

Amy was on halfway through the evening, so he could catch her set before heading home for an early night. She had rather more self-confidence than some of the performers, despite her age. When she was down by the pier, Les had noticed that she had engaged the audience between each song and, as a result, her collecting hat was fuller than that of the average busker. Many people can sing, but audience rapport was a much-practised skill which some never mastered. Good for you, girl, he thought to himself. And, of course, there was something else that his researcher from the theatre had discovered. She could dance. Indeed, she had won any number of school dance competitions. Isobel knew of her. Useful.

She was good enough to consider, but probably rather too young, he had thought. Good for a couple of years' time, maybe. Nonetheless, he introduced himself to her at the interval. You should always keep tabs on talent. He knew that from experience.

'You sing well. I enjoyed your set. Les Westley of the Cromer Pier Theatre, by the way,' he said, offering his hand.

She shook it tentatively, but then she realised that they'd met before.

'Sorry... we met by the pier in the summer, didn't we? You bought a CD. I hope you liked it.'

Short, dark-haired, slim build, with brown eyes and a pretty round face, she smiled brightly. Les found her personality quite charming.

'I did indeed. You've added to your repertoire. That Adele song is rather difficult. I thought you pulled it off well.'

She winced.

'My mum likes it, so I sing it for her really. It's not easy. That woman's a genius.'

'Well, with a little coaching, you will improve considerably. You're obviously local?' he enquired, rather disingenuously, as he already had the backstory.

'Yes. Born and bred in West Runton. There aren't many voice coaches there.'

'What's your ambition then? Musically, I mean.'

She thought for a moment and looked at him directly.

'If I said I wanted to perform professionally, would you believe me?'

Les smiled.

'Why not? Can you do anything else? In the entertainment line, I mean?'

Amy considered.

'Well I can dance a bit. I won a few cups at school.'

Les smiled.

'That's always useful in our business, Amy. Look, let's stay in touch if you will. Here's my card. I assume I can contact you on the email address on the CD?'

She took the card and looked at it. Les continued.

'No promises. Let's just keep in touch?'

But he'd telephoned Janet the next day, and had arranged for Amy to audition as a warm-up act to a star who was doing a one-night show in a few weeks' time. Let's have a look at her under the lights in a full theatre, he thought.

*   *   *

Paul Warren was having a seriously shitty evening. It had poured with rain all day, and he was standing on the side of the pitch, rain seeping through his tracksuit. He'd known that they would be up against it. They were playing the league leaders after all, and his team had lost the last couple of games. He was also angry that his star striker had sent him a text that afternoon, saying that he was injured. A bloody text message. A recurring groin strain, it said. I'll give him a groin strain when I see him, Paul thought. At that moment, they conceded a third goal, which finished the game off. It would be a long coach trip back after a heavy defeat like this.

He sat back down on the bench in the dugout, which at least afforded some protection from the driving rain. At times like this as the manager, you were helpless. He looked at the players behind him on the bench. They were all too young to make the slightest difference against a team such as this.

Devoid of inspiration, Paul's mind wandered. Things had been so different a few short months ago. At the time, he'd had so much to look forward to. Actually Carol had, too. Then it all happened out of the blue. He'd tried to be supportive when it happened. But somehow, things were never the same afterwards.

His mind was jerked back to reality. The crowd were on their feet, baying for blood. An opposing player was rolling around on the floor in apparent agony. The referee was waving the players away, but then, with maximum theatre, he flourished the red card.

His captain walked off disconsolately, his eyes straight ahead. The taunts of the supporters were as disgusting as they were racist. The coach, who had been sitting next to him, headed down the tunnel with the player. It was going to be a very long coach trip back home now.

And, of course, he'd missed his wedding anniversary, too. Just a fact of a football manager's life, he thought. His wife, Carol, understood as always. He'd bought her flowers. She liked flowers.

# 3.

## Spring

It was early evening on a spring Saturday. The unusually warm weather had brought some last minute tourists to the seaside for a long weekend. Above the sound of seagulls, a theatre organ recording belted out 'I Do Like To Be Beside The Seaside' from the distant amusement arcades.

The day trippers were heading for home, and the weekenders were heading back to their lodgings. Eager hoteliers quickly reopened rooms not used since last October. There was a whiff of fresh paint as the town got ready for the main season, and the seafront wore its Victorian heritage with pride. There were plenty of buildings bearing wrought iron and classical architecture, but these jostled for position with newer buildings whose design somehow lacked any real identity.

It was not, of course, the actual weather that brought the tourists in. What mattered was the BBC weather forecast. Usually conservative, the weather forecast had ruined many a weekend for hoteliers across the country. Once they had relied on two-week holiday-makers, but they now relied on short breaks, which were very weather dependent. Thus, as the BBC predicted a warm weekend, it triggered a rash of last-minute phone calls from tourists craving sunshine after a winter beset with recession. Whether the BBC realised that they had this power was unclear, but this particular weekend had been predicted to be warm and sunny, and the weather was, in fact, warm and sunny. For many a weekend, the reverse was true: resorts empty of customers despite fine weather, which arrived unexpectedly, fooling the meteorologists of the BBC and enraging those whose livelihoods were at the mercy of the weather.

On the pier, a Punch and Judy Show was just finishing. Cyril Brown was taking a bow, with his puppets in front of him. He smiled and bowed cheerfully, resplendent in black top hat and tails. He was sweating heavily from the unseasonably warm weather, the red rose in his buttonhole wilting.

He addressed his audience one last time, as they gathered their things to depart.

'Thank you, ladies and gentlemen! I hope that you enjoy the rest of the holiday. Thank you for coming! I hope little Johnny enjoyed the show, ha-ha-ha!'

His audience left and Cyril picked up assorted sweet papers and ice cream wrappers left by the young punters and their parents. He muttered and grumbled as he did so.

'Tourists. Bloody tourists. I've been doing this show for 30-odd years and I swear they get worse. That child today. I swear he's been to an Al-Qaeda training camp. ADHD his parents said.'

As he grumbled, his playful side took over. He picked up Mr Punch, his veteran puppet, a little frayed from his advancing years.

'What say you, Mr Punch?'

He lifted the puppet to his ear.

'Ah, yes. I agree, Mr Punch. Six of the best and then sent to bed without his supper. None of this Ritalin nonsense.'

Miss Judy appeared to be giving him an admonishing stare. He picked her up lovingly.

'What's that, Miss Judy? A breach of his human rights, you say? Oh, give me strength.'

The town hadn't changed much in his lifetime, but that's the point. We like the nostalgia, don't we? Cyril would doubtless agree, and assert that sometimes things should stay exactly as they were.

He lived alone, so he was in no hurry and packed up slowly. Time was not really an issue for him. He was quite lonely since Mary died, but he had Mitch, his dog, for company. He looked out to the east. He could see clouds in the distance. Sometimes he left his stand out overnight, but decided that tonight he had better not. He didn't need the BBC to tell him that the wind would pick up overnight and that the rain might come in with it.

Cyril finished packing up, mind still wandering, and still chuntering away to himself out of earshot of the dwindling tourists.

'What's that, Miss Judy? Why do I do it? Now there's a question. I suppose it's because I love the show and the town and, well, yes, I like the tourists, too. God bless them.'

He sat awhile and dozed off. He awoke a while later and sipped from a bottle of lemonade as he took in the scene. It was now evening and the sun was dipping over to the west. The wind had shifted to the east, and it was getting a little cold for his 73-year-old bones. There were fewer people on the pier now. Just a handful of fishermen.

Cyril recognised one of the fishermen as a local, Bill Challis. Another standing next to him was clearly a tourist. He had all the gear, but Bill was clearly offering him tips. A bit of local knowledge. Cyril waved politely, and Bill waved back. He then looked at his watch, and addressed the tourist.

'Well I think that's it for the day, then. We've seen the best of the weather,' he said.

The tourist agreed. 'Yes. Back to the missus, God bless her.'

They started to pack up, gathering up their gear.

'Back to work on Monday?' Bill asked.

'No. We're short-time working. It's worse now than last year. That's why we came here for a few days. No money for a Majorca break this year, but we had to get away. Haven't been over this way for a while.'

'Well, it's a change, isn't it? You're a long way from the sea in Birmingham.'

The tourist laughed.

'You're not kidding. Mind you, it's a bloody long way out here. Haven't you lot heard of motorways?'

'Oh, we don't have those things out 'ere. We might get some tourists if we did.' Bill replied affably in his heavy Norfolk accent.

'Has business not been good then?'

'Last year was awful but – touch wood – things have been a bit better so far this year. More short breaks and stuff.

They reckon a lot of people are staying home because of the recession. We're full tonight – a bit unusual for this time of year. Good weather, you see.'

'Have you always ran a B&B then?'

'Oh, no. Had to sell my crab boat a couple of years ago after I bust me knee and couldn't do it any more, not that there was much money in it anyway. Probably better off on the dole. Wife's always ran the B&B, but now she's carrying me as well. Not much work about here, especially in winter.'

'It's not that great getting work in the car industry either at the minute. No flipping chance. Oh well, at least this is better than working for a living. Time to go I suppose.'

'I'll walk back with you,' said Bill.

They collected the gear and headed back to the bed and breakfast. Bill would be on breakfast duty in the morning cooking the Brummie's breakfast. Then he'd try to change the beds to his wife's satisfaction, despite his knee. He'd rather have been out in a crab boat, but that wasn't going to happen anymore. He'd still be up early though. If he had time, he'd pop down to see the lads go off in their boats.

As they wandered down the pier, Bill nodded to Cyril who had by now completed his chores, and had sat down briefly. He was dozing off once again when he became conscious that he was being spoken to. He heard a woman's voice with a heavy Welsh accent.

'Excuse me,' she said.

He looked up and saw a tall, rather attractive blonde woman with piercing blue eyes. Standing at nearly six foot, she wasn't slim but simply well-proportioned for her height. Her hair looked naturally blonde, and was very obviously professionally styled. Her clothes were clearly expensive. Too expensive for Cromer. Bright red shoes completed the look. He knew her immediately.

'Yes?' he said.

She was pulling a large suitcase, too, he noticed. A designer brand. It must be her, he thought.

'I'm looking for the Pier Theatre. Mrs Janet Wells,' she said.

'Well, that structure at the end of the pier is quite definitely the Pier Theatre. We only have the one you see,' said Cyril politely.

'I'm sorry?' she said, a little perplexed.

Cyril smiled. 'That was my attempt at a joke. No matter. I haven't seen Mrs Wells though. Did you agree to meet her here?'

'Oh, yes. I'm a bit late though, I've got to admit,' she said, looking at her watch.

'Ah, the Saturday train late again? Cyril Brown, by the way.'

He offered her his hand. She shook it hesitantly, and smiled nervously.

'Lauren Evans,' she said.

'Ah, yes. I thought I recognised you,' said Cyril pleasantly. 'But don't worry, I won't let on. You've travelled a long way, I would guess?'

'Yes, from Wales. Via London actually. It's a bloody long journey to be fair. I'm pretty knackered now, to be honest with you.'

Cyril decided that Lauren needed cheering up. He picked

Miss Judy up from the box in which he lovingly laid his puppets, and pretended to listen to what she was saying.

'Ah yes. Miss Judy never forgets a face, Miss Evans. I'd heard you were coming. Quite a coup for us, I'm sure. Look, I suspect I know where Janet is hiding. If you wait there and have a seat, I'll find her for you. No need to drag your case any further. Just you give me a minute or two, and I shall return.'

With a flourish, he was gone. Lauren was suddenly quite alone.

She sat as Cyril headed off into the theatre. She held her coat tighter as the wind freshened. It was becoming chilly now. Her mind wandered. It had been a long day.

*Well, at least someone recognises me. And I'm here at last. A long way from South Wales. It's a long way from anywhere, to be fair. My God, it's not exactly the West End, is it? How did it come to this? My agent says go to Cromer. He gave me the spiel about consolidating my career. Maybe I've already had my 15 minutes of fame.*

She stood and looked out to sea. The best time was in Cardiff, at the rugby. She didn't really know much about the game but as the current hot property, she had to sing the anthem. In front of more than 70,000 people. Talk about pressure!

She stood at full posture as the wind strengthened, and gave her full soprano voice to an audience of two seagulls. 'Mae hen wlad fy nhadau yn annwyl i mi…' she sang.

Tears began to roll down her cheeks at the memory. It was one of the greatest moments of her life. At the end of the song, she sat once again, and thought to herself.

*A long way from home I am now, that's for sure. No use getting lonely and homesick. I've been from the Con Club to the National Stadium and now to Cromer Pier. What a laugh. Still, it looks a nice little town though. It's sort of old English – a bit of a throwback really. It's got its share of charity shops. Still, it pays the bills. Cromer Pier Theatre Seaside Special, here I come.*

The seagulls lifted off and flew overhead.

'Don't even think of crapping on me, bozo, this coat cost a fortune.' She glared at the seagulls as she spoke.

She moved her large case over to one of the Victorian shelters, noting as she did so that she could see the sea below through the decking boards of the pier. She found it slightly disconcerting, and sat on the bench out of the breeze, which was strengthening as the day came towards its end.

She fiddled with her phone, getting bored. She was tired and looking forward to a glass or two before bedtime. And a long, hot soak in the bath.

A few minutes later, a woman came out of the theatre entrance and strode purposefully in her direction. She was not quite as tall as Lauren, and she was dressed in black. Late forties at a guess, Lauren thought, and every inch a theatre proprietor.

Lauren got up and they shook hands.

'I'm Janet Wells, Miss Evans. I'm the proprietor of Cromer Pier Theatre for my sins. Welcome to Cromer. I'm so glad you've joined us. Did you come by car?'

'No, I came by train from Wales,' Lauren replied.

Janet was surprised. She'll be a bit isolated here without a car, she thought.

'Oh, I see. I'm so sorry, if I'd known, I'd have met you at the station. The sooner we get you settled in for the night, the better.'

Lauren shivered against the strengthening wind.

'Is it always this cold?'

'Only when the wind comes from the east,' said Janet.

'Is that very often?' Lauren quizzed, as they walked out through the pier gates, Janet pulling Lauren's case along.

'Well, if I'm honest, a bit more often than we'd like,' said Janet.

They headed off out of the pier entrance and up the slope from the promenade.

Stanley, the pier gateman, was preparing to do his rounds. He waved to them both, bidding them a good evening. Stanley's boss appeared at the entrance in his Jaguar with the personalised plate. Checking up on me again, Stanley thought.

'Good evening, Mr Pemrose,' Stanley said, more cheerily than he felt.

'Good evening, Stanley. All's well, I trust?' said Pemrose in reply.

'Yes, sir. Not many people out now. Getting chilly again.

Mind you, they say that it comes fine in the next few days. A bit of decent weather coming in, they reckon.'

Pemrose smiled cynically.

'Oh, I think it's going to get very warm in the next few days. For some people, that is. Goodnight, Stanley.'

With that, Mr Pemrose paused to clean a speck of seagull poo from the bonnet of his bright red Jaguar, before getting into the vehicle and driving away.

'Goodnight Sir,' said Stanley to the tail lights of the car as it drove away.

Stanley had heard that voice before, and seen that twinkle in his eye. It normally happened just before someone got hurt. He's a thoroughly genial man, our Mr Pemrose, thought Stanley. Well, most of the time. A pillar of the local community one minute and Darth Vader the next. The original Dr Jekyll and Mr Hyde.

Lionel Pemrose drove around to the car park of the Seaview Hotel. He dialled his home number and waited for his wife to answer. It went to the answering machine. Good, she wasn't back from London yet, he thought. He would just leave her a message.

'Hi, love. Just ringing to let you know that Derek's sick, so I'm afraid I'm staying over at the hotel tonight. Sorry about that. I hope Oxford Street was good, and you've spent lots of money. I'll see you tomorrow night. Love you.'

He rang off, then swiftly tapped another number. She answered on the second ring.

'Lizzie Honeywell?'

'Lizzie, it's me. Champagne chilled?'

'Of course.'

'Good girl. I'll be up shortly. I'm just checking that the evening staff aren't running off with the silver. I shan't be too long. I'm sorry… we'll be working very late tonight. Mim's away.'

He listened and laughed.

'Yes, OK, I know it's double time on Sunday, especially after midnight. Not to worry.'

He terminated the call and laughed quietly to himself. Double time after midnight indeed. Well he'd see about that. He was an Investor in People, after all.

Lizzie ran a bath and got in. She sipped on the champagne. She was only 26 and knew that she would probably have a limited shelf life with Lionel. 18 months seemed about average. But with what she'd have on Lionel by then, he'd better be a good boy or she could get very nasty. In the meantime, if she had to work overtime, at least she could do it lying down.

Downstairs in the main bar, Amy Raven started her set. Her real name was actually Amy Strutter, but she had thought that Raven was better as a stage name, and it matched her jet-black hair. She was due at an audition at the Pier Theatre the following Monday for a part in the Summertime Special Show.

She had done a short set as a warm-up act last winter after an informal conversation with Janet following an introduction by Les. She had had the foresight to ensure that her extended fan club – mostly her family – were in the audience. She had obviously done enough to impress, as Janet then invited her to attend dance classes throughout the winter months.

Her coach was Isobel Strong, the Pier Theatre Choreographer. A mixture of group sessions and some private lessons shoe-horned between her day job in an estate agents meant that Amy was now a very competent dancer, as well as a strong singer. She hoped that getting a chorus job for the season would be the start of a glittering career in musical theatre. Her CV was a bit thin right now, so she needed a break. She heard that none other than Lauren Evans was headlining this year. Janet Wells must have come into some cash to afford a big name like her.

As she bashed out her set, she saw Lionel Pemrose enter the half-full room. He waved to her briefly but she pretended not to notice him. Definitely a bit grabby, she thought. He had suggested dinner but she decided that she didn't want to wind up as his dessert.

# 4.

## Monday

It was Monday morning, and Les Westley was sitting at a desk on the stage. Auditions were due to start at noon, and he needed to begin to rehearse his own stand-up act, newly written for the season. But first, he needed to sort out the hapless Lech Wojiek who was standing in front of him.

'And cut out the Irish jokes, as well. I don't want the racial equality people crucifying us on opening night,' he said tartly.

'I am so sorry, Mr Les. I am troubling with the language at present, but it will be, as you English say, all right on the night, yes?'

Les shook his head in dismay.

'You don't want to know how many people have said that to me, Mr Wojiek. Judy Dench said that to me once long ago, but you're no Judy Dench.'

'I am not knowing this Judy Dentures. She has problems with her teeth?' said Lech, confused.

Les initially thought this to be an attempt at a joke, but then realised that Lech simply wasn't capable of any reasonable English comprehension. He almost laughed out loud, but this was simply too serious a matter for levity.

'Dench, you idiot. Look, Mr Wojiek,' said Les through gritted teeth-.

'Lech. Please call me Lech.'

'Trust me, Mr Wojiek, I could call you many things after that performance.'

'Was there a problem with show, Mr Les? I am thinking that I am, how you say, getting hang of it.'

'No, Mr Wojiek. That is my very point. You are not!'

Lech shrugged. He was clearly confused. Les tried to stick to facts. That might limit the confusion, after all.

'Now, what precisely happened with the rabbit? You see, in a normal magician's act in this country, we pull a rabbit out of the hat, not a mouse. And he doesn't normally release the rabbit into the audience, as you did with the mouse. We find it causes the audience to head for the exits. Not that they need much encouragement with your performance.'

Les sat back, not looking forward to the answer.

Lech clearly understood. 'Ah, yes, Mr Les. Just a leetle accident. I had to leave my rabbit in Warsaw. Your rabies laws are very strict. Mr Ryanair doesn't let them on the flight, unless you buy a ticket, of course. So I bring leetle mouse. I have lots of mice in my caravan. I train them good. Few days only. Is OK. No problem.'

Les nodded slowly. Understanding but hardly convinced.

'That accounts for the mouse droppings on your suit then?' he ventured.

Lech looked at his stage outfit and noticed the offending marks.

'Ah, yes. No problem. My friend Jan works in the beeg hotel. He get it dry cleaned. No problem, yes?'

Les smiled. In spite of everything, the Polish magician was annoyingly likeable. It might make the audience more forgiving of his limited technique.

'Oh, I suppose so. Oh, and one more point.'

'Yes?' said Lech, looking across intently.

'You must not play chase the lady with the tourists on the pier during the day, or any other game. It's illegal gambling and will get you arrested in this country.'

'Oh, I am so sorry, Mr Les. I'm just trying to earn a leetle extra to send home to my Tanya. You want see picture of her and my baby?'

Les declined to view the photographs, which he had seen before, as had the entire company.

'No thank you, Lech. Now, let me make it clear. You have only a few days. You must work very hard, yes? Your technique requires major improvement. Understand?'

'Yes, Mr Les, of course. Lech work very hard.'

Karen Wells entered, passing the disconsolate Lech as he headed off. She was Janet's daughter and a permanent fixture in the show, most recently as Dance Captain. At first glance, mother and daughter were rather alike in appearance, but Karen maintained a strict diet and was thin and wiry. She wore little makeup off stage, but her smile was as engaging as her mothers, and she had a naturally caring disposition, which everyone found endearing. She was, to put it bluntly, a decent all-rounder and the ultimate team player. Her voice was her main strength, but she was a trained dancer and could have a crack at most things. She wasn't keen on being sawn in half, but if it came to it, she would give it a go.

Les spread his arms in mock surrender.

'In all my born days, I've never seen anything like it. He's not much of a magician, but the audience will love him, I suspect. No talent at all but, hey, there's many I could name who have got away with that.'

Karen smiled. 'Ah, that makes sense. I thought Lech didn't seem too happy.'

'Well then, I must be getting through. I thought of taking Polish lessons. I wonder what the Polish is for 'you're an absolutely abysmal magician and I don't want you to darken my stage door any more, thank you'?'

Karen sat opposite him, rolling her eyes. It was that time of year.

'Come on, Les. You've said things like that about performers every year since I was here as a little girl with Grandpa. You know that Lech will have them in stitches. They'll think he's a comedian, not a magician. When he did the thing with the mouse, I nearly wet myself it was so funny.'

'You are, as always and highly regrettably, correct. The punters won't know the difference of course, although it pains me that I will.'

'Grandpa said patience was a virtue.'

Les laughed. 'Oh, yes? He didn't exactly practice what he preached much though, did he? I don't think our friend Lech would have lasted long with him in charge.'

'I suppose not. Did you know it's 10 years next month since Grandpa died?'

Les paused to reflect.

'Yes, I suppose it is, thinking about it. Have I been here that long?'

Karen nodded and smiled. Les was beginning to feel his age.

'I liked him, you know, although we had our fights. A skinflint old bastard I used to call him,' he said.

'And he would tell you that he'd been running this show for years and didn't need a lecture from a failed, wet-behind-the-ears comic.'

Les thought for a moment.

'To be fair, he taught me a lot. He was a great people person. Always stood front of house for the show to meet and greet the punters. Some theatres should take a lesson from him. He was a mean negotiator, mind. I see where your mother got that particular trait.'

Karen laughed.

'Tell me about it. I grew up in this theatre didn't I? I wouldn't have it any other way though. The applause of a packed house–'

'Then playing to an audience of 50.' Les interjected.

'Don't remind me. Flogging your guts out for the brave souls who made it to the end of the pier in spite of a force seven gale.'

She sighed and shrugged. She was now in her early 30s, but wise beyond her years. Les put his hand on hers.

'We are blessed to have you. Besides, you're cheap, I suppose. You're five percent poorer like the rest of us.'

Karen laughed. 'Oh, thanks a bundle for reminding me.'

'No problem! That's what you get for negotiating with Janet Wells. Just count your fingers afterwards.'

Les paused for a moment. He was about to tread on sensitive ground.

'You still have a beautiful voice, Karen, and you're a sublime dancer. You could still, well, you know, try again?'

'West End? No, I don't think so, Les. Been there done that… didn't get the T-shirt. No. That's in the past. This is my home.'

'Then so be it. Their loss is our gain. Now how is our star getting along? Our little Welsh firebrand?' asked Les with some trepidation.

'Ah, bit of a problem there. That's what I was coming to warn you about. Mum's a bit late in this morning and Lauren isn't–'

At that moment, Lauren Evans stormed onto the stage. A dragon in full fury.

'I assume you're Les Westley? I've been looking for you everywhere. Look, I can't possibly share a dressing room with her – no offence, Karen. But I am the star of the show, you know. I must have my own space.'

Les stood and shook Lauren's hand in welcome. This was not starting well, he thought.

'I'm sorry, Lauren, but we only have limited dressing room space. This isn't the London Palladium, it's Cromer Pier,' he said.

He looked up into her perfect blue eyes and his heart skipped a beat. Christ, she's absolutely gorgeous, he thought. Lauren, however, wasn't having any of it.

'Well, that's as may be. I'll speak to my agent about this and my accommodation, such as it is.'

Karen held back a laugh. She'd had this discussion with her mother.

'Mrs Bloomingdale's not up to your expectations then?' she said, suppressing her amusement. It was as well that she did, for Lauren was certainly not amused.

'It's a bed and breakfast, for goodness sake. Not so much as a hairdryer, and as for my hair straighteners in that en suite, forget it. I was told I'd be in a hotel. That new Majestic Hotel looks OK.'

Karen had heard enough. She was now standing, facing Lauren. Les looked on, realising at that moment that Lauren was several inches taller than the more diminutive Karen. She must be nearly six foot, he pondered.

Karen was clearly not in any mood to compromise.

'Well, I'm sure it would be, but my mother isn't called Andrew Lloyd Webber. I suggest you get over it Lauren, and get real.'

'Well I never!' she said in shock.

Karen continued, staying icily calm.

'This show is running on a shoestring this season to pay your fat fee, and we all have to muck in. I'm cleaning the kitchen and the toilet every morning now, because we can't afford a cleaner. It's just what we have to do. Now, if you'll excuse me, some child has thrown up in the ladies, so I'll go and clean that up, too.'

Karen shrugged, turned around and walked off. In fairness, she thought Lauren had a point, but her attitude wasn't what was required, and Lauren needed to understand that from the start.

Lauren certainly wasn't in the mood to listen to Karen. She glared at Les, who would have been intimidated had he not seen this many times before. Time for the good cop / bad cop routine, he thought.

'This is absolutely ridiculous. I can't work with amateurs like her,' said Lauren, her rich Welsh accent making her even more attractive.

'Well, thank you for that, Miss Evans. Now can I suggest that you sit down and shut up, if you please…'

He pulled up a chair and motioned her to sit. Lauren wasn't used to being treated like this, but she sat down anyway. She was close to tears. Ah, yes, Les thought, both the ego and confidence were seldom more than skin deep, even in people as talented as Lauren.

Les sat opposite her and calmly began.

'That amateur, as you put it, held a West End lead for six months, and is the most talented woman I have worked with in my long – too long – career in this business. Oh, and I've done it all, too. You probably won't remember me, but I did some big London shows. In this business, you don't stop learning. Ever. My advice to you is to watch and absorb everything. Trust me – you have much to learn. We are a team. We are in this together. Things will go wrong this season, because they always do. And when that happens, you rely on your mates in the show. This is not glitzy, fabricated talent show claptrap. This is real professional theatre, with real punters who pay good money to be entertained. Now can I suggest you take a break and get down to the rehearsal room in the town by two o'clock? Why not go for a walk to get acclimatised until then? Isobel will start your dance tuition today. We've set aside the afternoon for you to start the basics. You should be fine.'

With that, Les sat back, picked up a list of auditioning performers, and starting reading. As far as he was concerned, the discussion was over.

Lauren's mouth opened like a goldfish, but nothing came out. She hadn't been spoken to like that for several years. She was Lauren Evans.

'Well I never,' she eventually replied. She got up and headed not towards the backstage area, but out through the seats towards the front foyer. He waited until she was two thirds of the way to the door.

'And Miss Evans, Lauren?' he said.

Lauren stopped and turned around. She was in tears now. She brushed them aside, damaging the carefully-applied mascara.

'You sang beautifully in your warm up earlier. I like the fact that you were in early. I was sitting right at the back. And I did, of course, see you on TV. You have talent, and whatever happens, don't let those press cretins tell you otherwise.'

He collected his papers and walked off stage, leaving Lauren standing there. Lauren was surprised and humbled. She was lost for words once more. She paused. Then she headed out of the door into the daylight.

Janet saw her go and was minded to go after her. But then she thought better of it. She found Les backstage.

'Sorry I'm so late in. Was that Lauren I saw flouncing about?' she asked.

'Yes, it was actually,' Les replied. More casually than he felt.

'Still a bit full of herself, is she?'

Les nodded sadly. 'Aren't they always? Too much too soon, then the bubble bursts. It's a long way to fall. A lot of damaged pride and no underlying confidence.'

Janet frowned. 'She's an awfully long way from home, too. I should have been here to greet her, but got Karen to do it. Shall I have a word?'

'No, let her stew awhile. If I'm right, Miss Evans will come out fighting and will make this our best season ever.'

'And if you're wrong?' said Janet.

'Then she will be on the next train back to the Valleys.'

Janet frowned. She wasn't entirely sure he was joking.

'So I must trust your judgement then.'

Les laughed. 'Have I ever let you down?'

Janet was unconvinced. 'What about that Japanese knife thrower two seasons ago?'

'Oh. Well, if you're going to bring that up…'

'It's the first time we'd ever had a visit from the Health and Safety Inspector,' Janet said coolly.

Les ignored the remark and became serious. 'Look, I'm right about Lauren. Tough love is what she needs.'

'I think you're probably right. She's a steal for a show like ours. I heard what you said to her at the end. You're a good person, Les.'

Les shrugged. 'I didn't have much choice. Where would you get a replacement now?'

'What? Someone with a household name? No chance.' Janet replied dismissively.

'Exactly. And she really does have talent. She's just been a bit battered by our industry and the free press.'

'But that voice. My God. The range she has.'

'Quite unique, I agree. And what I might call eye candy, too.'

'Down, boy!'

'Well, if I was five years younger maybe.'

'Dream on, sunshine. OK, moving swiftly on. Is everything in hand for the final auditions?'

Les picked up the list and handed over a copy.

'Oh, yes. I'm actually looking forward to it. I do like to find newcomers, and this year we don't have much choice.'

'We've had one or two discoveries, haven't we, over the years.'

Les smiled. 'Indeed, we have. It's what makes the job worthwhile. Seeing people that arrive here with fledgling talent. Nurturing it. Like Melanie West?'

'Of course.'

'Came in off the street one morning and asked for an audition.'

'And you were too polite to turn her away.'

'She wouldn't take no for an answer as I recall. Then she sang.'

'And the rest is history.'

'She still writes to me from time to time. She has two children now.'

Janet sat down. 'But some come to Cromer Pier in the other direction. The escalator goes down as well as up.'

'Booze, drugs, alcohol, gambling. We've had them all. Some we turn around and others, well…'

'Don't remind me. It's still too painful.'

'How is Karen? Three months, isn't it?'

'Since she dumped our friend Karl? Yes, it is. Well, she has her days. Bound to, I suppose. Together for four years, after all.'

'Did he have a job in all of that time?'

'Only a few seasonal jobs. Let's be honest, he was a waste of space and it took a long time for Karen to accept it. She should have known better but well…'

'Love is blind after all? Not much of a gene pool in a small town,' said Les sympathetically.

Janet nodded. 'Exactly. But back to business. What about the rest of the show?'

'Well, Lauren we've spoken of, if she's still here after her little strop. Karen will be fine as Dance Captain as always. Signing Sven Karlson was a real bonus, too. I never thought you'd get him after what he said to me on the ship.'

Janet smiled.

'I can be very persuasive Les. He said that, having discussed it with his agent, he could see the advantage of gaining experience in British musical theatre. He sees it as a stepping stone to the West End.'

'Good for him. He might be right. He's a decent dancer, too, by all accounts.'

'Well he's a bit of a risk at his age, but given the budget–'

'Exactly! And his voice will work well with Lauren's for the songs from the shows.'

'And as for Lech, well…' she laughed.

Les shook his head. 'Lech is a disaster, but he's so likeably incompetent that the audience won't notice. Things are just a lot more difficult this season. He's going to need very careful management.'

'Yes, I know. He's a gamble, I accept. So we've just one more headline act to sign. Howard's been on the line again.'

Les flared. 'No chance. I've told you I'm not having that bloody dancing dog again.'

'Are you sure? He went down well with the punters a couple of years back, and at least he's reliable.'

'Until the dog crapped on the stage and I trod in it while singing my big number. No bloody chance.'

Janet laughed.

'As I recall, the audience found it hilarious. They thought it was a set up. Morecambe and Wise would have been proud of it.'

'Yes, well, they might have but I still have my standards. Although, thanks to you, they seem to be getting lower this year, along with my salary.'

'Come on, Mr Grumpy. It's nearly time to start. We still need a novelty act and we're a dancer short. Isobel's getting them ready backstage.'

'Talking of which, I've had George on the line pleading once again.'

Janet stared. 'God, is he still alive? The accordion player from hell?'

Les looked at her ruefully. 'Sadly, yes he is. I think I'd rather have the dancing dog.'

'Well, it's warming up later today and the forecast's looking promising. That's something at least.'

'Hottest place in Britain by the weekend they reckon, so maybe there's hope.'

*   *   *

Amy Raven arrived at the theatre at the appointed time. The sun was coming out and the day was turning warm. She carried her guitar, but wasn't sure what to sing. Was she better to go with one of her own songs or would they prefer a cover?

She had been sick that morning. She was OK when she sang her set in the hotels, or when she had started out busking on the seafront aged 13. But this was different. This was real theatre. She had rehearsed the dance routine, and her mother said it was great. But then her mum always thought she was great. What if she made a complete fool of herself?

She introduced herself at the stage door and was shown through. She was the last to arrive. Several dancers, a fire-eater and some sort of acrobat were all compressed into a couple of small rooms behind the stage.

Isobel had assured her that she was in the frame along with the rest, even though they seemed older and much more experienced. It helped that she had danced at secondary school, and her lessons with Isobel had featured the audition routine, so she was pretty confident she could hack that. But could she handle the routines day after day all through the season? In reality, she was as scared of getting the job as she was of losing the opportunity.

Eventually, she was called through. Les was sitting in the audience seats, and he introduced Janet Wells. They discussed the choice of song. They decided to start with the cover.

Amy sang 'You've Got A Friend.' She was slightly nervous, but knew the song so well that it was a safe bet. Then she sang a ballad that she had written herself. It was probably too high for her, Les thought, but then she was only 19.

Finally, they auditioned the dancers in a group audition, using the routine developed by Isobel. Amy did her best, but she couldn't help thinking that the others just appeared slicker than her. They all left together, with the others heading back to London or wherever. Amy felt so provincial. She'd only been to London a couple of times in her life. These guys had travelled in from far and wide.

After all of the performers had left Janet, Isobel, Karen and Les reviewed the performers one by one. Neither the fire-eater nor the acrobat seemed to add much to the show, run on such a tight budget. Janet was negotiating with a ventriloquist who had been a success in Brighton, so that seemed the best bet.

Then they discussed the dancers. Isobel's opinion was crucial. The dancers only had two full weeks of rehearsals to reach performance standard, and reliability was vital. With two shows per day in season and two different programmes to learn, this show was no easy ride, and the physical demands on the dancers were considerable.

Picking up her notes, Isobel summarised things as she saw it.

'It's a tough choice. Amy has worked very hard over the winter and has natural talent as a dancer. She's come on leaps and bounds, but she isn't as competent as either of the other two who are more experienced. She's very young and would be a gamble without a doubt. But we do have more time to get her up to scratch, being local.'

Janet agreed.

'As much as I like Amy, I'd agree with you Isobel. I'd go with Melanie, personally. What about you, Karen?'

'Well, I'd agree that Amy is a gamble, but I think we should try to go with local talent when we can. She is just so determined to succeed. She's not missed a Saturday class all winter, and I've opened up for her on Sundays from time to time, too.'

Isobel nodded.

'She's achieved an amazing amount in a short time. And she has a better singing voice by a country mile. My heart says Amy but my head says Melanie.'

Les was weighing his options.

'I don't want to take too many risks, Isobel. You're working with Lauren who can't dance a step, and I'm going to guess that Lech is probably just as bad.'

Karen shook her head and Isobel smiled.

'You've not seen him dance, Les. Whatever you think of his act, Lech is no problem at all on the dance front. He's seriously good, actually. He's better than you. If that's possible, of course.'

Les was aggrieved at the collective giggles, and his retort was swift.

'Well, that's a relief. If his dancing was as bad as his magic, even Isobel would be in despair.'

Isobel picked up the theme.

'And young Sven is no slouch either to be honest. Quite dishy, too…'

The girls exchanged knowing glances as Les looked on in mock disgust.

'Can you girls just put your lust for Sven the Viking to one side for a minute? He's gay, by the way.'

They giggled at Les and his haughty admonishment. He continued.

'So if I read you correctly, Isobel, you could live with Amy if we decided to go down that route?'

Isobel considered for a moment and then nodded.

'Yes, provided that Karen is content as Dance Captain, because Amy will need a lot of mentoring through the season.'

'I'm happy to take her under my wing. We need to support local talent and her voice is a real bonus, surely?' said Karen.

Janet was not so convinced.

'I'm not about to interfere in what is a creative decision, but you need to weigh the risks carefully. Melanie has a decent track record. She's a safe bet. But in the end, it's your decision, Les.'

Les nodded. It was his decision in the end. Local talent was good for the show. A bit more training and she would be a decent addition, probably for a couple of seasons at least. But not now. Not this season. It was too much of a risk in a show already top-heavy with risks.

Amy was understandably disappointed when Janet phoned her later, but understood the reasoning, and was reassured that she would have a better opportunity the following year. Janet enquired as to her real name. Amy Strutter, she said. Oh yes, thought Janet, the Strutter family. It made sense now.

*       *       *

For Lauren, the irritability about her accommodation spilled over during her dance lesson with Isobel that afternoon. While her coach was patience personified, Lauren struggled to comprehend the basic steps that she was shown. They laboured until early evening, when Isobel called time on proceedings.

Lauren wanted to eat, but decided she needed a hot bath to ease her aching limbs. She headed back to the bed and breakfast with a chilled bottle of white wine acquired in the Co-op. She needed a drink. A bath might need some negotiation. As she entered, she was greeted by a smiling landlady.

'First day dance routines?' she enquired, smiling sympathetically.

'It's a bugger, and that's a fact,' replied Lauren, grateful for the sympathy.

'You'll be wanting a hot bath tonight then?'

'If it's not too much trouble, er–'

'Elaine. Call me Elaine. All part of the service. Plenty of hot water. Bathroom's upstairs, second on the right. Did we not show you when you arrived?'

'Thank God. I'm knackered to be honest.'

They headed up the stairs and it was clear that Elaine had seen this all before.

'The first few days are the worst. You're just using muscles you don't normally use. You'll soon get used to it. Isobel will sort you out.'

'If I live that long,' said Lauren.

'I'm sorry I wasn't here to greet you. Sunday's my day off. We'll make you as comfortable as we can.'

Elaine showed her an immaculately refurbished bathroom. She turned on the taps to run the bath and, seeing the bottle in Lauren's hand, smiled once again.

'I'll be back with a corkscrew and a wine glass.'

Lauren stripped off her soggy clothes and put on a dressing gown, but then realised that she hadn't brought enough training gear with her for this kind of regime. Washing was going to be a problem.

Elaine opened the bottle and poured a glass for Lauren, then she scooped up the clothes.

'All part of the service, Miss Evans.'

'What?'

'All part of the service. We do your laundry. We always do for our Pier Theatre guests. You just have a good soak.'

She left and Lauren slid into the bath, sipping her chilled white wine. She had a livid purple bruise on her right knee, and judging by the pain she felt as she settled in the bath, she'd probably have one on her backside, too.

She looked at herself critically. She would never be skinny, and wouldn't want to be. She liked food and wine too much, and living in hotels was a nightmare. There were the tell-tale signs around her tummy and thighs. She was always on some sort of diet, but could never stick to it. She was a big, tall girl but singers like her often were. Overall, she'd like to be slimmer, but with the life as it was at present? Give yourself a break girl, she thought.

As she tried to relax, she was also terrified of what lay ahead. This was nothing like anything she'd done before. Instead of being treated as the star, she was now part of an ensemble, and having seen a couple of the dancers signed for the season, she was awestruck by their skill.

As the alcohol's depressive effects took hold, her mind wandered. There was silence save for the distant waves on the shore. She brought up a picture of her mother on her phone and wondered what she was up to now. They hadn't spoken for a while. In fact, she hadn't spoken to so many people in a while, stuck in her celebrity bubble in a different hotel every night on tour. She wondered what her mates were doing on an ordinary Monday night back home.

It didn't take much time for her to convince herself that this couldn't possibly work. She was so far from home, and somehow Elaine's kindness only seemed to make it worse. It contrasted with the stark, no-nonsense approach of Les Westley and Janet Wells.

She became angry as she drank a second glass. She had thought that she would be treated as a celebrity by these people. Just who did they think they were? She was entitled to her own dressing room and a decent hotel. It wasn't too much to ask. She was also an international singing star, not a bloody dancer. What they had in mind was ridiculous.

She'd drunk two thirds of the bottle by the time she got out of the bath – a bad idea on an empty stomach. She put on a smart top, just about managed to do up some designer jeans, and looked out towards the Pier Theatre. It was getting dark, and it was time to eat.

She went down into the residents' lounge and leafed through some leaflets placed in a neat stand in the corner.

'Feeling better now?'

Lauren turned to see Elaine smiling at her.

'Things are always better after a soak,' Elaine soothed.

Lauren laughed.

'Especially if you've drunk too much white wine on an empty stomach. I'm feeling a bit pissed, if you'll forgive my French.'

'Ah! And on Monday night, there aren't that many good places open where you can eat.'

'Frankly, I'm too knackered to care.'

'Well, we've a good pizza place open all week. They deliver, too, if you don't want to go out?'

Lauren thought about it for a moment, and decided that being spotted by some lecherous local in a tacky pizzeria was more than she could stand right now.

'Takeaway pizza is fine. Pepperoni. Sod the calories!'

And thus, Lauren dined alone on takeaway pizza in the empty breakfast room of a bed and breakfast in Cromer, with one last glass of white wine to wash it down. As she munched hungrily, she reflected that this time last year, she'd stayed at the Grosvenor Hotel in London and dined on lobster and champagne.

She dragged herself up to bed, contemplating the following day at the dance studio with the dreaded Isobel. She slept fitfully in a strange bed, with indigestion from the pizza and unforgiving aches in every joint. She woke up with a start convinced that Isobel was standing at the end of her bed, arms folded disapprovingly.

Dawn was a long time coming.

# 5.

## Tuesday

That morning, the hotels and bed and breakfasts swung into action all over town. It was a warm, sunny day, and with more good weather promised, bookings for Whitsun were picking up nicely.

But for Lauren, the disrupted night's sleep had only made things worse. She had gone round and round the whole situation in her head many times and, by early morning, she had decided that this job wasn't at all what she'd signed up for. She'd expected it to be a variety show where she had a self-contained set; not one where she had to sing and dance as part of an ensemble.

Better to leave now and let the Pier Theatre secure a new headliner for their season, she thought, rather than let them down later. She tried Mrs Wells, but her phone was obviously switched off and there was no option to leave a voicemail message.

Lauren bundled up her night clothes and makeup into her case. She was glad she hadn't properly unpacked. This was all a big mistake. She headed downstairs and explained to Elaine, who was surprised but said that she'd sort it out with the theatre later. Miss Evans was clearly upset, Elaine thought, and guests behaved erratically from time to time. Lauren went to the end of the terrace where a taxi was waiting. Elaine rang the theatre but it went straight to the answer phone. Then she rang Uncle Cyril.

Lauren sat on the outbound platform waiting for the next train. She sipped a strong black coffee from a cardboard cup. The words of Les Westley were still ringing in her ears.

*'I think you'd better make your mind up. If you want to go running back to Wales, fine. Trust me – I've had worse disasters. Now I suggest you take a walk and think about it.'*

She checked her watch. She looked at the magazine she had brought with her from Wales but couldn't concentrate. She'd never been treated this shoddily. Just who the bloody hell did he think he was talking to? He's just a washed up comic after all. He'd had his five minutes of fame years ago. Les bloody Westley? She'd never even heard of him. A total bloody nobody.

She took out her phone and rang her agent again. No response. Typical.

My bloody agent's no use either, she thought. Said he'd get back to me and he hasn't. Tosser. Happy to take my money when I did the arena tours, wasn't he? You really get to know who your friends are, and that's a fact.

She tidied her purse, and cleared some rubbish from her handbag to kill time. Then she took out her magazine and tried to concentrate.

It was not an attractive station. All vestiges of its heritage had disappeared, replaced by the utilitarian Network Rail look. There were a few pots with random shrubs strewn about the platform, attempting forlornly to lift the street scene. A couple of platforms and that was it. It was the end of the line. How appropriate, she thought.

She looked across at the small retail park opposite the station. An Argos store featured prominently alongside the usual suspects. She'd worked at Argos before her big break. Now it stood there, silently mocking her.

She fought back the tears, head down, sitting on the deserted station waiting for the train to take her back home. It was all over. Even the bench upon which she sat was the standard vandal proof design, reminding her of the one that awaited her in the job centre in Wales.

She became aware of a man walking nearby. He sat on the seat next to her, but at least at the opposite end of it. All she needed now was a pervert to deal with, she thought. She'd had one or two of those in the last couple of years. A couple of perverts and a stalker, she recalled. Don't look up.

He took out a newspaper and began reading, then looked across and spoke.

'Miss Evans, such a coincidence,' he said.

Lauren looked up, ready to blow this guy off. She wasn't in the mood. But she saw a friendly face.

'Oh, hello. Cyril, isn't it?' she said

'At your service, Madam,' he replied gallantly.

Lauren looked at her magazine, ignoring him.

Cyril paid no attention to the fact that he was being ignored. He quite expected it, and this girl was clearly highly strung at the best of times. Instead he continued to read his paper.

He paused for a minute or two and then read from his paper out loud, to nobody in particular.

'It says here that advanced tickets for the Summertime Special Show are selling fast. Someone's pulling them in this year. Bumper sales as Lauren Evans takes town by storm, it says.'

Lauren heard but stayed silent, briefly looking up from her magazine. Cyril continued to look at his paper as if nothing had happened. He waited another minute or so. He spoke once more, while continuing to read.

'You're their big chance, love,' he said.

'What?' snapped Lauren. She couldn't help but turn towards him.

Cyril looked across. His dark brown eyes were looking at her kindly.

'This town is struggling. The recession is deep and harsh. You can see that, surely?'

Lauren relaxed a little. 'Well, yes, I suppose I can. It's obvious really.'

Cyril resumed his paper reading.

'It was another lousy year last year. The weather was awful. The banks won't take it forever. We had two more hotels go into receivership over the winter.'

Lauren was thinking about where this was heading. Say nothing, she thought.

Cyril looked across at her, and spoke again. This time he was addressing her directly.

'You will bounce back, you know. The great talents always do.'

Lauren thought for a moment. It was as if someone had tossed a lighted match into her heart.

'How do you know? How could you possibly know?' she stared at him, clearly upset.

Cyril remained calm as he replied.

'Because I've been where you are now. A long time ago. You would only have been a little girl. You won't recognise me.'

Cyril folded his newspaper and got up. The announcer's voice declared that the arrival of the train to Norwich had been delayed by 10 minutes.

Cyril looked back at Lauren. She evaded his gaze, looking silently into space.

'Just think about it, Lauren. I suspect you need them where you are today, and they certainly need you. It's been a pleasure meeting you.'

He put his hand out and she shook it without comment. With that, he was gone.

A while later, Lauren watched as the train came in. Some people got off, obviously tourists. A little boy, no more than four at a guess, came running down the platform leaving his harassed mother struggling with the heavy case she was dragging from the train.

As the little boy rushed by, Lauren grabbed his hand.

'Hey, mister, that's no way to behave now, is it?' she chided.

The mother rushed forward, frantic at her child's antics but grateful to the stranger.

'Thank you so much. He does this all the time. I can't take my eyes off him for a moment,' she said, shaking her head as she caught up with her child.

'No problem,' said Lauren smiling. 'What's his name?'

'Luke. He's just turned two,' said the mother.

Lauren picked the little boy up kindly.

'You're a right little handful, aren't you, Luke? I have a cousin called Luke back in Wales,' she said.

Taking the boy from Lauren, the lady was about to move on, but paused. She smiled, but was slightly pensive. Lauren knew the signs.

'Excuse me for asking, but are you Lauren Evans?'

Lauren smiled.

'Bit of a giveaway the accent, isn't it?' she said.

'I voted for you. So did my mother and her friend. You should've won, we reckoned.'

Lauren had heard that comment a few times. She had her own thoughts on the voting that day of course, but would never share it with a stranger.

'That's life, I reckon. I had a great experience, even though I came second.'

'So what brings you to Cromer?'

Lauren had feared such a question. What was she doing in Cromer? It was a very good question. And she didn't have long to make a decision.

* * *

Miriam awoke. She had dozed peacefully for a while, pleasantly contented. She had nothing much to wake up for, despite it being mid-afternoon. She could hear the distant noise of the lawnmower. The gardener had resumed his duties.

She slipped out of the king-size bed. She was naked. Now where precisely were her knickers? At the bottom of the bed, no doubt. She fumbled and retrieved them. They were torn at one side.

'Bugger it,' she murmured to herself.

He needed to be more careful. These weren't your average Marks & Spencer sensible sort. She took out another pair, retrieved her bra, and collected the various other items of clothing that she had discarded rather hastily earlier.

As she looked across, she caught herself in the mirror. She was slightly flushed and her auburn-tinted hair was a total mess. Bugger it. She'd only had it done a couple of days before. But otherwise, she looked pretty good for her 50 plus years, or at least she thought so.

And, of course, that's what he'd said, too. Maybe he said that to all of his customers. Meldrum Garden Services. She called him Mellors, for obvious reasons. And she felt naughty. Actually, just naughty enough. Lady Chatterley? Well, not exactly.

She showered and dressed to become the prim and proper pillar of the community – her usual persona. Not the rather uninhibited woman she had been an hour earlier. He was just so good, she thought. He was late 30s at a guess, but he paid attention to detail. Important details. It was a better work out than she got at the health club.

She put on shorts and a strappy top, noting that she could now wear size 12 at a pinch, and that the new bra bought in Oxford Street rather flattered her. The swimming and gym sessions, coupled with a sensible diet, meant that she managed to look a little younger than her years. Stylish sunglasses hid the inevitable signs of aging around her eyes, and the expensive facials were worth it, she concluded.

She stood on the balcony and looked out. He was mowing the lawn into perfect lines, and she could see the sea in the distance. It was a gorgeous spring day. Very warm. She wondered where her husband was. Not that she really cared. He never came home for lunch in any event. And it's Monday afternoon, she realised, so he'll be playing golf. He was such a creature of routine. So predictable.

Gary Meldrum looked up from his mowing and waved. She waved back. It might be time this stopped. It had been going on for nearly a year after all. But he made no demands. No commitment. He just provided really good sex, and was anything but predictable in that department. He was a reliable gardener, too. So, why worry?

She came downstairs and made herself coffee. Flicking through a magazine, she then turned on the television. Various adverts tried to fund her funeral, reclaim her PPI, which, of course, she'd never taken out, or get her to save donkeys, snow leopards or the like. She turned over to the BBC but the news was still depressing. Exasperated, she snapped the television off, took out a trashy chick-lit novel and headed out onto the terrace.

*   *   *

Les Westley stood centre stage in his reserve stage costume. He had at last found rehearsal time for his new solo spot in the show, when it was finally quiet. He adopted his stage accent, developed during his time in the northern comedy clubs in his youth.

'Good evening, ladies and gentlemen, boys and girls. Welcome to Cromer Pier and the Summertime Special Show. My name is Les Westley and we've got a packed show for you this evening, starring the stunning and very beautiful TV star Lauren Evans!

Welcome to Cromer, gem of the Norfolk coast. Now, tell me, are we having a good holiday? Yes? Weather hot enough for you? I'll have you know that it were 'otter 'ere than Benidorm last week. Basking, we were! Oh yes... and they don't have fish and chips like we have here, do they? Or Norfolk Crabs, or proper English best bitter.

Eh... What do you mean, we don't have any night life? Have you not been to our latest night spot, The Pink Flamingo Show Bar? The only Flamingos you'll find around 'ere, let me tell you. Plenty of flipping seagulls, though. Bird poo everywhere. But somehow calling it the Incontinent Seagull Show Bar doesn't quite have the same ring to it does it?

And 'ave you been to the local bingo hall? We 'ave the world's first dyslexic bingo caller. Dyslexic Derek, they call him. Five and three, 35! He causes mayhem, he does. The only bingo hall where they have a steward's enquiry.

And we don't have a problem with those foreigners sticking their towels on our sunbeds like they do in Benidorm, do we? Oh, no! Mind you, we don't see many Germans in Cromer. Come to think of it, we don't see many sun beds either.

We have all sorts of entertainment here. Donkey rides, Punch and Judy... Have you met Gypsy Rose Lee, our resident fortune teller? Some kid tried to swipe her takings last week. Boy, did she tell him his fortune! Her case comes up on Tuesday. Grievous bodily 'arm. Got him by the crystal balls, she did. Very painful.

Mind you, it all 'appened 'ere this week, oh yes! We had to get the air sea rescue out an' all. Apparently a couple got washed out to sea on an airbed. Worse still, she wasn't his wife! Bet he'll have to LILO for a while! Lie low... get it? Oh, well, please yourselves.'

As he finished the punchline, he noticed Karen walking down the side aisle of the theatre. At this time of the season, she was normally found at the dance studio working with Isobel on the dance routines for the new show, so the fact that she wasn't spelt trouble.

'Something tells me you're not about to give me a belated Easter egg.'

'I'm afraid not.' Karen admitted.

'Lauren?'

'She hasn't turned up this morning. Gone AWOL, it seems.'

'Shit.'

'Yes, and there is more bad news.'

'Oh?'

'Melanie rang. She's pregnant.'

'What? Bugger it,' said Les. 'Hold on, didn't she know yesterday?'

'I gather not. Hard to believe, I know.'

'Oh well, you'd better ring Amy.'

'I already did. She's delighted.'

'Good. But what about Lauren?'

'Elaine says she checked out and headed for the station a couple of hours ago.'

'Is your mother around?'

'No. She's gone to London today,' Karen explained. 'I called her but her phone's switched off.'

'Brilliant!' Les said sarcastically. 'I'll ring Lauren's agent right away. I'll need to find his number.'

They headed up to the box office and into Janet's office. As Les hunted for the number, Karen looked at the leaflets her mother had been folding the night before. Each one showed a glossy, airbrushed picture of the great Lauren Evans. She didn't look quite so glamorous without her posh hairdo and stage makeup, mused Karen.

*   *   *

Lauren was plucking up the courage to return to the bed and breakfast. She had kissed Luke's mother on the cheek at the station, and posed for a selfie with her, having told her that she was in rehearsals for the Summertime Special Show at the Pier Theatre.

She went back to Bloomingdale's to apologise to Elaine, but instead encountered the landlady's mother. Peggy was 85 now, but still helped out at the bed and breakfast that still bore her name to allow her daughter to fit in another part-time job. In her time, running what were then holiday flats had been her full-time occupation, but things weren't like that anymore.

She met a rather reticent Lauren at the door and, upon seeing the young woman looking flustered, she had shown her through to the residents' lounge, empty at that time of day. She provided hot, sweet tea and they chatted for an hour or so as Lauren poured her heart out while shamelessly munching on chocolate biscuits.

What Peggy saw was an ordinary, vulnerable, late-30-something woman. This was not the starry-eyed, lip-glossed Lauren on the poster. This so-called international singing star with her posh clothes and glitzy hair was completely lost when it came down to it.

Peggy listened until Lauren had finished her story. She had some sympathy with the woman, but many people would have given anything to have had her opportunity in life, so Peggy wasn't about to mince her words.

'Well, I've heard the sob story, but what do you actually want?' she asked.

Lauren hesitated, not used to such directness.

'Well, I don't know really. I was terribly rude to them, and the dance session was a total disaster. I'm not a dancer. Fair play to me, I never said I was. I'm so far from home, too. I've missed Wales a lot, if I'm honest. I might just be better to jack it all in and go back to the clubs where I came from.'

Peggy nodded, although she rather doubted in her heart of hearts Lauren really wanted that. It would represent an end of the dream, and surely nobody who'd been where Lauren had would want that?

She went into the kitchen to replenish the tea, and to reflect. As she returned, she decided that she needed to stop this girl taking decisions that she might regret.

As she poured the tea, she looked at Lauren and smiled.

'Look, why not give yourself time to think things over? We haven't let your room yet. Stay over tonight and make a decision in the morning. I always think that it's much better to take some time to think things over rather than act in haste. What do you think?'

Lauren thought for a moment.

'I suppose so. I don't want to mess them around, though.'

'I've known Janet for a long time. She's very tough but also very fair. I'm sure that she would rather you give it proper thought if it helps you come to a rational decision.'

And that is what Lauren decided to do. She put on her oldest jeans and a strappy top, and walked for miles along the beach and coastal path. Peggy rang the theatre, and was put through to Karen.

'Aunt Peggy! Good to hear from you. Mum's away today so can I help?'

'Well, I hope so, Karen. I've got your star, Miss Evans, back in residence. It seems Cyril made her think again.'

'Cyril? Really? Oh, thank God. We were worried sick that she'd got back on the train to Wales.'

'Well, she may well still do that, but I've suggested that she stays over tonight and decides what she wants to do in the morning.'

'What's wrong do you think?'

Peggy thought for a moment.

'Pretty much everything and anything, I should imagine. She seems to be a very mixed up young woman who has had it all a bit too quickly.'

'Yes, I get that Peggy. Is there anything that we've done to upset her?'

'Well, I gather Les told her her fortune, which didn't make her like him very much, but was probably what she needed. Oh and she's scared stiff of dancing, from what I understand.'

'Really? Well, as you know, everyone dances in our show. It's a variety show, after all. What planet is she on?'

'Yes, but I don't think her agent made it clear what was expected of her, and she's in a strange town with no friends. I'm minded that she's behaving like a spoiled brat to be honest but there you are.'

'All right, Peggy. Thanks for talking her down for us. Why not suggest that she meets me for coffee at the Majestic

Hotel in the morning, say 11am, and I'll see if I can make a difference. I am the Dance Captain, after all.'

They agreed that getting Lauren to have a chat at a neutral venue with another cast member was the best chance of sorting things out, and the Majestic Hotel was the sparkly new place in town, even though it was owned by Lionel Pemrose.

Lauren returned in the early evening, and was pleased that Peggy had fixed for her to meet Karen to talk things through. Her long walk had cleared her head and the weather had lifted her mood. The beach reminded her of her childhood holidays in Tenby. She had an early dinner at a place Peggy recommended, owned by a friend who would ensure that she wasn't pestered. She returned for an early night and fell into an exhausted sleep.

# 6.

## Wednesday

The next morning, Lauren stole the bathroom once again, then went downstairs feeling refreshed and hungry. Sod the perpetual bloody diet, she thought, and decided on a full English breakfast. Elaine brought in her breakfast cheerfully but made no comment about the events of the previous day. It was none of her business. Guests were guests, after all.

Lauren had time to kill before the meeting, and wandered around the town this time.

She amused herself on the crazy golf, unrecognised by the tourists, but decided against the helter-skelter, which reminded her of her childhood holidays in Tenby. She sat on a bench looking out over the pier and its Pavilion Theatre. A plate lovingly dedicated it to Mr Brian James Robson, apparently a gentleman who loved early morning cliff-top walks. She could understand that, looking out to sea. Walking to the pier front, Lauren noticed that the banners were being put up declaring to the world that international singing star Lauren Evans was coming to the Summertime Special Show. She had never quite got used to seeing her name in lights or on billboards, but knew that she liked it.

She met Karen outside the Majestic Hotel at exactly 11am.

'Hi, Lauren.' Karen said, smiling. 'It's a lovely morning – shall we take a walk along the promenade instead?'

Lauren was rather taken aback. Karen behaved as if nothing had happened. They walked to a sandwich shop for a coffee and sat on a bench overlooking the sea as they drank their cappuccinos. It was apparent that everybody knew Karen, and Karen cheerfully greeted so many people as they strolled along. Karen made small talk with Lauren at first, breaking the ice.

'So, how are things? Feeling any better about stuff?' Karen asked finally.

'I just feel like a fish out of water, to be honest,' said Lauren.

Karen nodded and smiled.

'Look, it must be really difficult for you. You're such a long way from home.'

'Takes a bit of getting used to, and that's a fact. I'm sure Mrs Bloomingdale and her daughter must think I'm a right stuck up bitch.'

'Oh, that's no problem. Peggy and Elaine are friends as well as doing business with us. I even call her Auntie Peggy for no good reason. We've put a lot of our people there over the years. It's not posh, but she looks after everyone for us early on while they get used to things. Then they tend to find digs in the town.'

'I wasn't very nice to you, come to that. Sorry.'

'Don't worry about it. It wasn't the biggest wobbly I've seen in my life. It's a bit of a come down this, after what you've done. We do realise that. I overreacted. Things are a bit tough right now.'

'But you meant it, didn't you? About the pay cut?'

'Yes. But I should never have mentioned it. Mum had to cut costs after we made the loss last year. But never mind. If the weather stays like this, we should have a good season. How's Bloomingdale's? I know it's only a bed and breakfast but…'

'Peggy's absolutely lovely! Nothing's too much trouble. She said I can use their bathroom any time I want. I always feel better for a good soak. I'll need it after those bloody dance routines. They're doing my laundry, too.'

'Oh, good. They got used to our needs and habits a long time ago. Business hasn't been good for them either. They need the money.'

'Huh! Don't we all?'

Lauren sipped her coffee slowly, before continuing.

'Peggy was telling me her husband was coxswain of the lifeboat before he retired.'

'That's right,' said Karen.

'My cousin Tim's on the Tenby lifeboat. Gives us something in common, I guess. She told me about her cousin, the trawler man. Tragic that.'

'Yes, it was. Gosh, yes… the things you forget. I was very young then. He drowned off Yarmouth in a storm. I remember the funeral. I sang in the choir at the service. An awful, awful day.'

'Tim's had his share, too. Brave people, those fishermen. Lecherous too, mind. I got a few chat up lines from the guys on the beach this morning when I went for a walk.'

'I imagine you did! I'll bet they weren't after your autograph either.'

'Trust me, I've had worse in the clubs.'

'Haven't we all? Well, I did when I was younger.'

'It's a sweet little town though, isn't it? I went up the church tower this morning. It's a stunning view when the sun's shining. The rector was really nice. People are so friendly.'

'So you met Paul Bishop? His father baptised me in that church.'

'Really?'

'Yes, the Wells family goes back a couple of hundred years in this town. Mum did the family history.'

'I did mine recently – well, sort of – for that show on TV. They found we were just miners and steelworkers. They weren't interested after that, of course.'

They continued in silence. A few families were out on the beach. An ice cream van pulled up ready for a good day's business. The tide was coming in and the town was coming to life.

'One or two locals recognised me in town. I gave them my autograph and I might have flogged them some tickets.'

'Good for you. We need all the sales we can get. You're a real draw, you know, if you're staying on, that is?'

Lauren paused and looked across.

'Will Les have me back? He was bloody furious with me.'

Karen laughed.

'Have you back? Are you serious?'

'Well, I don't know. I know many people who wouldn't.'

'I think we need to understand each other first. We are

a variety show, which means that, however bad we are as dancers, we need to grasp the basic moves as an ensemble. I gather your agent didn't explain that?'

'Well, no, not really. All I've ever done is sing, you see. In the concerts, I had a backing band or a choir, so they did the moves. I just moved around the stage.'

'I gather you don't like dancing much?'

'It terrifies me, if I'm honest! They took the piss out of me at school about it. Two left feet and that's a fact. If I'm singing, I'm singing. I don't like the distraction.'

'Right. Well, Isobel was showing you the basic moves, so we need you to absorb them to do your bit.'

'But I was bloody useless, right?'

With that, Karen's phone rang. She moved to switch it off, but then saw who was calling. Isobel.

'Excuse me, Lauren, it's Isobel. I need to take this.'

Lauren listened as Karen's day got worse.

'So, she's OK? Nothing broken I hope?'

Karen winced upon hearing the reply.

'Broken? Her ankle? Are they sure?'

Karen shook her head and looked at Lauren.

She ended the call with a pained expression. Lauren feared the worst.

'You're down another dancer?' she said.

'Yes. Kathy this time. Fell off her mountain bike. Bust her ankle, poor girl. We've only just drafted Amy in to replace Mel. These things happen in a show like ours. Better now than later, I suppose.'

She pondered what they would do, but then realised that Lauren was a much more important matter.

'I'm sorry about that interruption. Let's get back to you. We want you to stay – that much is certain. We can move you from the bed and breakfast to a flat if you prefer it, and we'll do what we can to simplify the dance moves. But you have to take on board that we are a variety show so you're going to have to go through the mill a bit and learn the dance steps. I'll help you personally all I can, as will Isobel, but we can't compromise on everything, I'm afraid.'

Lauren nodded. It was as much as she could ask for in the circumstances, and she had signed a contract after all.

'Look, Elaine and Peggy have been very kind and have gone out of their way to make me comfortable, so if it's all right with you, I'll stay there. Let's see how it goes.'

'And the dancing?'

'Well it's a worry, that's for sure. I'm just worrying about messing up in a performance for everyone.'

'You'll need to train extra hard. Look, why not give it two full days of rehearsals and then we can both take stock? We'll explore the market in the meantime to see who could replace you, which won't be easy, but hopefully with a few days to acclimatise, you'll feel better about things.'

'Thank you, Karen. That seems very fair. I'll start this afternoon. No time like the present!'

They walked back to the theatre. As they entered, Les was sitting on the stage reading. He looked up as they came in.

'Hi, Les. Look what the cat's dragged in,' said Karen.

Les smiled.

'Hi, Lauren. Wait, I'll come down.'

They sat in the front row together. Karen decided to make herself scarce.

'I'll leave you to it, Lauren. See you at one o'clock at the studio. In the meantime, Lech wants me to help him with his act.'

'Good luck with that!' said Les.

'Well, he actually seems to be struggling with your sense of humour, Les.'

'I don't follow you, Karen. Where he's concerned, I don't have any sense of humour.'

'He keeps pestering me. To use his words, he wants to have the audience 'eating his hands'. Something that you said, I think?'

'Eating out of the palm of my hand is what I said. You might remind him that he's supposedly a magician.'

'Yes, but I gather you told him that he was a total comedian?'

'I suppose I might have. I was being sarcastic.'

'There lies our problem. He seems to have taken it literally. He wants to become the top Polish comedian in England. Lech Wojiek Live At The Apollo!'

Les closed his eyes.

'Give me strength. That man is becoming a bloody nightmare.'

Karen smiled and headed off backstage.

Les decided to take the initiative.

'I was rather abrupt the other day.'

'I guess I deserved it,' Lauren replied.

'I should have shown more compassion. You'd only just arrived.'

'It wasn't that. I'm scared stiff.'

'What?'

'I'm scared. I can't do this.'

'Why ever not? You sing wonderfully.'

'I know that but I can't do anything else. Most of these guys can do it all. Sing, dance, act a bit—'

Les laughed.

'They don't have a choice, Lauren. They have to in a show like ours. I guess we take it for granted.'

'But I haven't done anything else. I just go on and sing. Whack out a set, natter with the audience a bit, job done. Those dance moves Isobel went through first thing scared the crap out of me, but the rest of them knew what she wanted straight away.'

Les laughed. He suddenly realised that he'd been a bit stage struck by Lauren. He'd not made anything clear.

'Well, you don't have to do the complex bits, but you'll need to do some of the simple moves that Isobel showed you. The professional dancers do the full routine behind you. Nothing complicated, I do assure you.'

'Karen explained that now. I'd thought you wanted me to dance properly. I've never learned a step, if I'm honest.'

'You're a singer, Lauren, and a bloody good one. We need to get the best out of our headliner, if you're staying on, that is? Have you made up your mind?'

She looked at him squarely.

'I'm staying on if you'll have me. I've been a first-class bitch, but you've all made me so welcome. I won't let you down again. Promise.'

Les was more relieved than he cared to show. He'd been awake half the night worrying that his big star had got the next train home, but she was just a bit homesick and worried about a little dance routine.

'Well, that is good news. I know that Janet will be delighted. I know this is difficult – the place, the show. It's a bit run down, I'll admit. A bit of a come down for you.'

'Well it seems only yesterday that I sang the National Anthem at the Millennium Stadium. But you people have shown faith in me when others wouldn't. A deal is a deal.'

'I'm not going to say that isn't a huge weight off my shoulders.'

'Karen made me so welcome just now, treated me like one of the family. It's been a while since I felt I belonged anywhere, to be honest.'

Les nodded. He knew the feeling.

# 7.

## What Could Possibly Go Wrong?

Several days later, things were beginning to come together, or so it seemed to Janet Wells. At around 11am, Les entered Janet's office at the theatre. The word 'office' made it sound posher than the reality. It had barely enough space for a desk and, given Janet's slightly cluttered modus operandi, it seemed smaller still. He found her folding leaflets. Karen was sitting opposite Janet, munching her late morning cereal. Les addressed Karen.

'Good morning, Karen, or is it afternoon yet? I'm here to discuss the drunken dancer that your dear mother sent us this morning.'

Karen smiled. Her mother hadn't long arrived, and she hadn't yet had a chance to advise her that Les was on the warpath. Janet recognised the body language.

Les glared at her and leant forward to emphasise his frustration.

'Where have you been? I've been looking for you everywhere. Didn't you take your phone?'

Janet was immediately embarrassed.

'I'm sorry, Les. I had a meeting first thing, then I went out delivering leaflets to the hotels, it's probably in my handbag.'

'I'll bet you haven't charged it either,' said Karen.

'I'm sorry, darling. I should have stayed with that old Nokia I had rather than letting you buy me that Blueberry thing.'

'Blackberry, mother. Look, I meant to tell you. We've had a problem this morning. Angela De Gray.'

'Ah, yes. She got in last night. She started this morning then?'

'Sort of. She was a little worse for the gin.'

Janet looked up from her task, a concerned look on her face as the problem became clear.

'Oh, no. I'm so sorry, Les,' said Janet.

Les was not so easily placated.

'You know she has a reputation for the drink. What were you thinking of?'

'I know she does, but her agent insisted she had dried out.'

Karen laughed.

'Let's just say that she might have been dry at one time, but the tide came in this morning.'

Janet winced.

'Are you really mad, Les?'

'No, Janet. I'm bloody furious. Why didn't you discuss it with me first?'

'Well, we needed someone quickly as I recall, and I rather think she's the most capable dancer available at short notice. She knows how we work, so it seemed an obvious solution.'

Les leaned forward, placing both hands on the desk.

'First, you give me an incompetent Polish magician, then a homesick Welsh singer with delusions of grandeur, and now a faded, drunken soap star who talks about nothing but her past TV career. She brought her cat Tinkerbelle, too... who promptly peed everywhere.'

'Look, Les... I can explain.'

'So can I, Janet. She was cheap.'

'Well, if you remember, we discussed it and you agreed...'

'What? I did no such thing. I said it was very risky, as I recall.'

'She's got a decent singing voice, and she's still a good dancer. She's been back on TV recently.'

'When she's sober that may be so. However, when she tried to show me the dance she did on Strictly Come Dancing recently, she fell head first into the front row.'

'Is she OK?'

'Alas, yes, a bruised ego but nothing more. Her burgeoning backside cushioned her fall, no doubt. Sadly, Tinkerbelle did a runner.'

'And, of course, she's distraught?'

'Of course. She threw an enormous hissy fit and demanded that I find the little shit immediately. Now she's in the ladies dressing room sobbing her heart out. It will, of course, be all my fault.'

Janet rose from her chair and hugged Les by way of apology, then kissed him on the cheek. Karen laughed. She'd seen this so many times with her mother and Les.

'Come on, Les. Let's go and sort it out,' said Janet.

They left Karen laughing at the bickering couple's behaviour. There would be many more arguments before the opening

night, then a roller coaster of problems bigger than the Great
Yarmouth Big Dipper before another season was done.

\*   \*   \*

Janet returned to her office just after lunch. She noticed a
letter on her desk. The envelope boasted the bank logo and
a special delivery stamp. She had a very bad feeling about it.

She had been in discussions about the renewal of the
facility since October, but the bank kept referring to central
directions on bank exposure, whatever that meant. In the end,
the cash flow projections won her a six-month extension, but
she had been unable to pin them down further. As the clock
ticked down, she had explained how the summer show was
put together, and the up-front costs involved. The manager
had been sympathetic, but reiterated the banking platitudes.

Becoming ever more concerned, Janet had approached
other lenders on the quiet, but received the same response.
There was simply no appetite for new business. The managers
involved only seemed to care whether they would have a job
next week.

She had been to London, but it was the same story. She
wanted to tell Les and Karen, but feared that uncertainty
would scare off the talent. No talent meant no show.

She hadn't been able to sleep, and she needed sleep more
than anything. She resorted to her GP, who was sympathetic.

'I've had quite a few appointments from people in your
line of work,' the doctor had said. 'We can try the sleeping

tablets, but you know what the only solution to your problem is, and I don't have medication that will provide it.'

Karen knew her mother had not been sleeping. They had talked about it. Karen could see her mother visibly ageing, but Janet was an impenetrable wall when she wanted to be.

There it was. The letter. It was special delivery even though the branch was only a couple of hundred yards away. She finally took out the letter opener – an antique one inherited from her father. It was monogrammed with his initials, which were fading from continuous use.

'Oh my God,' Janet said.

The door into the box office was open, and Betty Allwood looked up in surprise.

'A letter from the bank?' said Betty, entering swiftly and closing the door.

Janet read it aloud, paraphrasing as she spoke.

'Following a review of your banking facilities, the bank is unable… requires additional security… I regret that… oh my–'

Betty took the letter from her and read it.

'Not good news with this season's rent due within days,' Betty said.

Janet looked up.

'Lionel Pemrose and his cronies, I suspect,' Janet speculated.

'Looks like it. But you said the overdraft was OK. They had the accounts?'

Janet nodded.

'Yes. The numbers for last year weren't great, but they seemed to be going with it. But now we get this.'

Betty shrugged.

'You'll have to talk to them, Janet. I doubt that Mr Pemrose will wait for his money.'

'I'm absolutely sure he won't. He's been trying to get hold of the theatre since he bought the freehold of the rest of the pier.'

Betty left and Janet called the bank. The manager was in a meeting, of course, and would ring her back as soon as possible. Janet tried to get an urgent appointment, but was advised that the manager had back-to-back meetings for the rest of the week, and was then on leave. Janet just about maintained her civility.

She put the phone down and leant her head back, closing her eyes for a moment to gather her thoughts. She'd worked with Betty on refining the projections, and although the figures were tighter than the previous year, things had seemed fine. She'd considered moving banks previously, but the Wells family had done business with the local branch for such a long time, and things had usually gone very smoothly.

When the Cedars Hotel went bust in November, she had been stunned. The family had owned it for years, but the rising tide of maintenance costs in such an old building had taken its toll. And, of course, the Cromer Pier Theatre Company had no freehold property.

Janet reflected that even her own house was mortgaged as far as she dared to risk it. Local gossip implied that the Wells family must be well to do, but both Janet and Karen needed the salary from the theatre.

When her father died, there were debts. Gambling debts.

He bet on horses mainly. The house in Burnham Overy Staithe, where Karen was born, had been the first to go, but re-mortgaging the family house in Cromer had been a necessity.

Then there was the long, slow decline in the holiday trade. Janet had taken that salary cut to keep the business above water. Now she wondered why she had bothered.

*   *   *

Lionel Pemrose left his red Jaguar in the hotel car park, and strolled down to the pier. He wore a cream-coloured jacket and a striped, short-sleeved shirt. In his lapel, he had a red carnation, plucked as usual from the display in the hotel foyer. It was his trademark. He had his Cromer Rotary Club lapel badge on, too. Lionel was a man who liked to be recognised. He was short and rather plump. His thinning hair betrayed that he was older than he cared to admit. He passed the time of day with both local people that he knew and tourists who he didn't. He'd never quite lost his London twang, which gave him the aura of a barrow boy.

He stooped to pick up an ice cream wrapper lost by a careless child, and put it in the bin. He noted that the paint-work in one of the original Victorian shelters was flaked and showed the tell-tale signs of rust. He made a mental note.

He had met Miriam when he was appointed as a regional manager to a national chain of bingo halls and amusement arcades along the east coast. Her dad ran one of his competitors. Years later, Lionel and Miriam owned the lot, but Cromer was his favourite place, and he and Miriam had built a house with a lovely sea view just outside the town.

As prime spots became available, Lionel bought them up. He had come to know the tourist trade well, and knew how to do a deal. When the pier ran out of money, he just had to buy it. The jewel in the crown of his adopted home. The refurbishment had cost a fortune, and to his frustration, he had come to realise that the Pier Theatre Company had what his lawyers had told him was an unbreakable lease arrangement. Others were reluctant to take on the investment, but Lionel convinced Miriam in the end.

Lionel was also convinced that, one day, the theatre would be his, too. He had learned to be patient. Everything comes to he who waits, especially if you can give fate a helping hand from time to time.

He smiled as a little boy ran towards him, with a mother frantically chasing behind.

'Whoa, young fella,' he cried, grabbing the child and swinging him aloft.

He handed the child back and smiled at the grateful parent as he did so. He'd have loved to have had children, but they couldn't. It was him, not Miriam. He'd come to terms with it. But just occasionally, moments like this happened, and brought a tinge of regret.

He reached into his pocket and handed the child's mother a discount voucher for the new Pemrose Ice Cream Parlour, and then he handed one over to the child, too.

'Buy mummy an ice cream,' he said to the bemused little boy.

He shook the mother's hand and smiled.

'Have a great holiday,' he said.

Most people encountering Lionel for the first time found him affable, personable and charming. He appeared to be a happy-go-lucky wide boy. A lovable rogue, if you will. Del boy meets Arthur Daley. But his persona hid a much darker, more calculating side.

Lionel continued to the end of his pier-based empire. Having checked that all was well, he retraced his steps, then reached enemy territory. The Pier Theatre box office.

He entered through the small box office, empty at this time. Ignoring the bell made available to prospective customers, he entered the inner office where Janet Wells sat, the bank letter in front of her, brow creased, deep in thought.

'Knock, knock. Landlord calling.'

Janet was jerked back into reality, the letter sliding from the desk onto the floor as she did so.

Lionel absentmindedly picked up the letter.

'A very good day to you, my dear,' Lionel continued. 'How is the new show coming along?'

Janet wasn't in the mood. Lionel was in the habit of show-ing up unannounced and poking his nose into her business as if he owned the place. Technically, as landlord, he did. She tried to retrieve the letter, but Lionel stepped to one side, ignoring her.

'Do you have business here, Mr Pemrose?' she said tartly.

'Why yes, my dear. Landlord's inspection. Always like to make sure my tenants are OK.'

'Make an appointment, Lionel. And give my letter back, please.'

Lionel feigned surprise. He'd seen the letterhead, and scanned the limited content as he handed the letter back to her.

'Oh. Oh, dear. The bank regrets… oh dearie me.'

Janet snatched the letter back. She was furious, but decided to let him play out his little game. Lionel was clever, but one day, he'd discover that he wasn't the smartest tool in the box.

He sat without invitation, further infuriating Janet as she sat, too, apparently impassive but quietly simmering.

'I'd like to help,' he continued again, 'but my own cash flow is very tight. Things are very difficult for all of us.'

Janet stared at him. She allowed the silence to continue. Let's see where this goes, she thought.

Lionel pondered, leaning back, arms behind his head, apparently deep in thought. Then, as if he had suddenly seen a great vision of the future, he continued further.

'Unless, of course… a partnership between us? Bingo on five nights, theatre shows on twice a week, with a matinee. Some real acts! Not the deadbeats you have now. Bit of investment, lick of paint–'

Janet laughed. She'd heard this all before.

'You're not serious. Now if you'll excuse me?'

She stood and showed Lionel the door. Lionel stood, taking the hint and smiling at her. He put his arm around her shoulder, as if in support.

'Why not think about it, Janet? Talented lady like you shouldn't be on your own. I could look after you.'

'Wouldn't Miriam have a problem with you looking after me?'

Lionel looked deep into her eyes.

'Oh, Miriam and I have been married for 30 years. We have a certain understanding. She has her charity works…'

'While you shag around?'

'I'll let that comment pass. I just think you and I, well, we'd make a great team. I could look after Karen, too. A talented girl, your Karen. Talented singer, great dancer and still very beautiful. With my management and financial resources, who knows?'

Janet smiled defiantly, pulling away.

'I struggle to find the words – ah, yes – get lost, Mr Pemrose. This is my show, my friends and my theatre.'

Lionel's grin disappeared.

'Only for a few more days, Mrs Wells. Either the licence fee is paid or it reverts to being my theatre. Think about it. In spite of your little emotional outburst, I am a reasonable man. When you've got that head of yours straight, why not give me a call?'

She followed him out of the door. He picked up a leaflet advertising the show.

'The theatre will make a nice little bingo hall. I'll show myself around to check on things, if that's OK? You'll have a lot on your plate, no doubt. Good afternoon, Mrs Wells.'

With that, he walked out through the box office and into the sunlight.

\*   \*   \*

Paul Warren was standing on the pier next to the theatre. It was the late afternoon of what was probably the worst day of his life. He'd changed out of his tracksuit at the bed and breakfast having arrived with very little in the way of clothing; just an overnight bag he kept in the car through force of habit, his briefcase, and laptop. He'd bought a few essentials when he arrived, but his knees still felt like jelly. He wanted to rewrite the last few hours and pretend they hadn't happened. He was still in shock. When he awoke that morning, things were normal, and by late afternoon, his world had more or less collapsed. He was still struggling with the new reality.

When it happened, all he could think of was that he needed to go far away. Go as far away as was possible. He found himself heading down the motorway. Then he had a thought: Cromer. Why? Why not? He might as well. As good as anywhere to disappear to for a while.

Cromer had been the family holiday destination. Every factory holiday fortnight every bloody year. It's what they did. It was here, or Skegness or Weston-Super-Mare. What a choice. They stayed at the same place every year, too. Mrs Bloomingdale's. He checked in there for old time's sake. It hadn't changed much since the 70s, although it was now a bed and breakfast. The painted Anaglypta wallpaper was still on the walls. They'd also managed to wedge an en-suite into the corner of the bedroom. It was certainly an imaginative

use of space. You had to laugh. He decided that the only way
to use the loo was to reverse in.

What on earth was he doing here? He sat down on one
of the benches as he pondered.

He was just feeling sorry for himself, he supposed.
Wallowing in nostalgia for times when life wasn't complicated. Family holidays of fish and chips, footy on the beach
and amusement arcades. Big copper pennies clunking into
the old one-armed bandits. Flashing lights, the bingo caller
in the background, the smell of greasy hot dogs, and the rock
with Cromer running through it.

As his mind drifted, he looked at a patch of sand some
distance away. The old breakwater where it had happened
was still there, he noted. Way back in the 60s. He became
oblivious to the world as his mind retold events of happier
times long ago.

*I remember a warm early evening, and a game of beach football
in full swing. It pitted my brothers – Tom and Mike – against
Dad, me and my friend, Ian. It must have been the first year
that I had been allowed to play – except in goal, of course. I was
probably seven or eight. Tom and Mike, being older, didn't like
playing with the little brother and his mate, but Dad insisted,
and his word was law. Four other kids were playing. I don't
remember their names – they just appeared, the way they do
on holiday.*

*Dad was a good player. At another time, he might have
played professionally, but too much beer and too many cigarettes*

*didn't help his cause. Anyway, this was a time when my elder brothers discovered that I could play a bit as well. I don't remember the real score, but Dad had called it level and, as I said, his word was law.*

*The ball was out wide, with Dad. Tom went to tackle him. A typical Tom tackle, in football as in life. Just dive in. No messing around. But Dad nipped past him on the outside. He looked up and crossed. I was in the middle. The ball went over the head of Mike, and dropped ahead of me. I couldn't head the ball then – some say I still can't – but I knew that I just had to do this. I threw myself full length as the ball dropped. I felt a bump on the top of my head as I made contact, eyes closed. I saw stars and took a mouthful of sand as I hit the ground. I heard a whooping cheer, and felt myself being lifted from the sand. My dad whirled me around his shoulders, a broad grin on his face.*

*'GOAAAAAAL!' he cried. Tom and Mike looked aghast. They'd been beaten by the little brother for once.*

*Time plays tricks on the memory, but I remember Cromer for those warm summer days, yet I know that there were countless times when a raw east wind ripped across the beach, making any pretence at sunbathing ridiculous. Somehow though, it didn't matter. As a growing child, what mattered was eating fish and chips and playing football, or cricket, or doing those countless other things that a beach and an imagination can create.*

*I don't really know why it was Cromer every year. There are hundreds of alternatives on offer. I know that Mum came to hate the place, but Dad wanted to go, and Mum put up with it. I suspect that Dad never actually realised how much Mum wanted to go somewhere else. It's funny how you can live with someone for years and still not fully understand them.*

*We stayed in the same flat every year, overlooking the pier. Mrs Bloomingdale's Holiday Flatlets. Red flock wallpaper, polished oak staircase, hot water of variable temperature from scalding to lukewarm, antique gas cooker, and exactly six of everything in the kitchen – no two items of the same brand. Oh, and the electricity meter that required the endless supply of shillings.*

*The front bedroom had a stunning view of the sea, and the kitchen a not so stunning view of the bingo hall. Two bedrooms. Mum and Dad had the bedroom with the sea view, and we had the other one, without a view at all. A set of bunk beds and a single bed with an iron frame filled the room.*

*We didn't cook much. I seem to remember it was fish and chips most days, except Sunday, of course. On Sunday, it was the café in the High Street for Sunday lunch. It seems funny, looking back, that the only apparent difference between the roast beef, pork or chicken was the colour. It was all thinly machine-sliced and tasted of virtually nothing. Still, the spotted dick and custard (all in the price, along with the pot of tea) made up for the mediocrity of the offering.*

He came back to the present. Both of his parents were dead now. They pretty much smoked themselves to death on 20 Woodbine cigarettes a day each. But he could feel the ghosts of them on the beach here. He wasn't sure what Mum would say about what had happened. Well, maybe he was. She'd never liked his wife Carol. Not good enough for her youngest son.

What was he going to do? Doubtless, people would want to speak to him. He just needed a day or two to think. Give it a few days and the whole thing would be yesterday's news. Seven missed calls on his mobile. But he didn't want to talk to her or to anybody else for that matter. Not yet. He needed time.

He sat there for a long time, then went to a fish and chip shop, and returned to the pier to eat. He had a beer at the pub, but when his face appeared on Sky Sports, he left swiftly. It was getting dark by the time he headed back. Not that there was much on the TV. Mind you, if it's still only terrestrial and two of the channels don't work, it limits the choice a bit, he'd thought. But tomorrow would be another day. Each day will get better, he told himself, even if he didn't see a future right now.

# 8.

## The Bank Regrets...

It was misty that morning but the sun was apparently going to break through later. Janet Wells entered the bank, her mood as gloomy as the weather. A traditional bank building of brick and marble of which Captain Mainwaring would doubtless have approved. She had bullied the customer relationship advisor into obtaining her an urgent appointment with Mr Hodson.

Peter Hodson had not been keen on a meeting ahead of his holiday, but didn't wish to appear unreasonable. He shook her hand as she entered.

'Good of you to drop by, Mrs Wells. How may I help you today?' he said, immediately aware that his standard opening to a client meeting sounded rather ludicrous in this case.

'I think you know how you can help me, Mr Hodson. You could start by telling me that your letter was a bank error definitely not in my favour.'

Hodson sought to recover from his rather crass opening. His hands steepled in contemplation, he then spread them wide as a gesture of sympathy.

'Alas, I'm afraid not, Mrs Wells. You see, Head Office has instructed us to reduce our exposure to the entertainment sector, and with the tighter conditions for bank lending, and the state of your balance sheet, I'm afraid the bank has no choice. Very regrettable, I'm sure.'

'But we are at the start of the season. The only way is up from here. Surely you must be able to do something? My family has had this facility for years.'

Hodson knew that there was nothing that he actually wanted to discuss. His mind was made up, and the conversation needed to be kept focussed and uncluttered.

'I'm acting under a direct Head Office instruction. The bank is simply seeking to reduce its exposure. I'm really sorry but there is nothing I can do. You will recall that the Cedars went under only a few months ago. A sign of the times, I'm afraid.'

'But can't you appeal? Can't I get the area manager to review the position?'

'I could, but sadly we're between area managers at present, and we're in the middle of a restructuring. I won't know if I've got a job myself for the next few weeks.'

'By which time, you will have shut my business down and handed it over to Lionel Pemrose.'

Hodson looked up. He became suddenly terse and formal.

'I'm not sure I follow you.'

Janet knew from his reaction that she was right in her assessment. The two men were linked and she was wasting her time.

Hodson decided to placate. He trotted out his de-escalation line that he'd learned on his customer relations course.

'Look, Mrs Wells, I can assure you that I've tried to remodel the figures to get Head Office to go on with supporting your business, but I'm afraid there is nothing more I can do. I did go out on a limb to get the extension over the winter, you may recall. I would point out that you lost money last year, and it's not the first time. I know it's a bitter blow for you, but that has to be our position. Of course, if you could provide additional security that would be a different matter.'

Janet knew that this was disingenuous, too. The bank had a charge over her house already. There was nothing more that she could put on the table.

She left with nothing and walked the short distance towards the pier. She paused to look out over the Pier Theatre. Her second home for so long. What could she do? How would she break it to Karen and to the rest of the cast? The weight of the world was on her shoulders, and she suddenly felt her age.

She did a few errands, dropping leaflets into hotel receptions, but gave up halfway round. She couldn't help but think that it was pointless in view of the situation. She went home and hit the telephone. Surely somebody would take on one of the oldest businesses in town?

\*   \*   \*

Peter Hodson took a call from Lionel Pemrose an hour later.

'Lionel? Good to hear from you. Mrs Wells left me a while ago. She was rather upset as you'll imagine. Says she's going to take her business elsewhere. I don't think any of my competitors will take a different view in the current climate. I spoke to most of them at your golf day last week. A wonderful gathering, by the way.'

'Glad you enjoyed it, Peter. Thanks for the warning. It'll give me time to develop a rescue plan. I can't let the iconic Pier Theatre go under. Let me give it some thought, and we'll speak when you're back from Malaga. I'll get Lizzie to get something in the diary.'

Hodson laughed.

'Ah, yes. That new PA of yours is a bit special, isn't she? Can she type as well?'

'Indeed, she can. Enjoy Malaga.'

'Thanks, Lionel, will do. It's so nice of you to lend me your place.'

Lionel put down the phone contentedly. His plan was coming together nicely.

*     *     *

Janet had a way of muddling through. She would often ponder over a matter for days, weighing up the pros and cons. She wasn't given to overreacting to anything, so it was completely in character for her to hold onto this bombshell. As it was, Karen had been out that evening, and her mother had been in bed by the time she'd returned.

As Janet reflected on how to break the news, she came to realise that she had always been her daughter's insulation from reality. As an only child born to a single parent, Karen was so precious. Janet might deny that she had spoiled Karen, but would probably concede that she had been there to protect her when things went wrong, which sadly, for Karen, they often did. Such a big talent wasted. She should have been a big star and yet she was now tangled inexorably with the woes of her mother.

But Karen had to be told, and was now sitting opposite her in the office at the theatre, shell-shocked by the news. The full implications of the letter she was holding were slowly sinking in.

Since returning from her meeting with the bank, Janet had made further phone calls to each of the local branches of the major banks once more. As a locally respected business woman, she knew a number of the managers, and each took her call. They expressed continuing sympathy, but the story seemed curiously familiar; they were not taking on new exposure to the tourism sector. The consistency was too consistent. She sensed a stitch up but had no proof.

Karen spoke having carefully read and reread the letter.

'But it's impossible! Surely someone will help us? We've been a part of this town for so long. There must be some way?'

'That's why I didn't tell you. I thought I could sort it without worrying you further. It's no use, Karen. I've been to every local branch manager, but none of them looks likely to help. And even if they did, we couldn't get the facility turned around in time. I tried the town council and the chamber of commerce, too. Lots of sympathy but nobody will help us.'

'Why? How come?'

'Well, it's the recession, or so they all say. But at a guess, Pemrose has some of them in his pocket. The banking crisis has made them all risk averse. Duck and cover is the order of the day.'

'Surely there are other banks? Ones that are not in town?'

'I've tried London. No go. They just weren't interested. Not at this time. Not ever, really. They had the full financial projections, the business plan, everything. They all said no.'

'If you hadn't bailed me out when I left London, you could have put the house up as security.'

'Don't dig that up again. Your grandfather gambled and dodged tax for years, and when the tax man caught up with him, we had to re-mortgage the place anyway. Your bit meant nothing in the grand scheme of things.'

'But what will you do? I can earn a crust somewhere. You've never known anything else.'

'I don't know. Get a job, I guess. Not much demand for theatre managers, though. Perhaps I'll accept Lionel's offer. At least that will keep some jobs going, including yours.'

'Over my dead body! I don't want to work for that oily creep.'

Janet leaned forward and put her hand on top of Karen's.

'We've got to be realistic, Karen. I'm not saying I want to. My God, I don't, but I don't have any options right now, and it's not only about you and me. There's the rest of the cast to think about.'

Karen looked across and shrugged.

'I suppose so. It's just that, well, I never expected the show to end. I thought of this as my job for life, as well as yours.'

'I know. I still felt I could sort things until that letter arrived.

The fat lady wasn't singing, but she was certainly warming up. I should have known. In denial, I guess.'

There was silence as they each had their thoughts. Karen smiled thinly.

'I remember singing on the stage out there when I was 14. Do you remember?'

'Of course! It seems like only yesterday.'

Karen put her head back and started singing.

'Somewhere, over the rainbow, way up high.'

'There's a land that I longed for, once in a lullaby,' sang Janet, joining in.

They had the natural harmony of mother and daughter. They sang it through to the end, drawing comfort from the age-old melody.

Les Westley entered as the song concluded, applauding as he did so.

'Bravo, ladies. If you're interested in an audition, please make an appointment,' he said.

Janet smiled. She would have to tell Les first. She owed it to him.

Karen decided to make herself scarce.

\*   \*   \*

Les stared at the letter. It was a death sentence. He was stunned and yet, why should he be? They'd had so many years of bucking the trend, watching the other end-of-the-pier shows disappear one by one, until Cromer was alone. Like the sea washing away the cliffs along the coast, the end-of-the-pier shows had been eroding and sinking slowly away.

But they'd been different. They had the quality. They had the star quality without some of the big salaries to go with it. They could spot the up-and-comers, or the ones who were damaged on the inside, but would still show their quality under the lights where it mattered. Like father like daughter, Janet was as tough as nails in getting deals done. Until this.

The bank had had enough and pulled the plug. He couldn't really fault the decision, in honesty. The recession was the final straw for them. The day of reckoning was here. Les was nothing if not pragmatic. Nothing lasts forever. But suddenly, the years had flown by. He was no longer the new kid on the block comic with the rubber-faced smile who had charmed the ladies and graced the Royal Variety Show. He was a fat, middle-aged comic who was becoming a comedy caricature before his very eyes.

Janet was sitting opposite him with her head back in her chair. Eyes closed. There was silence except for the sound of seagulls and the waves breaking some distance away.

'You need to take Lionel's offer, Janet. It's the only offer you'll get. He owns the freehold, so the licence will expire and he can do as he pleases.'

Janet stayed silent. Les was philosophical.

'Janet, I don't doubt that Lionel stitched you up, but the bank's position is logical in the times we're living in. I expect that Lionel just joined up the dots. He's wanted this place for years.'

Janet was thinking. He was right, of course. She'd been through all of the emotions. Lionel was a vindictive shit who had hated her father. The licence arrangement was watertight according to the lawyers, unless they defaulted on payment.

'If I sign up with Lionel, I'll be betraying you, Les. You know you're finished after what happened.'

'Yep. But better that than see the show die entirely. You need to look after yourself now. And Karen and the staff as far as you can. I'm just a hired gun.'

'Without you, we'd have closed years ago. If you hadn't stepped up when Dad passed away, I wouldn't have had a clue.'

Les weighed up her words and shrugged.

'You're doing yourself down as usual, Janet. I got paid, didn't I? It's a job at the end of the day. A job I love, for sure – despite the drunken dancers and Polish magicians – but a job nonetheless. I'll get another job. Do what's best for you and your family.'

'Thanks, Les. As you say, as much as I hate it, I will have to take Lionel's offer. But I'm going to insist that this season goes ahead, and whatever building works he wants can only take place in the winter. That way, at least we keep our reputation intact, and you have time to sort things out.'

'Do you think he'll accept that? I don't see why he would?'

'Because he cares about his reputation, and when he gets the Pier Theatre, I'll be in the photograph shaking hands on our new partnership while trying not to throw up. He cares about how things look, does our Lionel.'

'So he'd rather have a willing partner than a forced marriage?'

Janet grimaced at the analogy.

'If you think I'm sleeping with that bastard, you can forget it, Les. Miriam Pemrose and his numerous mistresses can have that dubious honour. No, I'll play a little hard to get. I reckon he'll give me a few weeks' grace on the licence while we sort things out.'

'So you buy yourself time. Makes sense to me. And in the meantime?'

'You say nothing to the cast. They don't need to know, provided I can get Lionel to agree that the show goes on.'

# 9.

## Good Times

The sunlight peeked through the curtains into the room and the solitary male figure blinked at the bright light slanting across his face. As he awoke, he felt the pain across his forehead and the sudden realisation in his gut that the awful events of yesterday were not a dream, but a grim reality.

Using the bathroom, he surveyed the rudimentary plumbing arrangements. He showered sleepily and felt better for it. His hangover was diminishing a little. He saw the half empty whisky bottle on the dressing table. Had he really drunk that much, he asked himself, ruefully. He looked at the bottle with disgust.

Throwing open the curtains, the brilliant sunshine blazed in. The pier stood below him, proudly advertising its wares. Flags fluttered from the towers at its entrance. The town was a picture-perfect sight, which, on any other morning, would have lifted his spirits, but not this morning.

For he was Paul Warren – an out-of-work football manager, and he must begin to face the reality of his situation. His world was now turned upside down, and all that he had worked for had been reduced to ashes, as of yesterday. He switched on his mobile phone. More missed calls. Not yet, he thought. He needed more time to think. He switched the phone off, as if in doing so he could switch off the reality.

He looked at the clock. It was 9:50am. He was up late, nearly missing breakfast. He went downstairs and ordered a full English, gingerly reading through the papers. There it was. Just a small clip in the sports section in two of the tabloids. A few days from now, it would be out of the press – at least for a while.

It could have been worse, he thought. He calmed down a little. He talked to himself as he often did. Take your time. Don't make rash moves. As mother used to say, things would be as they would be.

The breakfast room was empty now, as the other guests set out to make the most of the sunshine. The waitress came, so he ordered another pot of tea and sat looking out of the window to the seafront below.

She came back with his tea and smiled. He recognised that smile. A family trait.

'You must be a Bloomingdale then?' he said.

'Yes, well, sort of. I'm Chrissie,' she said.

'I was last here in the 70s. I was about your age. Thinking about it, I only knew the landlady as Mrs Bloomingdale,' he said.

'Ah, that would be my Grandma Peggy. She's retired now. Mum runs the place now. But it's still Bloomingdale's.'

'It's not changed all that much. The view's still just as nice.'

'It's not so nice in mid-winter,' she said, ruefully.

'Do you work here permanently?'

'No, I do a few shifts to help out. I'm doing a college course in hotel management.'

'Oh, that's quite exciting. You fancy taking on the family business then?'

'Something a bit bigger than a bed and breakfast I think, but we'll see.'

'Perhaps you ought to seek out this chap Pemrose? He seems to be the big cheese around here these days.'

'The less said about him the better,' she said, a dark look on her face.

She wished him a nice day and headed back into the kitchen.

Warren looked out again onto the beach below. A child was building a sandcastle far below. It reminded him – way back to his childhood – of a childhood romance, and his first love. Where was she now, he wondered?

He allowed his mind to drift once again.

*It must have been in the early 60s when I first met her. I remember that she was stark naked at the time, as was I. Although it wasn't quite as rude as it sounds, since we were only around five years old.*

*I was happily building an enormous dam to control the flow of water down the beach. I liked building dams, although what nasty bacteria lurked in the water I was paddling in I now dread to think. What I liked even more was engaging in simulated dam-buster raids, arms spread, aeroplane-like, with two enormous stones in each hand as simulated bombs.*

*I was preparing for my first bomb run, when I spotted this girl entering the line of fire, so to speak. I didn't really understand these girl creatures at the time, and recent events might suggest I still don't, but there she was, bold as brass, decorating my dam with flags and seashells. I watched incredulously as my dam then sprouted two perfectly round towers, each bedecked with a flag of St George.*

*Having watched this for a few minutes, I'd had enough. I commenced my attack, complete with simulated engine noise. I leapt over the little girl who was apparently unaware of the impending attack. I released the devices over the target, and noted with satisfaction that one tower was completely destroyed and the flags submerged.*

*Now you might expect that the little girl would burst into tears and run off to Mummy. But she was different. She ran across the sand to where I was standing triumphantly. She pushed me over, and proceeded to jump on top of me, her little fists whirling in fury. Tom pulled her off, and I was hauled from the sand by Mum, who spanked my wet bottom. I went off and both cried and sulked. The injustice of it! It was my dam, she interfered and I got the blame. Oh, well. I suppose it's a bit late to go to the European Court of Human Rights on that one.*

Warren smiled at his recollection. For so long, he had had no time to reflect on things. He was far too busy with the hustle and bustle of his career. But now, well, time wasn't an immediate problem. He didn't take time off very often. Doubtless that was one of Carol's more legitimate grievances.

He stood and put the papers in the rack. Let's walk off the full English, he thought.

He spent the day wallowing in nostalgia. He needed space and kept his phone switched off as an act of defiance on his part. He had no desire to contact his old life, which was so troublesome. That could wait, he decided.

He entered the Parish Church – the church where she had sung that morning so many years ago. She was 16 or thereabouts at the time. He'd made an excuse to his parents to leave the beach. He didn't want them to know. He was in love with this girl, but didn't need the teasing questions that parents always asked at his age.

He had only gone to the rehearsal that day. He didn't ordinarily go to church, so explaining a prolonged absence on the Sunday morning to his parents wasn't on. But he'd promised to go to her rehearsal the day before instead. His mind drifted back.

*She'd worn a bright yellow top and wide-flared, green trousers. She sang 'Amazing Grace' and 'For Those in Peril on the Sea'. It was for some seafaring gathering or something. I can't recall.*

*She'd smiled as I'd entered the church, and then she waved at me. I remember my stomach churning and my hormones racing out of control as I watched her, church or no church. Three renditions later, the vicar was satisfied, and she walked to the back pew where I was sitting.*

*The Reverend Donald Bishop. That was it. That was the*

*man's name. My memory has dug out the name from deep in its archives. Donald Bishop. A great name for a vicar.*

*The vicar had waved to me as he headed for the vestry and out of sight. It might have been a coincidence but the vicar was probably obligingly making himself scarce. I had stood up at the end of this very pew as she approached me that day.*

*'Glad you could make it,' she had said, smiling broadly.*

*I took both of her hands in my hands, and she had pressed her lips against mine. She tasted of peppermint. I recall the scent of perfume. We kissed again. Longer this time.*

Back in the present, Warren now found himself standing at the very spot where it had happened. He found himself wondering. What if things had been different? Where was she now? Probably far away from here, he thought.

He explored the rest of the church. It was beautiful. He realised that he had never really appreciated such things. His life had been football, and little else.

His eyes were drawn to a board in a side aisle. The names etched carefully for posterity. There it was. Donald Bishop, vicar of this parish from 1971 to 1978.

*She'd climbed the tower ahead of me. I remember it quite well now. Breathless, we finally reached the top and she showed me the local landmarks visible from the tower. The pier below us, stunning views towards East Runton to the west, and Overstrand to the east. Then, aware that we were alone, we had kissed once again, more deeply this time.*

*I'd reached under her top, undoing a button to gain access.
She chided me.*

   *'Not in church, Paul.'*

His mind came back to the present once more, and he re-emerged into the bright sunlight. After an enjoyable couple of hours, he went back to the bed and breakfast. He was perversely enjoying his freedom, but that awful feeling of impending doom would not leave him. It was simply a case of reality postponed.

He retrieved his training bag from the car, and changed into his training gear. He was still pretty fit, despite hitting the big five-zero last year. He could still play in a practice match, provided he was careful with his knee. The knee that had cost him his playing career all those years before. Nowadays, doing in a cruciate ligament was not career-ending, but it had been for him. He'd had surgery a couple of years ago, but it was all too late now.

A casual observer would have seen a middle-aged man of average height, but rather muscular and stocky. Hair short and cropped, torso bearing a slight beer gut. He looked athletic in spite of his years, and could pass for a night club bouncer.

He set out on a long run, initially along the seafront, then down onto the beach. There was still a good number of holiday-makers enjoying the sunshine, and the tide was out. He ran to East Runton, stopping at the local pub for a mid-afternoon pint.

They'd come here together, he remembered. They'd ridden there on their bikes. Two young people enjoying each other's company, away from the prying eyes of their parents. The boats on the beach seemed as if they were the same ones as all those years ago. In fact, they were. They'd just had a few more coats of bright red paint to preserve them from the march of time.

He ran back along the same route, but the sand was taking its toll on his ageing limbs. Eventually, he found himself walking past the beach huts, newly painted for the summer. His family had one every year, he remembered.

He found the hut they'd rented the last time they visited, although in reality, he suspected that the actual structure had probably been replaced.

At the time, he'd wondered if she would be there the next summer. She was a local, so he thought she would at least be in town. They'd both grown up, though. It had been a whole year, after all, so she might have got a boyfriend now. They weren't an item at all. It just seemed that each year, she was there, on that beach, a year older each time. And she was rather more attractive to an adolescent boy each year, too.

In honesty, he had more affinity with her brother, Ian, who used to like to join in the games the family played, be it football or beach cricket. Ian was a bit of a loner, but then so was he, when he came to think of it.

Anyway, they'd been playing football on the beach, as a family, and she was sunbathing nearby. She was wearing a bright yellow, one-piece costume, he recalled. He'd kicked a ball in her direction, just to get a better view.

He was still a bit tongue-tied, unsure of what to say.

She'd picked up the ball and held it tightly to her chest.

'Now, Paul, I think the words you're looking for are 'Can I have my ball back please?" she said, mischievously.

He said nothing, but she laughed and threw the ball back to him. He smiled and turned away. She followed.

'Whose side am I on?' she said playfully, getting up and pulling a top on over her swimsuit.

He shrugged his shoulders, so she joined in anyway.

A while later, his brother tackled him. As he stumbled, she grabbed him around the waist, dragging him down. Then she'd stolen the ball and made a run for the beach hut.

She'd tried to shut the door in his face as he chased her, but he was too strong. He'd fallen on top of her as the door opened. She lay underneath him, fresh-faced, gorgeous and laughing. He looked at her intently, and she looked back.

'Well?' she said.

He kissed her. More like snogged her, really. There wasn't much technique, just that rearing of adolescent lust. She was neither reciprocating the kiss nor objecting to it.

'Oh, I see,' she said, as Warren pulled away after a few moments. A serene smile appeared across her sun-freckled face. She lay back impassively, as if awaiting his next move.

He had retrieved the ball, and the game had resumed. She said nothing and he certainly didn't know what to say. They'd parted with a rather chaste hug when the holiday came to an end.

'See you next year,' she said.

There had been other girls back home, but nothing seri-ous. He was at a boys-only comprehensive school, which was football mad. It was his obsession, and in a nearly all-male household, the only feminine influence was his mother. It was thus inevitable that he found himself wondering if the girl would still be there the following year, and if so, would she recall their special moment?

As he looked at that very beach hut now, he laughed at the memory. His football career had taken him to many exotic destinations, and he and Carol had visited some far flung parts of the world. But now he was back, in sunny Cromer, wondering as to the whereabouts of his first love.

The following year, he was 17, and his parents were surprised that he didn't quit out on the annual holiday, as his older brothers had. If they suspected anything, they didn't let on. He wanted to go in case his first love was there again that following year. Mrs Bloomingdale was very kind. She waited until they were heading out that first morning, and slipped him a note without his parents noticing.

He promised his parents ice creams a while later, and slipped away to read the note.

*Dear Paul,*

*I heard you were coming again this year. I'll be finished at the theatre by two o'clock each day, if you want to meet up. I promise I won't steal your football this year.*

*Hope to see you.*

*Bremner xx*

Bremner. His favourite player. His pet name for her after she'd hauled him over during that game of beach football last summer. As in 'Who do you think you are? Billy Bremner?'

He made an excuse to his mother. She gave him the knowing glance, but said nothing. His father was asleep in the deckchair. He arrived at the theatre just before two o'clock.

She came out through the front door of the theatre, dressed in a black T-shirt and trousers.

He called over to her, and she turned.

She came over to him, smiling. She looked older, and simply gorgeous. He was taller than her now, he noted.

'Well now, Bremner,' he said.

# 10.

## Playing For Time

It was the oldest hotel in Cromer. The original hotel was built in 1830 and rebuilt in 1893. A symmetrical structure built of reddish stone, with original, white-painted iron guttering, and a roof capped with verdigris turrets.

Her decision to invite Lionel to meet there was deliberate. For this was one of the few iconic buildings in Cromer not controlled by Lionel Pemrose. As she walked up the slope to the Hotel De Paris, she began to think that her gesture of defiance was more than a little pathetic.

This was surrender after all. She'd had a meeting with her solicitor that afternoon, a favour from an old friend. They talked through her plan, but somehow, as she pitched it, the words sounded unconvincing. Why should Lionel give her an extension? The theatre company wasn't anything much, really. He had no sentimentality where the show was concerned. He could simply lock the doors and do as he pleased.

She had talked it over with her solicitor and, although between them they came up with the best line of attack, it would require more chutzpah than she thought she possessed to pull it off. The two ladies hugged each other as they parted.

The friend being the friend even though, as her solicitor, she thought the plan had a rather slim chance of success.

Janet entered the foyer and found the small meeting room set aside for the purpose. She poured a cup of tea and sat down. She was 15 minutes early, allowing her a few moments to gather her thoughts and set out her stall as the home team. She had certain documents drafted by the lawyer. An extension to the licence, a memorandum of understanding, which wasn't worth the paper it was written on, and a non-disclosure agreement.

Secrecy in this matter was vital. If the cast came to hear that the business was in trouble, it was probably game over. They were too far in for major cast changes, and what she hadn't told Les or Karen was that the costs of the show thus far incurred would leave the organisation insolvent if the show didn't go on. Her personal guarantees to the bank would trigger, leaving both her and Karen jobless and potentially homeless.

She thought about her father. He'd secured the licence on the theatre in this very hotel. When the pier came up for sale, he could have bought the freehold, but was too scared of the risk. It looked a wise decision when the purchaser went bust some years later.

When a much younger Lionel bought the pier for a song from the receivers, he thought he could break the lease on the theatre, but her father knew better. Since that time, Lionel had regretted his naivety, and was determined to own the iconic theatre one day. Now with her father long gone, Lionel would at last achieve his goal.

But Lionel had an ego. So the key was to feed the ego. Get him to be magnanimous in victory. Get him to play the pillar of the community, a crown that he had fashioned for himself, even though he was actually an outsider.

Lionel sprinted up the steps two at a time, and waved cheerily as he passed reception, not bothering to stop. He knocked on the door of the conference room, and entered without waiting.

Janet stood and shook his hand.

'Lionel. Glad you could make it. Do take a seat. Can I get you a coffee? Black without sugar, isn't it?' She said cheerily, rather embarrassed at her fake bonhomie.

'Oh, yes. Thanks, Janet. Many thanks.'

She was more cheerful than he expected. He sat and took out a lined A4 pad, with his trademark Mont Blanc pen.

She set his coffee down on the crisp, white tablecloth, then sat down herself. She sipped her tea, repositioned her papers one more time, then smiled a little nervously and began.

'Now, Lionel. I've obviously been giving a lot of thought to your proposal, and although I have a number of refinancing options to consider, I recognise that there has been bad blood between the Pemrose and Wells families going back to when you acquired the pier, and this is an opportunity to reconcile those differences.'

Lionel sat back. He tried to look inscrutable, but he was a poor poker player and Janet sensed she'd got the initiative.

'So I'm minded to take your proposition to the next stage and see if a partnership could work. You've added value to the town already and you've brought in substantial, much-needed investment—'

Lionel shrugged affably

'I do try, Janet. It's not always easy. Some of the locals, well, let's say they're slow to move things forward, to move with the times.'

'And I recognise that without having control of the theatre, you're not about to invest in what is the jewel in the crown of our town.'

'Well, exactly. My sentiments precisely.'

'It stands to reason. So obviously, if we formed a joint venture, investment could be forthcoming to create a state of the art facility at the end of the pier, befitting its status.'

'Go on.'

'I do accept that as little as bingo appeals to me personally, there is a demand, and therefore, bringing those two businesses together – the theatre and the bingo – could work. It uses the asset much better, after all.'

'Yes.'

'So I think we should move to a planning stage. It's going to need careful planning, and that will need some time.'

'Of course.'

'And we're in the middle of a show, with unbreakable legal commitments to artistes and contractors—'

'So?'

'… I need an extension on the licence, just until we're up and running for the season.'

'No.'

Janet looked across at Lionel, who was smiling benignly. This wasn't going to be easy.

'Look, you're buying into a business for no money. The reputation of the show is why it is the only surviving show of its kind. We have a nationally known headliner this year and people are flooding into our seaside town because of the recession. It's the year of the staycation. They're flooding into your hotels and my – soon to be our – theatre.'

Lionel was sceptical.

'Our bookings are up, for sure. But I'd rather shut the theatre now so we get a good run at the refurbishment. Then reopen with a fanfare next year.'

Janet shook her head.

'A refurbishment for which you have no detailed plans? Just some architect's sketches? On what is a listed building? That will take months to sort out with the planners.'

Lionel sat back. He was enjoying the fight. It was cat and mouse, and she was the mouse. She continued, retaining a measured tone to counter the nausea-like worry welling up inside her.

'And the partnership agreement will take time to sort out as well.'

She paused briefly, before going on.

'Look, Lionel, I'm just protecting the brand. Give me a two-month extension on the licence, which I can happily pay. That gets me through to opening night, after which you know we'll make money across the season. In that time, we can sort the partnership out and close at the end of the season when all the contracts wash out.'

Lionel looked up.

'Including that of Mr Westley?'

Janet returned his gaze. Beneath his benign façade, the steely and vindictive Lionel was bared at last.

'Mr Westley's contract is up at the end of the season and will not be renewed. It's time for a change. I will tell him when we mutually decide that the timing is right. Probably in September.'

Lionel nodded.

'I see. I'm glad to see you're receptive to change.'

'I always have been, Lionel. It's just that not owning the theatre outright has made it difficult. We have a first-class product in the theatre and you can leverage the investment. A partnership makes eminent sense.'

'Good. Yes.'

'And that is why we need to agree a limited lease extension. We need to get things right. We can't afford for our family feud to get in the way moving forward. We need to be completely clear and transparent. I need to understand my role in the new business, and there's a lot of detail to agree.'

Lionel was thinking. Maybe, just maybe, she thought.

'I've had my lawyers draw up a couple of documents. This one is the lease extension, and this is the memorandum of understanding, which outlines our discussions to date.'

She handed the papers over. Lionel leafed through them, putting on his reading glasses. The church bell rang in the distance as they sat in silence. She poured another cup of tea for herself and replenished Lionel's coffee. Her hand was shaking a little as she did so.

Janet tried to keep from fidgeting as Lionel read the papers for several minutes, and then set them down.

'So if I agree to the extension, what's in it for me?'

Janet feigned surprise.

'Well, of course, you get two months' rent.'

'And? It also gives you time to cut another deal with someone else. And don't say you won't. Anybody would.'

Janet laughed.

'Whatever. What do you need Lionel?'

'An exclusivity agreement preventing you from selling the business to anybody else for, shall we say, 12 months?'

'And if I agree, I get a two-month extension?'

Lionel smiled and leaned forward.

'No. Just until the day before opening night. Not that I don't trust you, but, well…'

She sat back, considering the next move, but decided that it would be the best she would get.

'OK, Lionel. It's a deal.'

They shook hands and discussed next steps, agreeing to sign the documents within the next day or so. Lionel returned to being cuddly Lionel once more. As they parted, Lionel seemed poised to hug her, but she deftly avoided it. Instead, a warm handshake was exchanged.

When he was gone, she sat down, shaking with a release of the tension. She could just about live with herself. She had delivered Les as the sacrificial lamb, knowing that it would give Lionel the additional prize he wanted. An old score settled. She rang her lawyer who agreed to tweak the papers and get them across first thing in the morning. Her lawyer knew Lionel's solicitor so, all being well, they could get things signed by tomorrow night. She knew that Lionel could change his mind in the meantime but, for all his faults, Lionel tended to follow through on agreements he made.

Lionel returned home to Miriam, but she had gone out for the day. Meldrum the gardener was mowing the lawns ahead of the expected showers later. A good man, thought Lionel. He was always punctual and reliable.

He decided to change his clothes and was surprised to find the bed unmade. He poured himself a chilled white wine in celebration. He wouldn't bother to tell Miriam of his triumph as yet. The subject of the pier was sensitive. Best not tell her until we've done the deal, he thought. There was nothing for Miriam to worry about, after all.

\*   \*   \*

Janet returned home to Karen, who looked up as soon as she came through the door to the sitting room.

'How did it go?' she asked.

'Make some tea while I get changed and I'll go through things. It's been a very long day.'

Janet changed into jeans and a polo shirt, by which time a pot of tea was awaiting her downstairs.

'Have you eaten anything?' said Karen.

'What? No. I'll get something in a while. I saw the solicitor today, and then I saw Lionel.'

'Lionel? You didn't say you were going to see Lionel! Whatever for?'

'To agree to enter into a partnership with him.'

'My God.'

'Yes.'

Janet sat, and sipped some tea. She looked up and shrugged.

'Look, love, I'm out of options. I've no chance whatsoever of finding the money for the licence and the company is all but insolvent without the overdraft. So I decided to play for time.'

'Oh. Well I guess…'

'No, let me tell you the plan. Then you can comment.'

Janet outlined the deal. She had protected their home and their jobs, for the time being at least, and the show would proceed so the cast wouldn't be let down. She would use the licence extension period to see if she could find ways of taking the business forward, although in reality that was most unlikely. She explained how the partnership would work, and how the new building would possibly look. She showed her the architect's drawings that Lionel had previously given her of the remodelled theatre. Karen was unimpressed.

'Pemrose Wells Theatre? What happened to Cromer Pier Theatre? The arrogant tosser.'

Janet smiled. Sometimes she wished Karen had the bigger picture in mind.

'Don't worry. The theatre is a listed building and there's no way they are going to agree to that redevelopment. It's too big for a start.'

'It looks like a bingo hall.'

'Because that's pretty much what it is. But take the wretched bingo paraphernalia out and it's a theatre four days a week, with dressing rooms far better than anything we have now.'

'That's something, I suppose, but the show won't work financially on that basis. The costs will be far too high without the current number of performances.

'Yes, I know that, but Lionel doesn't, as yet. Although it won't be long before he does the sums. He's not dumb, our Lionel.'

'Then what's the point, Mum?'

'It gives us time to think, and with the takings from this season, we should get out without the bank taking the house away. Then who knows?'

\* \* \*

It was evening and still surprisingly warm. Les had a couple of fishing rods cast from the end of the pier. He whistled 'Stranger on the Shore' as he fiddled with his rods. He sat down, and began singing quietly to himself.

'La mere, beyond the sea… she's there, waiting for me…'

He was unaware of a presence behind him until he heard her distinctive Welsh voice.

'I know things are tight, Les, but catching your own dinner?'

Les turned to see Lauren stood in her running gear. She'd obviously been out a while judging by the beads of sweat. She was a naturally big girl, and running was one method in controlling her weight. She would never be skinny, but all the more attractive for that, he decided.

'Oh, hi, Lauren. Here, take a seat.'

'My dad used to fish. River Taff. Good fishing down there. I used to go with him when I was younger.'

She sat, took a swig of water from her water bottle and wiped her face with a towel.

'See much of him?' said Les.

'No, not since… never mind. Beautiful this place, when the sun shines.'

'It is. You're out late.'

'Yep. Sod all to do so I decided that I need to get fit! I've got to get some brownie points with my dance tutor and I've a total bastard of a director to manage, and that's a fact.'

Les laughed as he checked the line. She smiled.

'I could get to like this place, you know.'

Les was suddenly reminded of his predicament. He was trying to forget about things, or at least come to terms with it, hence his evening fishing trip. Her comment made things worse somehow. Would the show go ahead at all? They could all be unemployed within a week. He wasn't convinced that Janet had any chance of persuading Lionel to extend the licence. He'd been after this prize for years, and now it would fall in his lap. The default on the licence would give him the theatre. He could just let Janet go bust, shut the theatre and do with it as he pleased. He didn't need the show at all.

He fleetingly wondered if he should he tell Lauren. She seemed to have so much to lose. But his loyalty to Janet was such that even though he didn't think she had a chance, he must give her time.

Best change the subject, he decided.

'Yes, it grows on you, and actually I've had some great summers here.'

'And you started here as a comic rather than as director?'

'Yes. I was here on a rebound. I needed to get away, make a fresh start. I've stayed ever since.'

'How did you become the director?'

'Janet's father died suddenly. He'd been the owner and director for years, and Janet was in a real fix. Karen was in the West End.'

'So what happened?'

'Well they were in a fix, and I'd seen how the show came together so I said I'd see it through to production, and I've been doing it ever since.'

'It's not an easy job, is it? When you've got people like me to deal with?'

Les laughed.

'No, it isn't at times, I'll admit. But I've had some fantastic seasons. Janet and Karen are lovely people and this is a great place to live, particularly on days like this. I've come to love it. It can be so peaceful. Then we have the hustle and bustle of the summer. I like it in winter, too. I come down here when it's blowing a gale and the huge waves roll in. It's a lot different to now.'

They sat a while in silence, enjoying the sound of the sea and the gulls. One or two people were still around, but it was getting late and dark. A brief gust of wind rattled the ropes on the flagpole from which a frayed Union Jack fluttered.

'As a child, we'd go down to the Gower,' Lauren said. 'Lovely beaches by there. I loved my bucket and spade, me.'

'As a kid, who needs anything more?' Les replied. 'There are too many computer games these days.'

He adjusted the lines, and generally tidied up.

'You're a good guy, though, as a comic, I mean. I remember you on the telly some years back.'

'Oh yes… I was up and coming, a new star in the making at that time.'

'So what happened?' Lauren asked.

Les was silent. It was as if he hadn't heard her. Lauren corrected herself.

'Sorry, Les… I didn't mean to pry.'

Les thought for a moment then turned to make eye contact.

'It was booze, Lauren. Other stuff, too, but mainly the booze. I'm an alcoholic. I got the job here as I tried to dry myself out. My agent knew Mr Wells. He gave me the space to sort myself out.'

Lauren laughed.

'That sounds familiar. I need space to sort myself out.'

'Yes, I suppose it does. But my wounds were entirely self-inflicted. Whereas yours…'

Lauren fidgeted with her water bottle. She looked out to sea as she spoke.

'So we've both stuffed up a bit, haven't we?'

'I guess. That's why I got so ratty about Angela De Gray.'

'Well, I've not had much to do with her but by reputation…'

'And in denial, too. I've seen it all before several times.'

'What will you do? You'll have to sack her, I suppose, if it's affecting the show.'

'I'll try not to. I'll get her to seek help. Janet knew, of course, but she's very loyal. Too loyal sometimes.'

'I saw Angela dance, though. She's dead good.'

'Yep. Nothing wrong there. That's the tragedy. She's a talented performer if she stays off the booze. Still believes in herself. Actually, quite often I think that success is as much about self-belief as talent, and persistence, of course. Sometimes you've just got to tough it out and work hard.'

'Yes, and you need luck. I've been a nothing most of my life, then suddenly I'm everything I wanted to be. Whatever it is that I'm having to do now, I wouldn't turn the clock back for a minute.'

'I wouldn't think that way. Stop looking back. Look forward. You are one very talented lady.'

'Thanks, Les. You're good for a girl's confidence.'

Les smiled. One of the lines twitched suddenly, breaking the moment. Les looked at Lauren and nodded.

'Looks like you just got lucky! Reel him in then.'

Lauren laughed.

'What me?'

Lauren grabbed the rod and tried to wind the reel in. She stumbled over the tackle box, but Les caught her, arms either side of her. There was a moment where both of them were wondering what might happen next. The line went limp and broke the moment.

# 11.

## Everlasting Love

Paul Warren spent the next few days visiting more old haunts. Surprisingly, little had changed. He couldn't really work out why he'd never revisited Cromer since he was 17. Then, as he recalled the events following his last visit, his mood darkened.

*My last contact with Bremner had been from a phone box. I'd been to Germany on a football tournament for several weeks. It had been my first trip abroad, and I was as wrapped up in my new career as I had been with my first girlfriend. She understood. Football was a precarious career, and I had to knuckle down and work hard.*

*We were trying to work out how we might meet up. We both had careers, and I'd made a surprise first team debut only weeks later, following an injury to two first team regulars. She'd been so excited, but hadn't been able to get over to see me play. She had her own life and commitments. I returned to the reserves a few games later. I'd done more than OK, though. One for the future, the local paper said.*

*While in Germany, me and the team had gone out on the*

*town, and amongst the alcoholic haze, I remember several girls and a seedy hotel with two of my team mates. I'm not proud. Sometimes things just happened.*

*When I got back home, I remember calling her number. Her father answered.*

*'She's not home, Mr Warren,' he had said, tersely.*

*'Well, could you let me know when it would be best for me to call her? We don't have a phone at home yet, you see.' I remember explaining.*

*There was a pause.*

*'I rather doubt I'd bother, Mr Warren. She's moved on. She's really not interested.'*

*The phone was put down. I felt puzzled. We'd been so close only weeks previously. I tried again the following day but, again, her father answered.*

*'I've told you, Warren, you're wasting your time. Please don't bother us again.'*

*The phone was put down. I wrote several letters, but they came back marked: return to sender.*

*I decided I'd go down to visit, but my mother advised against it. I clearly remember her words.*

*'Paul, it was just a holiday romance, at the end of the day. She's a lovely girl but she's clearly moved on. I know it hurts, but you'll get over it.'*

And to be honest, he had. He may have been shy, but being a footballer, he was a magnet for girls, and by the next season, he was in the first team. Cromer was forgotten as he headed for the Costa Blanca with some of his team mates, and then he went on a pre-season tour with his club.

But as he sat in the café of the Pier Theatre that day, he couldn't help but reflect on the matter once more. Looking back at what had happened, it made no more sense to him now than it did then. He thought about asking about her at the box office, but then thought it daft. She was probably long gone by now, and what was to be gained? He had enough problems as it was.

His phone was full of voicemails and text messages. They were mostly from Carol, although there were a few from his brother, Tom. He deleted those straight away. Tom always played the head of the family since his parents had died. He was a senior manager in a big six accountancy firm. He always referred to it as a proper job, unlike Paul's job in football. As far as Paul was concerned, he was a patronising bastard with a snob of a wife to match.

Paul Warren never forgot his roots. He was socialist and proud of it, unlike his calculating Tory shit of a brother.

He did open the last text message from Carol though. He'd have to face the music sometime, he knew.

'Paul, we need to talk. Please get in touch. The police want to speak to you but I'm sure we can sort things out. I miss you. Carol xx'

Miss you? Kiss kiss? Really, he thought. Bollocks to that. He deleted it and dared to pick up the tabloid paper left by a previous customer. He leafed through from the front first, but gave up after the first few pages. Then he looked at the back page, and moved a page further in.

There it was. He read it carefully, what there was of it. He put it down. His position suddenly felt so precarious. Wanted by the police, with no job, no wife and no prospects. His nostalgia trip down memory lane suddenly seemed silly and irrelevant.

He left the paper on the table, finished his coffee and headed out into the sunshine.

He spent the afternoon puzzling through the options. He had one piece of good news. He checked his personal email account on his laptop and the legal agreement was there, all agreed by his solicitor. A simple phone call and a signature and it was all sorted. At least the bastard had been good to his word, he thought. He'd agreed to pay up his contract in full without any hassle. It was conscience money. It was the least he could do mind, having sold him down the river. It was just as well he'd signed a new long-term contract before the start of the season when, of course, he could do no wrong.

He thought about going abroad for a while. It was unlikely that the police were watching the airports. His wasn't exactly a capital crime, when all was said and done. Money wasn't a problem. He could just leave Carol with all the sorting out to do. It wasn't his fault, any of this.

He wandered onto the pier and came across Cyril's Punch and Judy Show, watched by a dozen or so youngsters and their parents. It had been more than 30 years since he'd seen that show. The last time, he was with his new girlfriend as she had become, and he remembered them singing Gary Puckett's 'Young Girl' as they walked down the pier at the end of the show. They sang the chorus together as they walked and laughed arm in arm.

But otherwise, his mind was very much on the present. He had awoken late that morning, and was set in his mind that today was the day that he needed to face up to things. He had caught a Sky Sports news report in a pub. The correspondent was speaking outside a house.

It was his house.

'Police investigating the assault on United football star Enzo Mariano are understood to be keen to discuss the matter with Paul Warren, the former manager of the club. Nothing has been seen of Mr Warren since the incident, which has left Mr Mariano hospitalised. A spokesman at the hospital said that Mr Mariano was in a stable condition. Mr Warren's wife, Carol, is understood to be unharmed and staying with friends. United have made no comment at this time.'

It seemed bizarre, watching his life unfold on television. There was that ache in his stomach. Butterflies of the worst kind. He needed to go to the police before they found him. He had never transgressed in his life, save for a few speeding fines. But it was obvious that turning himself in was better than being arrested in the street.

He couldn't help but wonder when there would be a tap on the shoulder.

He found himself on the pier watching the Punch and Judy Show as an escape. Putting off the reality a while longer.

Cyril was coming to the end of his patter. Paul was struck

by the fact that as devoid of technology as the show was, the children were glued to it.

'… And they lived happily ever after!'

First, Miss Judy and Policeman Plod feigned a bow, and then Cyril himself emerged from the booth and bowed. Paul joined in the applause as parents and children departed.

'Thank you for watching, boys and girls. Enjoy the rest of your day!'

Cyril bent down and picked up the top hat containing his takings. As he did so, Paul tossed in some coins.

'Good show, Mr Punch. The weather is perfect for a change.'

'Ah, yes, the weather. It's so very English.'

They shook hands. Paul could see a slight look of recognition in the old man's face.

'You know, I last saw that show 40-odd years ago,' said Paul.

Cyril smiled and shrugged.

'They'd have been the same puppets but a different Punch and Judy man. That would have been my father, Cyril Brown Senior.'

'Have you done this show long?

Cyril considered.

'Over 20 years. My last week this week though. I'm moving on.'

'Oh? How come?'

'My dear landlord Mr Pemrose put the rent up.'

'Oh? He seems a bit of a local big wig, Mr Pemrose. I've seen his name on a few places around here.'

'Oh, yes. He's quite a man, our Mr Pemrose. What do you say, PC Plod?'

Cyril held the puppet to his ear, listening intently.

'Ah, PC Plod thinks Mr Pemrose is an unscrupulous rogue. I'd better not comment. A little bit quick with the writ is our Mr Pemrose.'

'In a genteel little town like Cromer? You surprise me.'

Cyril decided to move the conversation along. He knew this face. The man had a midlands accent and an athletic build. He'd seen him somewhere. Yes, that's it, he thought. On the television.

'So what brings you back to our little town after so long an absence?' he asked.

Paul pondered his answer.

'That is a very good question. What am I doing here? Just wallowing in nostalgia, I suppose. Childhood family holidays of fish and chips, footy on the beach and the amusement arcades. Big copper pennies clunking into the big, old one-armed bandits.'

'Then you've come to the right place. Nostalgia we can do well here. I imagine Queen Victoria might still feel quite at home.'

'Oh and I might see the end-of-the-pier show. We saw that every season back then, whether I wanted to or not.'

Cyril held up the other puppet to his ear.

'What's that, Miss Judy? Ah yes, that is true, Miss Judy. A big star is indeed coming this season.'

'Does old man Mr Wells still run it? No, I suppose he must be long dead by now.'

Cyril pointed to an advert glued to a billboard nearby.

'But the name lives on, old boy. His daughter Janet took over. Here, take a look. They have the stunningly beautiful Lauren Evans, no less.'

Paul looked across at the brightly coloured poster, and was taking it in as Cyril remembered. He held Mr Plod to his ear once again, and then he spoke.

'Ah, PC Plod has recognised you.'

'What?' said Paul, his face betraying concern for the first time.

'Yes, indeed, PC Plod. I believe that he is Paul Warren, the football manager. And he's wanted by the police to boot!'

Cyril smiled. Paul looked back, trying to find a suitable answer. Devoid of any, he shrugged.

'Yes, OK. It's a fair cop, PC Plod.'

'Don't worry, Mr Warren. Your secret is safe with me. My wife ran off with someone else, so I'm not about to judge your behaviour.'

'It's still in the news, I see. I was hoping that it might have gone away by now.'

'Today's news is tomorrow's fish and chip paper, old boy. I only recognised you from the initials and the logo on your shorts. You look a little rough, if one might make so bold.'

'I've not slept well. A strange bed and rather dodgy plumbing doesn't help.'

'It takes time, I should think. To come to terms with a shock like that, I mean.'

'What are they saying? The tabloids.'

'Well, of course, they are skirting around the topic as they don't have all of the facts. I rather suppose that the foreign chap was being naughty with the lady of the house. You had a pretty bad day. Fired in the morning… then that?'

'I've had better days, that's for sure.'

'Well, it seems like the foreign chap had it coming, so I rather doubt he'll want to make too much fuss.'

'I just saw red.'

Cyril smiled.

'Personally, I'd have chopped his balls off. Mind you, it's probably good to go to the old bill before they have to go to the trouble of finding you. Making their job easy might go in your favour.'

'You are very probably right, Mr Brown.'

'Cyril, call me Cyril. Where are you staying?'

'Bloomingdale's B&B.'

'Well, well. A very good choice. I'm related to Peggy. She's a cousin of mine.'

'We always stayed there when I was young. It's still a lovely view from the bedroom. I'll need a run every morning to work off the full English though.'

'Yes, I imagine so, and an afternoon one to deal with the fish and chips, no doubt. I'm afraid that Michelin Star cuisine is somewhat absent in this town.'

'From my recall, it always was. Not that I was much bothered when I was younger.'

'As a growing boy, I doubt you would have been.'

'Well, life was all a bit simpler then. Though I don't think I realised it.'

'I rather think you are right. I'm sure you've had better weeks here.'

'You could say that. Still, in my business, you need to be able to bounce back from adversity. It's an occupational hazard.'

Cyril put Miss Judy to his ear.

'Oh, I quite agree, Miss Judy. Miss Judy says to remember that it's always darkest before the dawn.'

'Well, she may be right. It might not be easy, but hope springs eternal. I'll take your advice about the police and face the music. I'll see you again, perhaps?'

'I'm sure you will. I'm not given to travelling far. I'll set up down by the beach at low tide. Mr Pemrose doesn't own that – at least not yet. Oh, Mr Warren, if you see the old bill, see if you can have him locked up, will you?'

Paul smiled.

'I'll do my best. Might not be enough cells though.'

They took their leave, and Paul resolved to return to the bed and breakfast to change his clothes before dropping into the police station, wherever that was these days.

At that moment, his mobile rang. Carol again. He switched it off.

Warren visited Cromer Police Station later that afternoon. The Sergeant was courteous, but as a man who had not the slightest interest in football, he was unaware of who Paul Warren was, in spite of him being in the eye of the national media. So much for joined up policing, thought Paul.

The Sergeant quickly realised that this matter was way above his pay grade, and sitting Warren down in the single interview room devoid of any furniture other than the utilitarian desk and chairs, he called Norwich HQ for guidance.

The Detective Inspector he spoke to was a keen football fan, and realised that this was a national story, albeit a fairly transient one, and called his colleagues in Cheshire for guidance. His equivalent at Cheshire Police took the call.

'So that's where he's gone! We wondered when and where he might surface. Cromer, you say? Where the hell is that?'

'In Norfolk. It's by the sea. Nice place. What's the SP on this? Do you want him back up north?'

The Detective Inspector thought for a moment. He'd got enough on his plate, and hauling Warren back for interview didn't appeal to him that much. He was due to retire in six months, and he was counting down the clock. He certainly wasn't about to generate more paperwork than necessary. He wouldn't miss the bloody paperwork.

'Well, I'm not sure we'll be pressing charges. Mr Mariano's left hospital. Cut his head open as he fell down the stairs. I'm not actually sure who he's more scared of, Mr Warren or Mrs Mariano. She was none too pleased with her husband when I met her at the hospital. Any antipathy he feels towards Warren is more than matched by his desire to get rid of this story as soon as possible. He said that he won't be pressing charges. Couldn't really recall what happened, or so he says.'

'Sounds like a classic domestic. He might just as easily have slipped down the stairs, don't you think?'

'Well, you might think that. It would be better for all of us that way.'

'Shall I just get him to write a statement and send it over to you? Then you can make your mind up.'

'Sounds like a plan. Let's see what he has to say.'

'Looks like a police caution. A shot across his bows in case he tries GBH for real next time?'

'Yep, that would certainly help me out. All's well that ends well in my book.'

And thus, the Sergeant supplied Paul Warren with a statement form and a pen with which to complete it.

Paul sat alone in the austere meeting room, trying to work out how to write the statement, not wishing to dig himself further into trouble. It felt worse as he recalled in detail the painful events of that awful day, and committed them to paper.

He'd arrived at the training ground as usual. It was after the end of the season, and most of the players were off on holiday, so it seemed like a day for thinking about next season. The Chairman had arrived unexpectedly just before 10 o'clock, having flown in from his home in Jersey. The closing day defeat a couple of weeks before had confirmed their relegation, having only been promoted in the previous May. Warren had not thought that his position was under threat, in view of press statements the Chairman had made. They'd agreed to meet up after Paul had returned from a well-earned holiday.

But the same Chairman who had been so supportive, and been on the open-top bus with him as they circled the city centre in triumph under a year ago, was now formal and unflinching. Warren couldn't remember all the platitudes. Results were unacceptable to the board. They'd concluded that they needed to make a fresh start after relegation. There were signs of a loss of confidence in him from the players. He was very sorry to have to take this decision.

Paul had simply shaken his assistant's hand, put his training kit and a few belongings in the car and headed for home. He pulled onto the drive and opened the front door. He was about to call out when he heard a woman's voice. Puzzled, he ascended the stairs and saw a trail of clothes as he went up. They were women's clothes. His wife's. Then he saw a United training top. A man's training top, and not one of his. It had the initials EM on it. He knew those initials.

He opened the bedroom door as the woman cried out. There on the bed was his wife with his team's so called star striker, Enzo Mariano. Paul recognised the tattoo on his back. The sex act can appear anatomically ludicrous, and the sight of a giant hairy backside humping up and down might have seemed that way to him, had his wife not been lying underneath screaming so lustily.

On reflection, what made it worse was that Mariano had been injured for most of the season, yet he didn't seem injured at all at that moment. As he was injured, he'd been excused from training for several weeks, too, the lying bastard.

Paul couldn't really explain what happened next. He recalled dragging Mariano off, and throwing him against the wall, hitting his head as he did. Carol screamed as she covered herself. Then in spite of their relative size difference, he had man-handled the dazed Italian onto the landing and thrown him down the stairs.

There was a loud crash as Mariano hit the hall table, and his head had thudded sickeningly against the glass panel by the front door.

Much else had been a blur. Carol was screaming as he headed down the stairs. He fleetingly thought of kicking the Italian's exposed face as he headed out of the door, but such violence was not in him. Mariano was certainly seriously dazed, if not out cold.

He remembered gunning the car down the road, passing Mariano's red Porsche discreetly parked in a layby near to the bypass.

He committed the account to paper as best as he could remember it, but was savvy enough to be vague as to how Mariano had come to fall down the stairs. He handed the document to the Sergeant, who scanned it without comment. Warren signed it and was given a copy. He was free to go, but required to attend again later the following week to meet Detective Inspector Clark.

As he headed out into the sunshine, Paul wasn't sure what to think. He had fully expected to be heading back north the next evening. The low-key response surprised him. Unsure of how things would work out, he headed back into town and went shopping for some clothes, given that he had arrived with virtually none at all. He thought about a solicitor, but knew nobody locally. He decided just to see what the next meeting brought first.

He wandered rather aimlessly around the town, looking for anything that vaguely resembled a men's clothes shop. A snappy dresser he was not. He'd always regarded suits as a restriction on his freedom and wore a tie only if mandated to do so. He had a dinner jacket for awards ceremonies, but despised wearing it. Carol loved such events – just about the only thing about football she did enjoy, and chided him for spurning the dinner jacket whenever he could.

He eventually found an old-fashioned gentleman's outfitters, complete with a counter and shelving fashioned from polished wood. Warren forced himself to enter, reasoning that getting the chore over with was a necessity.

A balding gentleman, doubtless Mr Brice, the proprietor, smiled and asked if he could help him. He looked rather like Mr Rumbold from 'Are You Being Served?'

After a lengthy consultation, Paul left with suitable apparel. The old-fashioned nature of the shop was not matched by the prices, which were very definitely up to date, thought Paul, as he winced at the final bill.

Mr Brice bid him a good day, and the bell jangled enthusiastically as Paul left the shop. The avuncular owner was a bandit, he thought. He returned to the bed and breakfast and changed his outfit. He switched his mobile phone on, and inevitably, there were a large number of voicemail messages. He could have checked emails had he set the phone up to do so, but he was a bit of a technophobe. The telephone rang while he was holding it. He looked. Carol again.

'You can bloody wait, you ungrateful bitch,' he murmured, turning the phone off once more.

He enjoyed the break. He felt relieved of the pressure

of his work, which had been so relentless through the years. He was also content to have at least addressed things with the police, and delighted that his legal agreement with his ex-employers was signed and sealed following a brief trip to a local solicitor. A huge amount of cash would shortly arrive in his bank account. He was beginning to look forward.

He walked extensively around the beautiful north Norfolk coast. Cley, Brancaster, Burnham Overy Staithe. As he did, he felt more relaxed than he had in a while. He found himself reviewing the career that he'd had as a player, and now as a manager. He thought about Carol. What had possessed her? How long had the affair been going on?

In honesty, Mariano had basically been foisted on him by the Chairman after promotion. He was out of contract and the wrong side of 30, so just the sort of signing the Chairman could afford, given the need for a big signing.

It turned out that Mariano's legs were gone. He had injury niggles throughout the season and had scored only twice. Inevitably, he'd scored on his debut – a spectacular volley, of course. But for most of the season, he was rather underwhelming. He was moody and prone to temper tantrums, too. His effect on the dressing room was disastrous.

The team that had achieved promotion were a mix of experienced journeymen professionals and great young talent from the youth set-up he'd created, drawn largely from the local council estates. There were no prima donnas, but promotion changed all that.

Carol had only met Mariano a handful of times. Paul

hadn't noticed anything. He came to realise that there were many things he'd missed, given his long working days and many evenings away through his career in football management. After many long miles of walking, he had chewed over the anger he felt towards Carol and her betrayal. What had possessed her? They had a happy marriage, didn't they? He had provided well for them both. She had never actually needed to work, had she?

There was a long email from her in the inbox of his email. He had deleted it in anger. He thought that maybe he ought to retrieve it from the recycled bin and read it. He had moved on a little from a desire for revenge to a search for answers.

Another morning, he went for a run, passing a sports field where a game was in progress. Two local Sunday morning teams. 13 year olds at a guess. He was drawn to it like a moth to a flame. A clearance came to him on the touchline. Instinctively, he chipped the ball up, cushioned it on each knee, headed it, and volleyed it neatly to the waiting player.

He laughed as their jaws dropped. He shrugged as he wandered on. You've still got it kid, he thought with pride. He began to ponder the future. Even after tax, his payoff was extraordinary. The Chairman had been keen to warn off clubs from poaching him after they'd won promotion, and he had signed a five-year contract. Even after a few days, he'd had some offers. Mostly from English clubs, but one or two from Spain, and a potentially ludicrous offer from a Gulf State backed by a Sheik with money to burn.

He decided to take his time. It was the closed season, after all. Take time out from football. Initially, he had determined to divorce Carol and give her as little as he could get away with. He'd make her suffer. He'd make her wait. But now the anger was being replaced by the need for answers and a feeling of unfinished business.

But something else gnawed away at him as he returned to Cromer, a place so full of memories. There was another very unsatisfactory ending to a relationship long ago. Bremner was still here, or so the poster said.

It was just after lunch a couple of days later when he found himself outside the Pier Theatre once again. He had no real plan. You couldn't just ask a stranger about a person who had probably long since forgotten him. He went into the booking office, but it was lunchtime and the desk was empty. He was just leafing through some tourist leaflets when he heard a familiar voice behind him.

'Can I help you?'

Janet had heard movement out front, and left her office to investigate. She'd been planning for another meeting with Lionel. It was later on that afternoon at a neutral venue. She was worried sick.

As she entered the booking office, a stranger was facing away from her. He was stocky and dressed in a sports shirt and shorts.

'Hello, can I help you? I'm sorry, the box office doesn't re-open until two o'clock. If you–'

Paul turned around. 30-odd years couldn't disguise who it was.

'My God. Hello, Bremner,' he said.

Janet was confused, at least for a moment.

'I'm sorry, I'm not sure I know who…'

Paul smiled.

'I recognise you, Janet. Look, I'll admit I've put on a bit of weight.'

Janet was shocked. A mixture of realisation and fear showed on her face.

'Oh… my word.'

Paul moved towards her. He thought of hugging her as you would an old friend, but it suddenly seemed inappropriate. Her body language was wrong. It was very wrong.

'Yes, Janet. It's been a long time. I rather think that I've aged a bit. I think we both have.'

She didn't smile. She stared.

'Paul Warren. Long time, no see.'

'Yes. 30-plus years, if my maths is correct.'

Janet was struggling. The words wouldn't come out.

Warren smiled and shrugged.

'30-odd years since you, er, dumped me,' Paul said. 'If that's the modern word for it?'

Janet couldn't believe his nerve.

'I beg your pardon?' she replied.

'Well, I honestly thought you'd dumped me. Look, it's not a big deal. I was just in town and thought I'd get in touch. Look, it really doesn't matter.'

'Not now, Paul. Please go.'

As Warren pondered this rather surprising reaction, Karen entered through the door, a bell jangling as she did.

'Hi, Mum. Oh, sorry, I didn't mean to interrupt.'

'Oh, no problem, Karen. Mr Warren was just leaving.'

'Yes, of course, I must be off. Well goodbye, Janet. It would be good to catch up, if you'd like to? I'm at Mrs Bloomingdale's. Here, take my card. The mobile still works. Maybe some other time?'

'Oh, yes. Goodbye, er, Mr Warren.'

Paul left quickly, feeling confused. The conversation was most bizarre.

Karen was equally confused at her mother's abruptness. As the owner of a theatre, she was normally totally at ease, even with strangers. It was part of the job.

'Who's that? A secret lover?' she asked.

'What? Oh, no. No, certainly not.'

'Are you OK, Mum? You look like you've seen a ghost.'

# 12.

## Moving On

Several days of rehearsals had passed, and Lauren was getting used to the routine.

It was nearly lunchtime when Karen caught up with her. They were both dressed in T-shirts and jogging bottoms, and sweating profusely after their efforts on stage. They sat out on the pier to get some fresh air.

'How's Les been with you this morning?' said Karen.

'Oh, he's been lovely with me on the whole. I'm a bit low on confidence, to be honest. Fluffed an intro this morning. I'm still learning some of the songs, you see. But he's saying all the right things.'

'He's a lovely man, most of the time. Trust me, Lauren, if you listen to Les and put the work in, you'll be great. He really does know his stuff. He's been in the business a long time.'

'I suppose I'm not used to being part of a team. Just turn up and sing, me. There's nothing to it really.'

'Did you have singing lessons?'

'No. What you see is what you get. I had a bit of coaching for the show, but nothing else. To be honest, the coach filled my head so full of crap, I blew him off. I did it my way in the show.'

'Huh, it's all right for some! I can't get close to you and I had years of flipping lessons.'

'Les says you're brilliant.'

'Mum and Les are my biggest fans. But I didn't win a national talent show in front of 14 million people.'

'Neither did I… good enough finishing second though.'

'Most of us are here because we finished second or worse at one time or another, Lauren. We've all got our stories.'

'There's some juicy gossip then?'

'Yep. But people will tell you in their own good time. Some of us have worked together for a long time. We know where our no-go areas are.'

'It's not easy for Lech, poor man. Les was giving him a really hard time. He's still struggling with the culture, the language and all that.'

'Well, if you're hired as a magician and you flunk your tricks, then Les won't show any mercy.'

'I got that impression. He doesn't take any prisoners, does he? Put me in my place for starters that first day when I did my high and mighty bit.'

'Well, we can't afford to waste money on people who aren't up to it. If Lech doesn't shape up, Mum will deal with it. There's no shortage of people wanting work.'

'Tell me about it. So it's a case of best friend, worst enemy?'

'That's about the size of it. Directors can't afford to make friends sometimes. But he really knows how to go about getting the best out of you.'

'He was the life and soul of the party last night though,

wasn't he? He's just so effortlessly funny. Do you do that every year?'

'Yes, it's a tradition. It breaks the ice for the newcomers, in particular. A good bit of team bonding. We were delighted you came down.'

'It took me back to the valleys. A big sing-song around the piano in the back room of the Con club. It made me feel at home.'

'I didn't know you played the piano. Some of those songs you did, I'd never heard them before. Not on your albums?'

'No, you won't have. I wrote them myself a while ago. Way before the show came along.'

'Really? That 'Maybe' is a really lovely song. It sounded a bit autobiographical at a guess?'

'Of course. The best songs have to be, I think.'

'Making up with a boyfriend?'

'Yes. My first love until he buggered off to uni. Then he came back to me for a time. I thought we'd make a go of it.'

'What happened?'

'He changed. He grew up, didn't he? He left Wales and me behind. He works in IT in London now.'

'You're a pretty good pianist.'

'Not really. I can pick out a tune. I don't get to practise much, so when I do, I play the stuff I wrote. It's the only stuff I know how to play, to be honest.'

'Well, it doesn't show. It seems very natural.'

'Thanks. You and your mother are so alike, you know. That 'Over The Rainbow' duet was lovely. It's obviously very special to both of you.'

'Yes, it is. We normally sing it when we're drunk, actually. Mum used to sing it in the show when I was little.'

Les came out of the theatre at the pace of a man with much to do.

'Sorry, Karen… Lauren, do you have a moment?'

Karen stood.

'No worries. Jobs to do…' she said, beating a path back into the theatre.

Les sat on the bench beside Lauren, and looked at her intently.

'It was last night I wanted to discuss, Lauren.'

Lauren pulled her cardigan around herself defensively.

'Look, I know I drank too much.'

'And smoked…' said Les.

'Yes, I know it's bad for the voice. But it's the nerves, you see. I've always smoked. I cut down a lot recently but well–'

Les cut in, raising his hand in apology, realising that he'd gone off track.

'Oh, I'm not being judgemental. It's not a good idea to smoke, of course, but I've smoked a few in my time, and some other stuff besides.'

'Really?'

Les smiled.

'Oh, yes. Frankly some years were a bit of a blur, if I'm truthful. Clinton might not have inhaled but I most certainly did. But I digress, it wasn't that I wanted to discuss.'

'Then, what?' said Lauren, a bit perplexed.

'The songs, Lauren. The ones you sang last night.'

Lauren seemed to become defensive.

'What of them? I only played them for fun. They're not in my set so, whatever.'

'Did you never think to record them on your albums?'

'No, the show said covers were what the voters wanted. Then the second album had new songs commissioned by the record label. I didn't get much of a say.'

Les shook his head in despair.

'Record labels… give me strength. The second album was dross, Lauren.'

Lauren flinched, her confidence deflating.

'Well, I wasn't much good I agree.'

Les shook his head.

'I mean the songs were dross, Lauren. They picked the wrong songs. The right songs for you are those you sang last night.'

'What?'

'Your songs are beautiful, heartfelt ballads. Unsurprisingly, they suit your voice perfectly. They're… believable, credible. They tell stories. People have been where those songs have been.'

'But my management said…'

'Oh, they would have. Another cloned product of a sausage machine industry, no doubt. How would they know any better?'

Lauren shrugged.

'Well, I can't say I gave them much thought. I wrote most of them when I was a bit younger. Breaking up and making up, dumping one bloke and being dumped by another. The usual stories of growing up.'

'But you can read music?'

'No, not really. Well, maybe a little. I play by ear mostly.'

'But you can play the piano. You had lessons?'

'Oh, no. I just had a few lessons from Auntie Gwen, nothing formal. Then I just made up songs. There was nothing much to it. I only play when I'm sad, or want a bit of nostalgia. I only played them last night as you'd heard all my other stuff.'

Les smiled once again and shook his head.

Lauren spoke again, uncertain but intrigued,

'So you think they're OK then? The songs I mean?' she said.

'Yes, I do. I'd like to put a couple in the show.'

'OK, if you say so Les. Were there any particular ones?'

'We'll finish your closing set with 'Maybe' I think. There won't be a dry eye in the house. We'll need to get some proper musical arrangements. I'll talk with Gerald, our Musical Director. Then we can go with your one-hit wonder for the encore. 'Maybe' will be a solo, just with Gerald's piano arrangement. For the big hit, you'll be accompanied by the full musical arrangement to close the show. We'll drop another of your songs into the first half just ahead of the interval.'

Lauren felt herself welling up.

'That would be great, Les. I'd love it.'

*　*　*

Paul arrived at the police station at two o'clock sharp, and was introduced to Detective Inspector Clark. He had read Paul's statement already, along with a copy of two other statements supplied by Cheshire Police – those of Enzo Mariano and Carol Warren. There were no real factual discrepancies whatsoever. All three statements were rather vague as to the precise circumstances of the afternoon's events.

It had taken a few days to get the facts together, but he'd eventually managed to talk with his opposite number in Cheshire, and they agreed the line of questioning.

'You had a bad day, Mr Warren?' said Clark ironically, referring to Warren's statement.

'I've had better, I must admit,' he replied, deliberately keeping his answers short.

'But throwing Mr Mariano down the stairs could have caused him a very serious injury. We could be looking at a charge of causing grievous bodily harm.'

Paul thought for a moment. Nice try, Inspector.

'Well, I can't recall pushing him at all. I can't really remember the sequence of events precisely. It was all a bit of a blur. Mr Mariano hit his head on the wall. That much I do remember, but as I say, there was a bit of a scuffle and he wound up falling. He must have lost his footing on the stairs. It's all I can remember. Then there was a loud crash. Look, I'm sorry, I'm not being very helpful.'

'So you deny pushing Mr Mariano down the stairs?'

'As far as I can remember, there was a scuffle on the landing and the next thing, he seemed to slip and fall backwards.'

'I see. So having seen Mr Mariano fall and clearly sustain a serious head injury, you ran off, leaving him to his fate?'

'Well, I panicked, and my wife was still around at the

scene, of course. Look, I appreciate that I could have helped. I do apologise. You will understand that the circumstances were, well, a bit out of the ordinary.'

'So what brought you down here? It's a bit out of the way.'

'Yes. I know. As I said, I panicked. I haven't been here in years.'

Clark questioned him for a further half an hour as a secretary took notes. Warren was guilty, without a doubt. He'd acted like a jealous husband would and thrown the bastard down the stairs. Then he panicked and ran from the scene of the crime. Clark equally knew that with none of the witnesses wanting to upset the apple cart, there was no way any judge or jury would convict him.

Eventually, he leant back in his chair, and nodded.

'All right. Well, there seems to be no material discrepancy between what you've said and what Mr Mariano and your wife said.'

'Well, as I said in the statement, I do regret my behaviour in running away. I reacted to the circumstances and had to get away. But, of course, once I had come to terms with things, I gave myself up, if that's the term I should use.'

Clark pondered. This was really quite straightforward, but he didn't want Warren to think that.

'I think you are very fortunate that Mr Mariano is not pressing charges, because had he done so, you would be heading straight back up north this evening charged with causing grievous bodily harm.'

Warren nodded. He had nothing more to say, and he

recognised a bit of theatre when he saw it. As a football manager, you learned to read people, especially body language. Clark was too relaxed.

Clark looked at him intently.

'You are a very lucky man, Mr Warren. I've checked with my colleagues in Cheshire, and as everything you've said checks out, we can let you off with a formal police caution, which will remain on file. Any repetition of this behaviour and any further contact with Mr Mariano and you will be charged with this offence and the subsequent one. Is that clear?'

Of course it was. Just 15 minutes later, the paperwork was done and Warren headed out into the sunshine, feeling incredibly relieved. He wondered what to do next. He could head for home, but frankly he wanted Carol to stew for a while, and he hadn't had a holiday in ages. He decided to stay a few days. He sent Carol a text saying that he would be away for a while, reflecting on things.

\*    \*    \*

Carol Warren was sitting in the lounge of their home. The home that she and Paul had shared since his appointment three years ago. It had been her pride and joy when they bought it, brand new on a select estate in the suburbs of the city.

Sitting opposite was her next door neighbour, Melanie Clark. It was Mel who had kept watch on the house when she had left in haste to avoid the media. So it was Mel who advised her that, as the last of the reporters had left a few days ago, it was now safe for her to return home from her sister's holiday cottage in Wales.

She was glad to be home. Now she was trying, almost literally, to pick up the pieces of what had happened. She had spent the last hour hoovering up the glass fragments from the glass vase that had broken in her lover's fall down the stairs, and caused the bloodstains on the expensive Sanderson wallpaper by the door. She'd moved a table into an optimal place to hide the worst of it, and a glazier was booked to sort out the cracked glazing.

Practical Carol liked things in their place, and in this worst of all crises, her instinct was the put things back to how they were before the calamity itself had occurred. She could not immediately deal with the appalling consequences, but at least restoring order in her home was cathartic.

Mel was her best friend. The two couples were close. Mark, Mel's husband, was an international salesman for an IT firm, and was away a lot. As Paul was working away a lot as well, they had something in common. They'd bought their houses at the same time, and had become firm friends.

Carol leaned back into her comfortable settee and momentarily closed her eyes. Mel had been a nurse, but hadn't needed to work, and had a couple of children, who seemed to absorb all of her time. She listened as Carol rambled on, the stronger than average white wine served in ridiculously-sized glasses only adding to the disjointed drivel that her best friend was talking. Mel had not been entirely shocked by events. She had guessed about the affair. She had seen the swarthy Mr

Mariano in odd places at odd times. She was only really surprised at the sequence of events. But she liked Carol, and for that matter, Paul, and figured that at this time, listening to Carol was the best chance of helping both of her best friends. Her Irish mother might not have been quite so restrained.

In Mel's eyes, you could write a film about what had happened. It was the bored middle-aged housewife story, husband away a lot, and flattery from a younger, sexy Italian man.

Carol opened her eyes, and looking through the wine glass at the meniscus of the wine, she thought for a moment.

'I've been a total idiot, haven't I?'

Mel shrugged. It was not the time to chip in. Not yet. Carol knows. She doesn't need telling. She's been wriggling around with self-justification but she's just too intelligent not to know.

Carol sipped once more.

'I mean, he's 10 years younger. Who was I trying to kid? It was always going to end in tears, wasn't it?'

Mel shrugged. If she thinks I'm going to sympathise, she is very much mistaken, Mel thought.

'I was just so absolutely bloody bored. Bored of football night after bloody night, Sky bloody Sports, Match of the bloody Day with overpaid presenters… day after bloody day.'

Mel smiled. Carol never swore. Gently does it.

'So you go and shag a footballer, of all people.'

'Yep. And you know what? He was sensational. I mean, he was sensational at sex, right?'

Mel sipped her wine. Slowly. Carry on, girl.

'Then, of course, his lordship was never home. He even went to stupid mid-week away games. A 200-mile round trip to see some such striker or other.'

Mel allowed herself one barb.

'Well, his current strikers weren't scoring, were they? Not on the pitch, anyway.'

Carol paused. If she spotted the sarcasm, she ignored it.

'It didn't do his lordship much good though, did it? He still got fired, the stupid twat.'

Mel said nothing. She was trying to keep some perspective, and hold onto some sympathy for her best friend. But her husband was away more than she cared for, and she had two kids to look after. Get real, lady.

Carol suddenly crumpled and the tears started to flow. She wanted to throw the glass to the floor in frustration, but it would have made a mess on the carpet. She set it down and looked across directly at Mel.

'Oh, God, what have I done, Mel?'

Mel went to the settee and took her friend in her arms as she sobbed. She reasoned that Carol was not the first victim of a workaholic husband. It's not actually their fault, she thought. They are just men, and men get obsessed with being the best they can be and nothing else matters. They live in a work bubble. She'd had enough rows with Mark to understand where Carol was coming from.

And football, as an industry, was something else again. All four of them had been at Wembley last summer. The adulation, the TV hype, the open-top bus. The big, new contract with the flashy new car, then the relentless unfolding disaster that followed. Playing in the biggest league, but still on a smaller club budget.

The happy, fun-loving Paul Warren, who her own kids idolised, became a distant and phone-obsessed shadow. The Saturday night meals at each other's houses died as Paul was mono-syllabic in defeat. He was simply not fun to be married to.

But Mel chided herself for not doing more. While she hadn't been absolutely certain about the affair, it was a bit obvious. Carol would disappear during the day wearing a new dress, carrying an overnight bag. She thought she'd seen her at the Hilton with Mariano one day but hadn't been sure.

Carol pulled herself together eventually, and Mel smiled.

'You'll be needing black coffee now?' she asked.

So they drank the black coffee and Carol answered the question that Mel had decided not to ask.

'I want him back, Mel.'

Mel nodded, and munched a second chocolate chip cookie. Sod the diet, she thought. This is a crisis.

'Well, that's a start, I suppose. But do you have any idea where he is?' she said.

'No. I've tried ringing him and texting him but he doesn't reply.'

Mel laughed, a soft Irish accent drifting through her next words, as the blood began to rise a little.

'Like you're surprised? He goes to work, gets fired and comes home to find his wife shagging someone in his own bed? Poor bastard's probably suffering from post-traumatic stress, I shouldn't wonder.'

Carol smiled thinly. It was fair comment. At that moment, her mobile pinged, and she grabbed it, reading Paul's text.

'I'm going away for a week or two. Need some time. I'll be in touch. P.'

Mel was matter-of-fact. 'At least he's responded.'

Carol hit the redial before Mel could comment further.

'Voicemail… again. Coward.'

She tossed the phone aside in frustration.

'He can't solve this by not talking to me.'

Mel shook her head.

'The man's just lost everything he cares about and you want him to talk it over?'

Carol flared.

'If he cared less about football and more about me, this wouldn't have happened.'

Mel looked back.

'Well forgive me but it might not be the best thing to point that out to him right now.'

Carol shook her head and fell silent. Mel pondered a moment or two.

'The police must know where he is. What are they saying?'

'Not much. Took a statement from me and I haven't heard a dickie bird since.'

'Will they press charges? Mariano was injured, so he could presumably claim an assault took place.'

Carol stared at her.

'Enzo is too busy explaining things to his wife, I would think. He won't want the fuss.'

'OK but the police will presumably know where Paul is. How do you think that Paul will react? I guess he's a wanted man. It said so in the paper.'

Carol thought for a moment. Her practical self was returning.

'I don't know. His parents are dead and he doesn't have much time for his brothers. He's not big on building real friendships. He likes your guy, though. He's not in the football goldfish bowl, you see.'

'So he's alone and he's running away. Where would he go? Back home to the Midlands?'

'I doubt it. There's nothing there for him now. He went back to his old secondary school with the trophy last year, but he's no friends there. In fact, he has no real friends other than you guys. What does Ian think?'

Mel laughed.

'Well Ian is Ian, so it's all been a total shock. He thought about ringing Paul but men don't do that in the way we girls would.'

'Not much help there, then.'

'What do you expect, Carol? They're just men, after all. Let's have another cookie.'

# 13.

## Flaming June

The show seemed to be coming together at last, thought Les. The dancers were getting better by the day. Amy was a quick learner, and when Angela De Grey was sober, she could still pull it off. Lauren was at least moving in sequence with the others, but was never going to be a dancer. Her voice was still absolutely amazing.

There was, however, something he needed to attend to. Les and Janet were ensconced in Janet's office, where Janet was dealing with a grievance form submitted that morning.

'Yes, Les. Lech does know he's up against it. I've given it to him straight. But he does work hard, doesn't he? No sickies. Always turns up on time. Nobody leaves later than Lech, do they? And his dance moves are pretty slick.'

'That's as maybe but—'

'Give him a break, will you? Do you realise that he's been doing shifts as a night club bouncer and bingo caller as well? All the hours he can do. No wonder he fell asleep in that rehearsal. He wants to ship money home to Poland, apparently.'

'OK, OK, but you can't forgive him this, surely? The female

cast are up in arms. It's a clear case of sexual harassment, apparently. You're a woman. Do something.'

'Apparently he wanted to saw a woman in half.'

Les looked at her sarcastically.

'Trust me, a lot of us have those feelings from time to time. Most of us just drink, or at least, I did.'

'Well apparently, in Poland, it's his best trick, sawing ladies in half,' explained Janet. 'He tried to speak to you about it, I gather?'

'Yes,' replied Les. 'I said we called people who liked that sort of thing serial killers.'

'Les, you are an idiot sometimes. You should have sorted someone from the chorus for him. He tried himself but he couldn't explain himself properly.'

'I'll admit being sarcastic didn't really help the conversation.'

Janet glared at him, arms folded. Better move on, thought Les.

'I take it he asked Lauren?'

'Yes. Apparently her exact words were 'Piss off, you degenerate pervert."

'He went into her dressing room then? Did she have any clothes on, by any chance?'

'Who knows? Probably not much. He said she had a tattoo in a very strange place.'

'Really? I must check that out!'

'We're in enough trouble as it is.'

'So having been rebuffed by Lauren, he went into the ladies dressing room, too?' asked Les.

'Well, yes. He simply went to find someone to saw in half.'

'Of course. The sawing a woman in half trick doesn't really work without a woman, does it?'

'Then according to the grievance,' Janet continued, 'let me see now...'

She referred to the grievance document that had landed on her desk earlier.

'Yes... he evidently encountered a somewhat under-dressed Amy. It says here she threw her hair brush at him and called him, and I quote, a 'lecherous pervert."

'So the chorus has filed a grievance alleging sexual harassment? Brilliant. So surely you're going to sack him now?'

'Actually, I think I've managed to patch it up. While you were having your usual leisurely lunch, Lauren has played peacemaker. She's told him his best bet is to get some flowers for the girls, and a nice card to apologise. Oh, and some chocolates, too.'

'Well, on your head be it. Frankly, what with Angela De Gray and Lech Widget...'

'Wojiek!' corrected Janet. 'Pronounced 'Voy Check!"

'Lord, help us. I can think of two people I'd like to saw in half right now.'

Les smiled, and Janet smiled back. They hadn't talked about the future. Les was resigned to the fact that this season would be his last, but somehow this re-energised him, making him determined that this would be his best season ever.

Janet picked up on this, placing her hand on his.

'You're loving it though, aren't you? Really?'

Les shrugged.

'I guess. I'll miss it, you know. Any developments?'

Janet pondered a moment.

'Well, Lionel has commissioned architects to come up with some new detailed designs, so that will take a while. You'll see one or two wandering around… just tell the cast they're concerned with the roof.'

'OK, fine.'

'He's going to have some private conversations with the planners and the conservation people,' Janet explained. 'Then, of course, I'll find fault with everything he does. He won't be able to submit anything until at least the deadline to our licence extension.'

'But then what? Any ideas?'

'I'm talking to a few people. Not the banks. I'm looking at grants and so forth.'

'Good,' said Les.

There was silence. Janet shuffled some papers. Les was unsure how to proceed, but then continued.

'Look, Janet, you don't need worry about me. I'll go back on the road. I've got the cruise ships. My needs are pretty modest.'

'I'm still not happy about offering you up as a sacrificial lamb. I'm not giving up.'

'Look, I know you'll try, but I'm more concerned about the future of the theatre. We're the last one, remember? The last end-of-the-pier show.'

'Don't remind me.'

'Well, I've been mulling it over and the fixed costs of

putting on this show means that it needs lots of performances to get the money back. It simply won't work in its present form on a few nights a week.'

Janet looked up.

'I know.'

'Then what's the plan, Janet?'

'I don't have one,' Janet admitted.

'One season, maybe two. Then it's done.'

'Yes. He'll find a reason to wind up the show. One-nighters only from then on.'

'And Karen? And you?'

Janet shrugged.

'Who knows? Maybe things will work out. He has some good points, does Lionel.'

Les laughed.

'Name one.'

'I know you've had a bit of previous with him,' said Janet.

'Well, not many people remembered what happened to me, but Pemrose did.'

'Don't beat yourself up, Les. It was a long time ago.'

'He splashed my criminal record around after others had forgotten. The vindictive bastard.'

'I know. Les, why relive this? It's not–'

'I had to rebuild my career, and your father had a job going here. He said that he didn't really give a damn what others thought. He said that the job was mine.'

'Now that sounds like my father. He did have a stubborn streak a mile wide.'

'Stubborn and single-minded. He told me later on that he never expected me to stay more than a couple of years. He thought that once I had stabilised my career, I'd move on. But I never forgot his confidence in me when I was at my lowest ebb.'

'He got a bargain, Les. You made this show. You still do, actually. When he died, I had to take the theatre on, but without you, I'd have stood no chance.'

'I know that. But recent events bring home how much this place means to me. Here… it's not much, but it's what I have, and if it helps, take it.'

He handed over a cheque. Janet welled up as she took it. The sheer kindness of this lovely comedian never ceased to amaze her.

'Oh, my. You are a truly good friend. It doesn't solve the problem, you know it doesn't. But be sure that if I can find a solution, I will cash it.'

She stood up as they hugged each other. Janet sniffled into his shoulder, Les only slightly less emotional.

'Look, why didn't you tell me about the bank? You knew a long time before you told me. I could have helped.'

'Because I thought I could fix it,' Janet said.

Les wasn't buying it.

'I say again. We've been friends for years, why didn't you tell me?'

'Because you and I know that our friend Mr Pemrose is responsible, and well…'

'You thought that I might get drunk again and go after him.'

'Well, yes, I did.'

'Look, I only do the sessions because you're only ever one drink away from… whatever.'

'I couldn't take the chance, Les. Remember what happened?'

'I hit him, you know, Pemrose. He called me a drunken has been, and I snapped. I struck him with a perfect right hook. Went out like a light. Hand hurt a bit, I recall.'

Janet laughed.

'Really? That I would have liked to have seen.'

'It's as well you didn't. In fact, nobody did. If they had I'd have been back inside. But he's hated me ever since. It's not only personal between you and him, but between the two of us as well.'

'Yes, I can understand that, Les. Ah, it looks like my next appointment's arrived. I need to go.'

Paul Warren entered the foyer.

Janet had decided that she would need to get this over with. She had contacted him late Sunday afternoon. It was unfinished business, both for her and for Karen, too, she recognised.

She had tried to put it out of her mind because the future of the theatre and their livelihoods had to be a priority, and yet it kept coming back to haunt her.

She recalled the shame of it at the time. All of the subterfuge and secrecy. The obsessive, controlling behaviour of her father, and the meek deference of her mother. The perceived reputational damage to the family of which her father spoke seemed so ludicrous now. Did people really give a damn about it, even then? She wasn't alone but it felt like it at the time.

So she had decided to deal with it. A one-off meeting, then move on. Then you can focus on the now. The important stuff. So she had contacted Bloomingdale's and arranged this meeting.

\*   \*   \*

Paul sat motionless. He couldn't believe what Janet had told him. It was an incredible story. She was stiff and formal. Almost matter-of-fact. How could she seem so detached? She seemed devoid of emotion as she told the story, almost robotic.

'I got you pregnant. My God.'

'Dad wanted me to have an abortion but I refused point-blank and Mum reasoned with him. You will recall that teenage pregnancies weren't exactly all the rage in those days.'

'But didn't you get my letters? I wrote a dozen then gave up.'

'No, I didn't get any letters at all. Dad said I was to have nothing to do with you.'

'And I rang from a call box. We didn't have our own phone then. Your father said he didn't want to hear from me again. I was upset for weeks.'

'I wrote, too. Not surprisingly, I was pretty desperate to speak to you.'

'But this makes no sense,' Paul said.

'Well, let's be honest, your mother never approved of me, did she? Thought I was leading you astray. More than a bit ironic after what happened.'

'And I went away on tour. I'd just turned pro. That youth

tournament in Munich, if I remember rightly. First time I'd been abroad.'

'And as soon as I was obviously pregnant, they shipped me up to the holiday home in Burnham Overy Staithe. That's where Karen was born.'

'But why did he not share the problem? I was so in love with you, I'd have married you in a heartbeat.'

'Not Dad's style. I was in disgrace. I'm not sure I was ever forgiven. Sleeping with a tourist, of all people, made me a right slut.'

'So… Karen is my daughter…'

'Yes, biologically she is. But she doesn't ask and I don't discuss it. I really want it to remain that way. Are you clear about that?'

'Of course. I've no desire to make things worse.'

'Well, that's understood then. Look, I'm sorry I was so rude the other day.'

'Well, now it all makes sense. It must have been a terrible shock, me turning up out of the blue.'

'Yes it was, after such a long time.'

Later on, each reflected on their meeting in their separate ways. For Paul, the irony was so apparent. If only Carol hadn't miscarried. Would things have been different? Now he had knowledge of a daughter with whom he had no relationship, and had only fleetingly met.

Bremner was still Bremner. She was a bit plumper than at 17, and her hair was professionally styled, which flattered her. But peel back the years, and Janet was still Bremner to him. As they shook hands rather awkwardly, she had smiled. The lines on her face were evidence of her age, but underneath she was still his 17-year-old first love.

As much as he had agreed that there would be no further meetings, and agreed also that what was said and done should not be revisited, he was left with a sense that this simply couldn't be the case. It didn't feel right.

Janet Wells was too stiff and formal. Too business-like. You couldn't just file this matter neatly in a box as she wanted to do. Karen had rights, too. She had a right to know her father. But he sensed another agenda. Janet was so distracted. As they spoke, he sensed something else. There was something bigger on her mind. None of his business, of course, but the outcome of their meeting was unsatisfactory, and he wondered how best to move things forward.

Janet had been adamant that this was an end to it. But although he had acquiesced at the time, he now knew that it just couldn't work.

And Janet knew it, too. As hard as she tried to get her mind back to the future of the theatre, she couldn't help but reminisce about the past. She had cried herself to sleep so many nights in the early days. She wrote letter after letter, and cursed the fact that there was no telephone number she could ring him on.

She had telephoned the club asking for him to ring her, but there had been no contact. Football clubs protected their players from girls, of course. Girls were a distraction. She had followed his career sporadically. She had no interest in football, but from time to time, he made the news and she would take an interest. But time healed things a bit, and she had a child to bring up, and then a theatre to run.

She was bitter at the time. He'd mugged her into a one-night stand and she had paid the price. Knowing footballers by reputation, she was probably one of a string of girls he'd bedded, their head turned by money and fame.

In fairness, he'd put on some weight but he was still Paul. He'd always been different. He had emotions. Blokes didn't cry, but Paul did. She'd sung to him one night on the pier, it was Harry Nilsson's 'Without You.' His mother's favourite. He'd applauded and hugged her at the end. He couldn't sing a note, but loved theatre. He'd cried at the movies, too, she remembered. What was the film they'd seen? She couldn't recall.

He had been riddled with self-doubt at the time, yet somehow, she knew that he would succeed. He'd talked about the game in a language she didn't understand. It was apparent that he was driven and would blow away the doubts through dedication and passion.

Now when they had met all these years later, he'd apparently been shocked by her revelation, and she had been both bitter and clinical as she spat out her story. The pent up dam of her feelings was gradually released, but in a controlled and unemotional way. She flared only occasionally, keeping her anger in check most of the time.

Did she believe him? At the time, she had fabricated a story for herself that Warren was just a typical footballer high on testosterone and low on morality, and knew perfectly well what he had done.

But now it seemed that, on the face of it, he knew nothing of her predicament. Could it actually be true? Did he really not get her letters? Did he really ring up? Surely after her father died, her mother would have told her the truth? It was too late now. Both were long dead.

But that night, she told herself that she had dealt with the matter once and for all. Focus on the theatre. The impending disaster. She had obligations to herself, Karen and the staff.

But it wouldn't go away. She slept poorly once again, craving rest but none would come. She had been in control of her life for so long. She had isolated and dealt with problems as they occurred. But now two emotional tidal waves had arrived at once and she needed to focus. And to focus, she needed sleep. But it still evaded her.

# 14.

## Girls Will Be Girls

Karen joined Lauren and Angela for an al fresco lunch. Angela, as the cast elder, roped in a reluctant Amy Raven to join them. Now several drinks later, they were swapping stories.

'So, that's my story girls,' said Karen. 'Old maid before my time, I reckon. What about you, Lauren? I watched that final on TV. I really thought you were going to win.'

'It was fixed, I'm sure. I got beaten by that 16-year-old girl. Butter wouldn't melt in her mouth would it now? Let me tell you, that little madam was a right little slut. She shagged at least one of the judges. One of the crew caught them at it.'

Angela smiled.

'I've met one or two of those. It's been going on for years. Mind you, I'm not going to throw too many stones in that particular glasshouse.'

'You didn't?' said Karen.

Angela shrugged.

'A girl's got to eat.'

Lauren nodded sadly and continued.

'They even made me change my name. They didn't think Lauren Butt was a good name for a singer.'

'Fair point,' said Amy, who had already made the same journey.

'Fat Butt, they called me at school. Get your fat butt over here, they'd say. It was typical comprehensive school stuff. I didn't do very well at school.'

'I'll bet you've been singing all of your life,' said Amy.

'All I ever wanted to do was sing. I started in chapel at seven years old. I did a few clubs when I was a teenager, and worked as a checkout girl after I left school.'

Amy sipped her drink slowly. She was star struck by Lauren, and yet this woman was so easy to get to know, once the star left her tiara behind.

'How come you didn't get a break back then? Your voice is just awesome.'

'My parents said there was no money in singing. They wanted me to settle down. Had a couple of flings with Darren, the guy from the song I wrote, then I married a real meat-and-two-veg guy who expected his tea on the table at six o'clock, then buggered off to the pub all evening.'

Karen laughed.

'Ah, yes. I know the type. There's still one or two of those around.'

'He didn't lift a finger around the house. Then the factory shut, and he was on the dole. He was a total waste of space so I dumped him.'

Amy continued, fascinated by this journey, which had been such a roller coaster. Life with Lauren would never be dull.

'But you never stopped singing then?'

'No way! I always sang on Friday and Saturday nights. Then years later, just as I was thinking of giving up, I got on the talent show, and suddenly everyone is my best friend.'

'Sounds so very familiar,' said Angela haughtily.

'Suddenly everybody knows me. They all flogged their stories. Told the papers we were best mates at school, dug out pictures and all. Bloody cheek.'

'People love a celebrity,' Karen offered.

'But the press lapped it up. Then I got drunk a couple of times.'

'As you do,' said Angela, looking disparagingly at her mineral water.

Lauren halted for a moment.

'Well, yes, and I smashed that bloody photographer's camera when he stuck it down my cleavage as I left a club. I accepted a police caution for that, then the wild-child stories started. Darling of the press I was. One minute, they couldn't get enough of me, then next minute, bad girl Lauren dumped by record company.'

Amy leant forward.

'But what about your parents? I'll bet they were delighted by your success.'

'Of course. I've never seen them so happy. But last year my dad hit my mum once too often, so they split up. It's desperate when that happens. Didn't see it coming see. Still, whatever, I can't really complain. I got a recording contract, cut an album. The new Charlotte Church, they said. But then the second album flopped, and the record company dropped me.'

'Such a familiar story,' said Angela.

'Then the bookings dried up and the money ran out. I'd have been on the dole back in Wales, if I'm honest. So now I've come here. Cromer Pier Summertime Special Show.'

Karen understood. Now it made sense.

'So when we came along…'

Lauren shrugged.

'My agent said to go to Cromer. He gave me the usual bullshit about consolidating my career, that sort of stuff.'

Karen nodded. She had been there, too.

'You're a long way from home, like I was in London. Stuck in cheap hotels and rented rooms. But Mum was always fantastic. She supported everything I did.'

There was a brief silence, but then Lauren asked what the others were thinking, but wouldn't ask.

'No father then?'

Karen paused. She was suddenly less assured.

'No.'

There was silence.

Karen shrugged as she continued.

'He left mum when I was a baby. I never knew him. I've often wondered what he's like. Mum doesn't really want to talk about it. It's just difficult for her to talk.'

Angela had found the situation puzzling. The mother and daughter were clearly so close, and yet this topic seemed off limits.

'You do have a right, you know? Janet should talk to you about it. It's not really fair on you.'

Karen nodded.

'I know. I've meant to have the conversation but never got around to it. I certainly don't want to make things more difficult for Mum. She's working so hard as it is.'

Karen had nearly gone too far and realised it just in time. Lauren decided they had ventured into one of those no-go areas to which Les had referred. Move on, she thought.

'She does have a point though. More wine anyone?'

'I'll stick to mineral water, thanks,' said Angela, pondering her glass with distaste.

'Dance routine after lunch?' ventured Karen.

'Don't remind me, darling. I don't think I'd get into Pan's People anymore.'

Amy looked puzzled.

'Pan's People? Who are they?'

'Oh, I'm sorry. It was before you were born, at a guess. I was a brilliant dancer at one time, now look at me. A fat arse and hot flushes to go with it.'

Lauren laughed.

'Oh, I don't know about that. You're still a much better dancer than I'll ever be.'

'It's only practice, Lauren. Piece of cake, the basics. I'll teach you, if you like. It's like getting married. Really quite easy if you've practised it as many times as I have.'

Lauren topped up the glasses. No dancing for her this afternoon, and she wasn't planning on learning any more than was required either. She set down the bottle and looked at her glass.

'I think I've given up on blokes. Unless they're stinking rich, of course.'

Karen smiled.

'You could always go after Lionel Pemrose, if Angela doesn't bag him first.'

There were collective giggles. Lauren punched Karen playfully. Amy wasn't so impressed.

'He groped my backside as I went on stage at the hotel for my last gig. He gives me the creeps.'

Karen looked at her sadly. If only you knew, Karen thought.

'You don't have to put up with it, you know. Put him in his place.'

Lauren flared. Her Welsh blood rising.

'I find a good knee in the balls lets them know you're not up for it.'

There were collective laughs. Amy was enjoying the company. These people had seen it all. There was much to learn. This was to be her apprenticeship, she decided, as they went their separate ways.

Karen and Angela continued their conversation on the way back to the rehearsal room. Karen was keen to understand the situation.

'Are you on the wagon now then?' Karen asked.

'I've no choice, Karen,' Angela replied. 'Les gave me a right bollocking. I've decided that the booze is over for good. Directors like people who they can rely on. Don't worry about me. I do get the message.'

'Thanks, Angela. Given that we've got to help Amy a bit, I need you to be rock solid through the season.'

'Look, if I was Dance Captain, I'd want the same. I need this job. My phone doesn't ring any more. I'm too old and with a less than reliable reputation. I owe your mother one, that's for sure.'

# 15.

## The Show Must Go On

'What planet are those people on? Don't they want new jobs in this town?'

Lionel was not amused. He was sitting at the conference table fiddling with the cheap hotel ballpoint pen, snapping the cap in exasperation.

It had taken weeks to even get a meeting with the planning officials, and all they had done was come up with objection after objection. He'd even given up his afternoon's golf to accommodate these people at the Majestic Hotel.

Nobody in the room wanted to speak next. Lionel's face reflected the pent up fury bubbling underneath – a cauldron of rage that had simmered throughout the meeting. Fortunately, he had just about kept his true feelings in check until the meeting ended.

He needed the loo urgently, too. Far too much black coffee. He left the meeting room, leaving just Tyler and the Finance Director, Jim Cameron, a calm and pragmatic counterbalance to the aggressive Lionel Pemrose. The architect, planning advisor and solicitor had all left as soon as the meeting ended. Tyler couldn't help but notice their rather quick departure.

'Those property advisors scuttled off a bit sharpish. I don't think they wanted to hear Lionel's post mortem.'

Cameron shrugged. His calm demeanour and soft Scottish accent were rather like a Scottish GP, thought Tyler. Cameron always thought things through before speaking, in marked contrast to his boss.

Cameron stood looking out of the window towards the pier as he spoke.

'I told him this wouldn't work. It's a listed building, for Christ's sake. You cannae just smack it around and double the size of the place.'

'But the jobs created? I thought Lionel's presentation was very strong. The town deserves a big focal point and the pier is it.'

'Maybe so, but that's not how conservation officers will view it. There was no way that they would accept it but Lionel's Lionel. He wouldn't be told.'

'It might have helped if Janet Wells had come. She is supposed to be his partner, after all.'

'I doubt that it would have made the slightest difference, and besides, that was never going to happen.'

'Really? How come?'

'She's playing him. Buying herself time.'

'But why? I've not been here long enough to understand the politics.'

'Well for two reasons, as I see it. I was suspicious when she refused to hand over the costing information on the show that I requested. I pulled the published accounts, of course, but they don't help much. I don't know much about theatre but a show of that standard is so expensive to put on. It's a west end level show with costs to match, so you need plenty of bums on seats for it to turn a buck.'

'Well, yes. Obviously.'

'But Lionel wants to use it as a bingo hall most of the time, so the show as it stands just won't work.'

'So what does Lionel say about that?'

'Not much, really. This is a vanity project for him.'

'I had that impression. Was that your second reason?'

'Lionel Pemrose hated Jack Wells, so even though Wells is long dead, Lionel wants the theatre.'

'I knew that bit. Wells screwed him out of the theatre, according to Lionel.'

'That is probably true. Wells was a Freemason, and there were plenty of masons involved in the botched up decision they made, leaving Lionel owning the pier and Wells with a licence on the theatre. Bonkers.'

'But why did Lionel go through with such a stupid deal?'

'Because Lionel always takes the long-term view in business. I quite admire him for it, actually. He believed that if he got hold of the pier, the theatre would be his one day.'

'And I guess now is the time. But he could simply have followed through when the bank pulled the plug and taken it back.'

'Which is what I told him to do. Instead of which, he's allowed her an extension and agreed to her insistence of confidentiality.'

'Then why? I don't get it.'

'I'm not totally sure. Lionel's a bit old school, so if he can get control the nice way then why not do so? He doesn't understand the theatre game so keeping Janet Wells on makes some sense, I suppose.'

'But suppose she finds someone else in the meantime?'

Cameron smiled and helped himself to a scotch, handing one to Tyler.

'Well she can't. Not for 12 months. Pemrose has exclusivity. And in this financial climate, who would want it?'

Tyler smiled and shook his head as he spoke.

'You don't sound entirely convinced. You think there's another reason?'

Tyler liked Cameron, and was learning a lot from this wise older man, but sometimes his game playing became annoying.

Cameron smiled.

'Well he's fancied Janet Wells for years. She was quite a stunner when she was younger. And if you cannae screw the father…'

Tyler nodded, finally understanding.

'You can screw the daughter? That's pretty sick. What about Miriam?'

Cameron smiled.

'Oh, you can bet Miriam Pemrose won't be told about this at all. Only you and I, plus the advisors, know about this. Lionel will keep this a secret.'

'Which is why he agreed the extension? Keeps it all confidential until he has it all buttoned up?'

'Precisely. But of course, Mrs Wells is just biding her time trying to find the money to keep going.'

'It's still crazy. It would have been so much simpler to pull the plug and act the white knight keeping the theatre going after it shut in the recession. He could have put a gun to the planners' heads. He could have said 'let me redevelop or it stays shut and I don't spend a penny.''

'Which is exactly what I advised him to do.'

At that moment, Lionel came back in, reading some correspondence. He looked up and smiled.

'Where's mine then, Jim? Drinking my scotch again?'

Cameron laughed and poured an extra glass. Lionel sipped it and motioned in the direction of the theatre.

'Never mind. I thought I'd chance my arm. I've got the architect doing a more modest scheme, which I've had blessed by the Norfolk Conservation Trust, no less.'

Cameron smiled and they clinked glasses.

It was typical of Lionel, he thought. He'd always have a plan B.

'And I'll bet you haven't shared that with Janet Wells,' said Cameron.

Lionel laughed.

'Well, I'm sure I'll get around to it. The theatre will be a little smaller, of course.'

Tyler was puzzled, but then realised.

'So there won't be a summer show at all then?'

'Oh, I rather think not. After all, there are plenty of profitable one-night acts available. I've a couple of London promoters keen to get involved. I just needed a bit more time to line things up. They can rehearse all they like but they won't see opening night.'

*   *   *

With the show now in hand, it looked like there would be one more good season before the Wells' period of sole ownership finally concluded. Janet was aware that the extension was coming to an end and could not really stall very much longer.

One by one, her possible sources of funding were falling away, so she was becoming resigned to her fate. She'd had several evenings at home alone, and decided that she needed to get out for the evening.

Peggy Bloomingdale told her that Paul Warren had moved on, taking a holiday let for a while in leafy Overstrand while he pondered the future. Janet had given the matter much thought, and decided that she ought to at least have one more meeting with him before he headed off to a new life, wherever that might be.

She called him, and they met up one warm evening for dinner. A new fish restaurant had opened, run by a friend of hers, and she wanted to show her support. As she looked at the brand new décor, she couldn't help but wonder how much the refit had cost.

It was awkward at first. Did they have anything left in common? But to her surprise, she found Paul easy company.

The sense of humour was still there, and he seemed remarkably relaxed considering the circumstances.

From Paul's perspective, Janet added some pleasant social company to his new solo life. Having a night out was a rare and welcome treat for him, in any event. Carol would doubtless have approved had he taken her out more. He was not under any pressure for the first time in so many years. There were no disaffected agents moaning about player contracts, no new signings to be courted, and football was on holiday for a while longer anyway.

He'd had no shortage of offers of employment, and no money problems thanks to the enormous severance payment sitting in his newly-opened investment portfolio. He'd decided to allow himself the luxury of time. With money no object, he'd hired a lovely holiday let on the cliff-top with a fine sea view, and loved his morning run along the cliff path. He knew it was reality suspended, but decided to allow himself some time out.

'Thanks for a lovely dinner, Paul. I'm glad I rang you now,' said Janet smiling, sipping a particularly nice glass of Sauvignon Blanc.

'It was great to catch up. Surprisingly, I didn't exactly have a hot date this evening.'

He realised that, although she had aged, her eyes were as bright as he remembered, and her smile was still as radiant.

'Has Carol called lately?' she asked, picking at her dessert.

'Yes. She gets full marks for trying.'

There was a pause. Then she looked at him directly. She was picking her words with care.

'You're going to have to talk to her, you know. You were married a long time. Actually, you still are. It's none of my business, I'm just saying.'

Paul shook his head.

'She's only after her share, that's all. She knows I got paid off.'

'With respect, you can't possibly know that. You haven't spoken to her.'

Paul nibbled some cheese and thought for a moment. Janet was just as direct as he remembered.

'I suppose that's true, but as far as I'm concerned it's all over after what she did.'

Janet looked at him surprised.

'So you were never tempted? You must have had offers. All footballers get offers. It goes with the territory. It's just like in show business.'

Paul shrugged and smiled a little.

'I guess that's true. Look, I'll admit I was tempted a couple of times but I never strayed or played away, so to speak.'

Janet was puzzled. She found that she still cared about him. He was still the Paul she fell in love with so many years ago. As much as she knew it was none of her business, she couldn't leave it alone.

The restaurant was thinning out now. They weren't alone but there were only one or two couples finishing up.

'Paul, you've been married so many years. Don't give up. What you have is worth fighting for, surely?'

He thought for a moment, and set his napkin down.

'Look, it's not just the affair, it's the disloyalty. I worked my butt off to try to keep the team up, and she has an affair with that lazy gigolo Mariano. A lazy, good for nothing bastard. Talk about eats, shoots and leaves.'

He rather realised as he said it that his comment was more than a little ironic. Janet seized on it.

'Oh, yes? I might say the same about you.'

She leant forward, placing her hand on his.

'I'm sorry, I didn't mean that,' she said.

'It's me who should be sorry, Janet. That was a stupid thing for me to say.'

He put a second hand on hers, and she clasped his. For a moment, he thought of leaning forward and kissing her.

She paused, then leaned back and took another sip of her wine.

Paul looked across at this still very attractive older woman, wearing a burgundy top, which showed just a hint of her cleavage.

Janet decided that she couldn't leave this be.

'OK, let's take a step back for a moment. Let me look at it from Carol's point of view. Suppose you were so much into saving the club that you didn't give any attention to her or your marriage?'

Paul shrugged. He knew she was right. He'd had the same thoughts during more cerebral moments.

'I hear that, but it still doesn't justify her behaviour.'

'No, it doesn't. But think about it.'

Paul nodded slowly. Janet knew she had said enough. Move on.

'Let's change the subject. How exactly did it go with Inspector Corner of the yard in the end? They obviously didn't cart you off in a van with a blue flashing light on the top.'

Paul smiled, recalling his relief at the outcome.

'Well at least that's sorted out,' Paul said. 'Mariano isn't pressing charges so I've accepted a police caution.'

'That must be a relief. Have you been spotted by the press at all? I suppose it's a few weeks ago now, so not much of a story?'

Paul smiled.

'Not by the press at all. The only one who spotted me was Mr Punch.'

'What?'

'Mr Punch. Cyril Brown.'

'Cyril? Oh, yes. He's a lovely man. You know, it doesn't surprise me that he was the one who spotted you. A very perceptive old boy is our Cyril.'

'He's left the pier, I gather. His rent has gone up or something. Shame after all these years.'

'Tell me about it.'

Paul hesitated.

'I think I already know, Janet.'

Janet looked up. Fear and concern took over and her whole demeanour became defensive.

'What do you mean?'

'I borrowed some clubs and played a round of golf yesterday. Mr Pemrose was in the Club House when I stopped in for a drink after. He was in an adjoining room with some banking pals holding court. It sounds like he has big plans for your theatre from what I overheard.'

'Oh.'

'Want to talk about it?'

'No.'

'Pemrose stitched you up, too, by the sound of it. Along with Cyril.'

'I said I don't want to talk about it.'

'Like I want to talk about my marriage?'

'I was only trying to help.'

'So am I, Janet. Look I don't want to spoil a lovely evening but, well, you didn't only come out with me for old times' sake, did you?'

'What do you mean?'

'You phoned because you needed to get away from reality for a bit. Something's been on your mind all evening. And the last time, too. You can't bullshit me, I'm a football manager. I'm paid to be a mind-reader.'

'Ex-football manager. Maybe you're not as good as you think.'

'But I'm right, aren't I?'

She hesitated.

'All right, yes, you're right, as it happens.'

How quickly conversations change, Paul thought. The boot was on the other foot now.

'Come on, Janet. Spit it out. Problem shared and all that.'

'I don't know where to start.'

She was welling up, struggling to find a tissue in her handbag. Her voice became brittle.

'Basically, I'm about to lose the theatre.'

'Go on.'

'Everything my father built. My career, too. Every dream Karen had. And all of the people I care about. Lionel has kippered me and there is nothing I can do. Put bluntly, I'm about to lose …the whole… sodding… thing.'

Paul moved around to her side of the table and put his arm around her. Fortunately the last diners had just left and they were alone.

'It's OK. You don't have to be indestructible with me.'

'Thanks, Paul.'

'For what? I haven't done anything.'

'I just needed to cry. I'm so used to being in control. It's just, well…'

'The way you've had to be. Indestructible Janet always has the answer?'

'I guess. The thing is, I just didn't see it coming. I've been plain stupid.'

Paul laughed kindly.

'I doubt that. I've met cretins like Pemrose before. He reminds me of my Chairman. This time last year, I was on top of the world. We won the play off final at Wembley, new contract, lovely house, lovely wife. Magic.'

'And Lionel? I don't understand the similarity.'

'Well it sounded to me like he had everybody stitched up. He is hooked into the Local Council, Rotary, Round Table, Golf Club. He gets things done through the cronies.'

'So?'

'He will have a weakness. You just need to find what it is.'

Janet thought for a moment.

'Well, he's a womaniser. He even tried it on with me.'

'Forgive me but so did I, with rather more success than he did I hope?'

Janet stared at him.

'That's so very helpful. What do you suggest I do, lure him onto the beach with a bag of chips and some cider for a quickie? Forgive me but I'm a bit old for that now.'

She smiled briefly and he smiled too, at her black humour.

'No. But I assume he has a wife. She's not likely to approve?'

'Miriam 'Pillar of the WI' Pemrose? Rock solid, their marriage. They've made a lot of money together.'

'So you couldn't talk to her? Tell her what Pemrose did?'

'No chance. She probably approves. And don't get me wrong, some of his ideas are good. It's just that, well, the little people do tend to be squished underfoot.'

'So what's your best option?'

'Look, I've said too much already. There's legal stuff.'

'Whatever. Come on, Janet. I'm not going to spill the beans. I hardly know anybody.'

'Oh, what the hell. He's offered me a partnership. Keeps a reduced number of shows interspersed with bingo.'

'Ah, I can see your problem.'

'No, I'm not so precious about bingo, but Pemrose won't accept some of my staff because of previous issues.'

'And you feel a big loyalty to them?'

'Exactly. But it's the only fall-back position I have.'

'You need investment, Janet. I can tell the theatre's seen better days.'

'I know. I've known it for a while, to be honest. It needs a total refit and Lionel's got the money to do it. He just won't when he doesn't own it outright.'

'Well it's a tough call, all right. But you will see it through. You're one strong lady.'

'Yes, you're right, I will because I have to.'

She put away the tissue and sipped her wine. Paul did likewise. She thought for a moment and spoke softly, her voice recovering.

'Look, Paul, about tonight. I'm sorry if you feel used. You were exactly right. I just needed to escape from the reality for a while.'

'No problem. I've had a wonderful evening, Janet. I needed some company, too.'

'But no sex for you this time, Mr Warren.'

'No, I rather thought not and, of course, I'm still married. At least for now.'

They paused for a moment, and Paul asked for the bill. Janet thought for a moment.

'Look, Paul, I said some harsh things the other day. Forget what I said about that night. To be fair, I was tipsy, but I wasn't drunk. I wanted you so badly it hurt. We were both to blame. We should have used a condom.'

'I tried.'

'What?'

'I tried to buy one. Trouble was that every time I tried to

use the machine, someone came in and I got embarrassed. Then when I did get to use it, the machine swallowed my money.'

She smiled and shook her head. How ridiculous it had been.

'What happened, happened. Let's live and let live. I wouldn't change Karen for the world.'

'So we're friends?'

'Yes, Paul. I'd like that very much.'

# 16.

## Carol

By now, Carol was pretty fed up with the whole situation. Days had turned into weeks and Paul had just gone AWOL. He wouldn't communicate. Day after day, she emailed and telephoned but he ignored them all. Just a terse email saying that he had ensured that the bills would continue to be paid while he was away. Away? What did he mean by 'away'?

Hadn't she done everything to try to make things right? She'd been a fool. She admitted that in writing. She'd apologised, begged forgiveness even. Now she was just getting mad. This was always Paul's response to things. Bury his head in the sand. If he didn't like a topic, he'd just stop communicating.

Thinking back, it was always the same.

Take a holiday? Talk about it some other time. Start a family? It's the transfer window now – let's talk next month. He'd just got worse and worse.

This season, things were worse still. Monosyllabic, preoccupied. He wouldn't go out to socialise. He forgot both their anniversary and her birthday this time. Even forgot his own birthday.

But how could she have been so stupid? Mariano the

gigolo. The toy boy 10 years younger. The Italian stud. Where was it ever going to lead? It was just a tawdry affair. Just sex, never anything more. It was always going to end in tears. She knew that but did it anyway.

So she would fight. She would fight to get her husband back. The old Paul who loved her, who bought her spontaneous presents, who called her every night when he was on tour in the early days, even left her little notes with kisses on when he left early in the morning. The Paul who proposed so romantically in St Mark's Square one warm summer's evening as the sun set with the day trippers long gone. Her Paul was still there, she knew, deep within that hardened shell into which he had receded.

But to fight, she had to find him. The police had been unhelpful, telling her the matter was closed and they couldn't identify his whereabouts due to data protection. In desperation, she'd spoken to his brothers. They had become as distant as brothers sometimes did.

The only thing that they had mentioned to her was Cromer. Mrs Bloomingdale's, they said. Some sort of guest house on the seafront. Their childhood holidays. But they had no reason to suggest that Paul had gone there. He could have gone anywhere. He'd vaguely mentioned it a long time ago when he reminisced about his childhood, but had never suggested visiting.

She telephoned Bloomingdale's on the off chance. As she dialled, she felt nervous and embarrassed. This might call for deviousness – a skill she had never really needed to develop.

They would probably decline to discuss their guests, respecting their privacy. A young female voice answered the phone and Carol began to explain.

'Hi, I would like to speak to Paul Warren, please. It's his wife, Carol. It seems his mobile's on the blink again.'

She had clearly got hold of the most junior member of the Bloomingdale household.

'I'm sorry, Mrs Warren, but Mr Warren checked out a while ago now. He rented my aunt's holiday home in Overstrand as a matter of fact.'

Carol had just got lucky. Any hotelier would have claimed client confidentiality, but 13-year-old Clara was just being helpful, as Grandma Peggy had said she should be.

Carol scribbled down the address, thanked the young lady and put down the telephone in triumph. She Googled the address the young lady had given her. There it was. It looked a very nice place. Nice view of the sea.

It was too late to leave that day, but she packed her bag and was on the road south by nine o'clock the following morning. It was a warm summer's day. She recalled that it was the time of year when they were normally on holiday somewhere hotter still, but not this year.

It had been so different after Wembley last year. The Chairman had insisted that they used his villa in Tuscany as a reward for promotion, and Paul had signed a five-year contract the day before they flew out, business class, of course.

The four-bedroomed villa was traditional, but the patio

had lovely views over the Tuscan hills, and had a large infinity pool. It stood in the grounds of a vineyard, and was both secluded and private.

There was no mobile signal, and feeble, if any, broadband, so they spent several days around the pool, reading trashy novels, eating pizza, enjoying a daily gelato in the village, and sipping red wine on the terrace late into the evening.

Life had seemed perfect. They swam naked late at night, made love then slept late in the mornings. It felt like a second honeymoon. After a tough season, she thought that they had taken the clock back to when they had first met. At that time, he was being talked of as a future England international and she was a part-time waitress while studying for her degree. He was the seasoned professional and she was so much younger. She remembered tipping soup down him the first time they met. She apologised profusely, but he smiled, and later asked for her number when she brought his dessert.

He was injured at the time. His right knee was playing up. So he had time for her then. It was a wonderful whirlwind romance. In Tuscany, it seemed that their love for each other had returned.

A few weeks later, she was violently sick and had vertigo. Until the GP said it, she had not dreamt that she might be pregnant. Not at her age. It couldn't happen to a 40-something, could it? It seemed daft in hindsight, but they had tried for a baby for years without any success, and it seemed that although the doctors couldn't really find anything wrong with either of them, it appeared impossible for her to conceive. They'd talked about adoption, but the nomadic nature of a career in football seemed to limit their opportunity.

They were both shocked and overjoyed by the pregnancy. It seemed that their life would now be complete. Everything was coming right now. The years of effort were paying off. Paul's bonus for achieving promotion made the mortgage history. His team were playing in the biggest league in the world.

Then she miscarried.

\*   \*   \*

Lauren returned to Bloomingdale's that evening, satisfied that she was getting the hang of things. The rehearsal had featured her full set, with the dancers on stage behind her. The steps she'd rehearsed worked well, and her two duets had gone well too. Les was pleased.

She felt so much fitter now. The dance routines required so much physical effort, and she had run for miles along the coast each day. The full English breakfast was a thing of the past and Bloomingdale's had agreed to cook her an evening meal to a diet managed by Isobel. She had subsequently lost nearly two stone. The hard-pressed costume department was now adjusting her dress sizes accordingly. She also went to the gym with Karen and Amy. They had brought in Karen's voice coach to make sure that her voice would stand the pressures of a full season. She was singing better than ever. All in all, she felt great.

As she entered her room though, she saw the bundle of

post in a brown envelope, obviously forwarded from Wales. The official-looking letter at the top caught her eye. She'd seen a couple of these before. But this one was registered post.

She sat as she opened it, and her heart sank.

She would be heading back to Wales first thing in the morning.

\*   \*   \*

Les allowed himself a quiet smile as he sipped a glass of ginger beer while sitting at a table on the pier. He'd completed a full run-through of his own comedy set, and it was clear that he was in good form. It was so difficult when only performing for a couple of cleaners and some part-time bar staff, but he knew that his new stuff was working.

Earlier that afternoon, he'd sat in the theatre watching a first run through of show one. He was joined by Janet Wells, who sat impassively throughout. They both applauded as the cast left the stage at the end and only then did he turn to her.

'Well, Mrs Wells?'

He saw that she was crying. She wiped away a tear and hugged him spontaneously.

'It's lovely, Les. The best yet,' she whispered into his ear.

'You say that every year, Janet.'

'No, I mean it, Les. It's just beautiful. Lauren just seems, well, just so different somehow.'

'Smaller in physique and bigger in voice, perhaps?' he said.

'Yes. I think so, somehow. Karen said she'd lost some

weight but I lose touch with the show with everything else that goes on. And her solo set just works so well. The new stuff is so right for her.'

'That's because she's singing about her life when she sings them. It's her life story, from when she was a little girl. Of course, Gerald's arrangements are spot on, as always. Even her agent's impressed.'

'Even Lech was good.'

Les smiled.

'I must admit he's just charming, isn't he? He has the makings of an all-round entertainer, God help us.'

They had parted contentedly, knowing that although this was their last season, it was indeed likely to be their best. Ticket sales were strong, ironically, a combination of the big star and the British staycation brought on by the recession.

Les had not recently mentioned the negotiations with Lionel Pemrose, because they were not his business, after all. His contract was up at the end of the season and would not be renewed. That was certain. What Pemrose and Wells did with his theatre after that was up to them, although the idea that the end-of-the-pier show might die with his leaving caused him great sadness.

He'd spoken at length with his agent about the future. He could spend his life cruising the world, if he wished. A major cruise line had even offered him a full-time contract as both a show producer and comedian. But Les wanted more than that. He'd written some stuff for others, and had an idea for a sitcom, the pilot for which was nearly complete.

He thought that, in spite of things, the show was in good shape and he could look forward to an exciting future. If he had to spend his life cruising around the world, he could think of a worse fate.

# 17.

## Lauren

Lauren caught the early train to London. She couldn't bring herself to talk about it to the staff at the bed and breakfast who had been so kind. She penned a handwritten note to Les, and dropped it through the box office door for his attention. She was so embarrassed to be letting them down after all the kindness that they had shown, but how things would turn out she couldn't say, so she needed to take a few days. Whether she'd be back at all, she had no idea.

She stood on the same platform as she had weeks before. But things were different now. Then it had been a nondescript seaside town, one amongst many places she had visited in her relatively short career. Now she felt she was leaving a place which had some feeling of home.

She was letting everybody down, but the letter that she had received required that she did so. The wording was clear. She needed to be there by 10 o'clock in the morning of the day after. She had seen other letters. So many from different people that she had just thrown them all away as if by doing so they would go away. She'd become blind to the issue because it told of her fall from grace, her total extravagance and irresponsibility. Nobody wants to face up to their shortcomings.

She boarded the train and watched the coast recede into the distance. She nodded off briefly, as she hadn't slept the previous night. She'd spoken briefly to her agent who, although horrified, had said that he would arrange for her to meet a solicitor at nine o'clock in the morning to review what papers she had ahead of the hearing. He realised that Lauren was in no fit state for a detailed conversation about what had gone on. He was as reassuring as he could be, and had he not been in meetings all day, he'd have met her in London and gone down to Wales with her.

He put down the telephone and allowed himself some muttered oaths. How could anyone be so totally stupid? How could you ignore such things? And just as he was getting her back on track. He'd kept in touch with Janet Wells on a regular basis to make absolutely sure she was settling in OK. Only the day before, Mrs Wells had said how well things were going. Now this.

He rang another solicitor friend for advice, and he agreed to find a colleague to meet her first thing in the morning. They needed to stop the ball rolling, and then work out how bad things were. Having reassured Lauren that she had not been abandoned, he was about to ring the theatre when the telephone rang. Janet Wells was on the line. He had the call put through at once.

'Good morning, Janet, I think I know why you are calling.'

'It's not exactly a good morning, Frank. We've received

a handwritten note from Lauren. Frankly, it's rather hard to read and grammatically awful, but I think that we get the gist. I assume she's made you aware of things?'

'Yes, she has. She rang me from the train in tears. I was just about to ring you.'

'You'd better explain the details then, because the note is virtually incoherent.'

'She's acutely dyslexic, Janet. As you've probably gathered, it appears that she is facing imminent bankruptcy. The hearing is in the morning in Swansea, hence her immediate departure. I'm so sorry – I really had no idea. She simply buried her head in the sand or so it seems.'

'Well, that clarifies things. Les Westley is on a train now. He'll be there in support. What are you doing about it?'

'I've got her a solicitor who will meet her ahead of the hearing, but to be honest, I'm not in full possession of the facts. It seems there are a number of creditors petitioning for her bankruptcy. They've all got court orders, or so it seems. It's a bloody awful mess.'

'And a bloody PR disaster, Frank. I hope you've got a plan for that, too.'

Frank Gilbert had anticipated this. Any drop in ticket sales just before opening night would be potentially disastrous.

'Look, I'm alive to the issue, Janet. But I'm only just responding to the matter so just give me some time. Hopefully we'll get the situation stabilised.'

'I hope you're right, Frank. I'll let Les know what's happening. Perhaps he can help.'

Frank thought for a moment.

'Well, the solicitor won't know her, and Les does, of course. It will obviously be her decision but I agree it could help. She's very emotional at the best of times. I'm so sorry about this. I know that this is all you need.'

'You're not wrong, Mr Gilbert. Without Lauren, the show is done. Finished. Understand me?'

'Of course I do, Janet. I assure you I'll attend to it personally.'

Janet put the telephone down. She was deeply worried. Whatever Lionel did or didn't do, if she was forced to cancel the show, the losses would render her insolvent. She could sue for breach of contract, but it would be all over by the time that the case was heard.

Les was on the train, trying to work out which train Lauren had caught. He reckoned that he was probably a couple of hours behind, but his train stopped less frequently. He wondered if he might get the same train from London, but it seemed unlikely. So when he got to Swansea, how would he find her?

His mobile rang. Janet Wells.

'Yes, Janet?' he said, as quietly as he could. Janet brought him up to speed.

'I've spoken to the agent. He's arranged for a solicitor to see her ahead of the hearing. At least she'll have representation.'

'Good. That's helpful. What about the PR though?'

'Well, he'll do what he can, but if a reporter sees her name in the court list, there's not much he can do.'

'She won't be listed as Lauren Evans though. She'll be listed as Lauren Butt. We might just get away with it.'

'I hope so, Les. I've given him your number, so if Lauren agrees, you can be there at the meeting.'

'I'm hoping that she's not in too deep, poor girl.'

'Poor girl? Forgive me if I don't cry too much for her given the shit that she's dropped us in.'

'Fair point. But I nearly went there myself remember? I'm not about to judge.'

'Well, I will if you don't mind, since I'm the next in line for the bankruptcy court, if you don't pull your finger out.'

'Have I ever let you down?'

'It's not funny, Les.'

\*     \*     \*

Lauren arrived in London and went to a cash machine. A card she'd used previously was declined. She tried another. Declined. She was getting looks from people behind her but she shuffled the cards and, third time lucky, she managed to get one to dispense some cash.

The game was up, she realised. She'd juggled and juggled the cards, getting new ones even as existing ones were cut off. Now even the new ones were getting declined. Tomorrow, she would face the music in court. A final humiliation.

She headed from Liverpool Street to Paddington, but she had plenty of time to kill when she arrived. She wanted to hide away. Ordinarily, she could handle being recognised. Most of her fans were lovely, and just wanted her autograph. One or two could be a bit wearing, but that was the price you paid. Today though, she had dressed down and her hair was just scrunched into a bun. She didn't want to speak to anyone. Her mobile buzzed as a text came in. Les. She'd ignored his three phone calls because she couldn't bear to speak to him knowing how difficult things could be for them. But she picked up the text.

'Lauren, I've been where you are now, so no need to panic. I'm a train or two behind you, so tell me where we can meet. Chin up. Les xx'

She smiled briefly. At least someone's still talking to me, she thought. The agent had taken the news as might be expected, but at least he was there for her. She'd been contacted by the solicitor, from a local firm in Swansea, who'd agreed to take the case. They would meet at eight o'clock in their office in Swansea. He needed all of the correspondence and a full list of her debts.

She texted Les back, still not able to talk to people she had let down.

'Seeing solicitor in the morning. Will you come with me? Shit scared. Lauren.'

He replied shortly after.

'Happy to. Let me have details. I'm happy to buy you dinner if you can face it.'

She declined dinner. She'd fixed to stay with her cousin and didn't want to risk being recognised.

Les was relieved that Lauren was at least communicating. Some in her position often didn't, he knew only too well. Some didn't even attend court. He knew the drill. The solicitor would act fast.

More than anything, he was happy that she was alive. People in hopeless situations sometimes took the only route out that they could see. That's what his friend Paul had done. Les still believed that, looking back, he could have done more.

He remembered another girl, too, many years since, in a similar situation. She was a dancer in the show. It was high tide and late evening. She had left the theatre upset, and colleagues were worried. He'd gone around the back of the pier and found her standing by the rail, one foot raised to climb over.

'Jane, it's OK. We know about it. We can help. Don't worry.'

He had talked her back down, but it still sent a chill up his spine. Suppose Lauren had taken that route, he thought.

He rang Janet back. She was at least reassured that Lauren was safe and the matter was in the proper hands. She also knew that Les, more than anyone, knew how to deal with it.

\* \* \*

The following day was miserable and grey. It matched Lauren's mood. They agreed to meet an hour before the meeting. Lauren threw her arms around Les as they met, to his surprise. He smelt her designer perfume, and she seemed thinner than he remembered her being. She wiped away a tear as she released her bear hug-like grip.

'Thanks for coming, Les. It means a lot.'

They headed to a coffee shop that Lauren knew from her

younger days. Her friend was the owner and there was an upstairs section unused at that time of day. Tea arrived and they sat down on two comfortable settees.

'Is Mrs Wells OK?' she said as she poured the tea into two cups.

Les tried to smile, but failed rather badly.

'She's certainly been better, Lauren.'

Lauren looked down at the tea, stifling tears.

'I've been bloody stupid and that's a fact. I'm fired, right?'

Les picked up his tea, went to sip it, but then set it down. She continued.

'Nobody hires a bankrupt. It was hard enough before. My agent told me that this was my last chance. I've blown it.'

Les smiled at her naivety, and shook his head.

'We don't fire people for missing a single rehearsal, Lauren.'

'What do you mean? I'm all washed up. I'm bankrupt. Or will be in a couple of hours.'

Les put his hand on hers, trying to calm her down.

'That is a legal matter for you, and no business of Cromer Pier Theatre. Unless, of course, the story damages the show, which we won't allow it to.'

She seemed perplexed. Les brought her back to earth.

'Lauren, you just need to focus your mind on this morning. You need to give the solicitor a full picture. Every debt. Nothing held back. Every last detail.'

'Yes. I've pulled it together. I'll show you.'

She went to her voluminous handbag, but he stopped her.

'I don't need to see it. Just make sure he gets the whole

picture. He'll have done any number of these. It's going to be a massive number. It always is at this stage.'

'But I can't pay it. No way. I've nothing to sell! The flat's rented and the landlord's not been paid either.'

'I should have guessed when you didn't bring a car with you.'

'Repossessed months ago. Candy apple red Mini, she was. Lush.'

'OK.'

She leant forward.

'Will court be awful? I've never been to court in my life.'

'Your solicitor will take you through it, but if I'm right, he'll try to buy some time.'

And buy time is exactly what the solicitor did. He spoke with a court official and said that he was working on some proposals to creditors, including those petitioning for bankruptcy. His junior took all of the papers and went through them with Lauren separately as he made some calls.

Les might have been surprised had he not seen it all before. The junior, a young woman in her 30s, was business-like and, to Lauren's relief, not judgemental. Leafing through the receipts such as they were, the young woman smiled at one point.

'Just how many pairs of Jimmy Choos do you have exactly?'

Lauren was embarrassed.

'Around a dozen, I suspect.'

Les was aghast.

'More shoes than I own in total.'

'You're a bloke, Les. You wouldn't understand.'

The junior smiled and went about her business. Finally, she handed the summary to her boss.

'Well?' asked Lauren.

The solicitor looked up from the summary.

'I've seen worse. Not many, but some. You've been rather naughty, haven't you?'

Lauren was confused.

'So? Shouldn't we be going to court? I wouldn't want to be late.'

The solicitor shook his head.

'Oh, I've got the hearing adjourned. I've got 14 days to put something together.'

'Meaning?'

'Meaning that we need to put forward a proposal that your creditors will accept.'

He turned to Les.

'Mr Westley, I gather that Miss Butt has a contract with Cromer Pier Theatre?'

'Yes, that's correct. The show opens this month and runs until the end of September, and we have every intention of honouring it. Her living expenses are being reimbursed.'

'That's very helpful at least. What about the winter season?'

'Well, that's for Miss Butt and her agent to decide, of course. But with Miss Butt's talents, I should have thought a season in panto would be logical. As the headliner, she should command a substantial fee. Cruise ships would also want her after that. I have some contacts.'

'Good. We can work on that with her agent. Now, Lauren,

you were telling me that your contract with the record company had expired.'

'Yes, that's correct.'

'But you'll still have royalties from that, and from personal appearances?'

'Yes.'

'Good. Now I'm going to hand over the files to a colleague who specialises in personal insolvency. He will work out how much you can repay and over what period. You'll need to keep up those payments to creditors once agreed, come what may, and live within your very restricted means during the period of the agreement. Hopefully that will get your creditors to stay bankruptcy proceedings, although there is just a chance that they won't agree. It is unlikely but possible.'

Lauren was still trying to keep up with a world that she didn't understand.

'So when do I have to go to court?'

The solicitor smiled.

'Hopefully you don't, Lauren. But I emphasise you will need to live within strict financial limits for many years to come. It won't be easy.'

It was agreed that Lauren would meet the insolvency expert the following day, and that was that.

They left shortly after, and Les bought her an early lunch. Lauren was quiet. She was still working out what had happened. Les did his best to explain.

'You're basically going to agree to pay people what you owe over a very long period. They'll probably agree to waive interest

on the debt, and possibly some of the debt itself. They'd rather
have a voluntary agreement than risk making you bankrupt.'

Lauren smiled.

'That sounds a bit too good to be true.'

Les shook his head.

'It's not that easy. It means you'll have to work your socks
off. You'll be working for them for years, and you can forget
all about designer handbags, shoes and so forth.'

'Were you, well, bankrupt then?'

'Nearly. I'm out of the woods now, but it took me a long,
long time.'

'What happened?'

'Let's hold that one for another day, Lauren.'

They moved on. Lauren said she'd come back to Cromer
the following day, so she could the make Friday rehearsal. Les
was more realistic.

'Take the extra day, Lauren, and make sure you tie up all of
the loose ends. Do some family stuff. When the season starts,
you won't have time to come home. We'll see you on Monday.'

She looked up at him, her sparkling blue eyes filling with
tears.

'Thanks, Les. You guys, well, I've just never known such
kindness.'

She went to the station with him, and she kissed him on
the cheek as they said their goodbyes.

He took out £200 and gave it to her.

'No cards now, Lauren. Make it last,' he said.

'I couldn't possibly, Les. You've been too kind already.'

'But you must. Don't forget that every card you have is now dead. Everything is cash from now on, even paying for your train ticket back to Cromer.'

She paused, then nodded and took the money.

Les hugged her again, and turned to get his train.

'See you on Monday.'

'See you, Les. Thanks for everything. And thank Mrs Wells, too. She's an absolute star.'

With that, they parted company.

Les rang Janet to confirm that Lauren was coming back. Janet was intensely relieved, but it was clear to Les that her mind was still preoccupied. About the deal with Lionel, no doubt. But he didn't ask and she didn't mention it. One day at a time, Les, he thought, falling into a welcome sleep on the seven-hour train ride back to Cromer.

# 18.

## Personal Affairs

Carol drove down to Cromer, but traffic delays meant that it was late afternoon before she arrived. She had no idea where she would spend the night, so she rang Bloomingdale's, only to find that they were full.

She went online and booked some place called the Majestic Hotel. It looked swanky, with an indoor pool and spa. It cost a fortune, and doubtless Paul would have thrown a fit at the cost, but she found that she really didn't give a damn.

Maybe she'd had enough of playing nice. Maybe she'd apologised enough. How many more grovelling emails and texts did it take? Besides, how long had she tolerated his moods and tantrums beforehand?

She checked in and was offered a cheap upgrade to a sea view room. She took it. Why not? She was shown to a beautifully decorated room, with simple furnishings and a dash of art deco thrown in. Nice. Clearly someone with taste had designed the décor in the room. It had a lovely sea view looking out towards the pier, and a pristine white bathroom, so she stripped off and ran a bath. She put on the complimentary bathrobe and sat for a while looking out. It was quite peaceful, as a grey sky took over from earlier sunshine and the tourists headed off for the day.

There was a minibar with hideously expensive white wine. What the heck? She poured a larger glass than was sensible. As she lay in the bath, eyes closed, her thoughts drifted. As a place to escape to, this wasn't half bad, she reflected. The food in the restaurant looked inviting, and she had every intention of eating whatever she fancied for once.

She looked at herself. She was quite a bit younger than Paul, and although the afflictions of middle age were telling tales, she didn't look bad, considering. A diminutive lady of five foot, five inches, she had short, blonde, highlighted hair, and stylish designer glasses. She had recovered from her miscarriage, and the repeated gym sessions with the club physiotherapist were paying off.

She thought briefly about Enzo. Whatever his faults, he knew how to treat a lady. More than Paul did. Enzo remembered her birthday when Paul had not.

Enzo was there for her. It had started after she miscarried. Paul initially said the right things, but as they entered a frenetic pre-season, he'd become preoccupied in every respect. The romance of Tuscany was forgotten. She'd attended a welcome party at the club, and that was where she first met Enzo Mariano. He was away from home, and she was flattered by the attention. Paul was heading off after the event, some scouting mission or other, but she was staying over. What happened shouldn't have happened but she was angry with Paul, and Enzo was charming. The drink just made it easier to go with it.

She was thinking about this when her mobile rang, and she answered it, hoping it was Paul. It wasn't. It was her friend, Mel.

'Hi, Carol. So how are things at the seaside? Bought your bucket and spade yet?'

Carol laughed.

'No. And I haven't bought my kiss-me-quick hat either. In fact, I'm lying in the bath drinking some hideously expensive white wine.'

'Are you alone?'

'Meaning?' said Carol indignantly.

'Meaning that hotels have young Italian waiters and you're prone to shagging Italians in strange hotels as I recall.'

'Sod off, Mrs Clarke.'

'Language, darling. I just wanted to wish you well. When will you do the deed?'

'Tomorrow morning, I think. Best time to find him, I should have thought. Late morning, probably.'

'I guess. How are you going to play things?'

Carol hesitated.

'Not sure. Play it by ear, I suppose. But I'm done apologising, I've done all that, I think I'll just see what he wants to do.'

'That's very sensible. Getting your Paul to discuss his emotions won't be easy, though.'

Carol pondered. The thought of it welled up inside her.

'No, I'm dreading it, to be fair. He could even have another woman by now. Maybe he was shagging someone, too? He had plenty of nights away.'

'Oh, well, I hadn't really thought about that. Surely not. I don't think he's stopped loving you, Carol. No, I don't think I buy that.'

'Well, we'll soon find out. There must have been some reason to take a bigger place. I don't suppose he's cooking much.'

Mel pondered for a moment.

'Maybe he just needs time and space to think, Carol? He's lost you and his job. He's certainly got a lot to think about.'

'Maybe. Either way, I'll soon find out.'

They chatted a while longer and said their goodbyes.

Carol had already had plenty of time to think – and overthink – her problems, which is often unwise. She got out of the bath, lay down on the big double bed and nodded off. When she woke, it was getting dark, so she threw a dress on and went down to dinner.

She took out a trashy novel and ordered a main course only, hating eating alone in a half-empty restaurant. She enjoyed the food as far as one could in the circumstances, then she saw a dark-haired young lady setting up on the little stage area in the corner.

She liked live music. It was something that she and Paul had in common. Shows and concerts.

A short, balding older man took to the stage in a white dinner jacket. He kissed the girl on the cheek and adjusted the microphone.

'Ladies and gentlemen, my name's Lionel Pemrose. The Pemrose Majestic is proud to present our headline act for this evening. Let's have a big welcome for Cromer's own Amy Raven.'

\*    \*    \*

Miriam Pemrose had the contents of the brown envelope strewn across the coffee table. She tried to come up with an alternative explanation to the obvious one. She wasn't given to excessive emotion, but to her logical mind, there was no real doubt.

She briefly held the telephone between her cheek and shoulder as she skimmed them one more time, then coughed and continued.

'Yes, I've been through the pictures, Julia. It's Lizzie Stack, his new PA. She probably spent most of the time looking at the ceiling while I was away in London.'

'The things we have to put up with, Miriam. I'm so sorry to share the sordid details but, well, that's what we hired the guy for. What do you want me to do?'

Miriam tossed the pictures onto the coffee table.

'Just file it with the rest, will you? If and when I choose to, I can chop his financial bollocks off.'

'Fair enough.'

Miriam was managing the hurt well. She continued as if nothing untoward had happened.

'Are you still good for lunch tomorrow? We can talk more then.'

'Yes, fine. Where do you fancy?'

'You choose, Julia. Anywhere but the bloody Majestic, if you don't mind.'

'Shame. It's rather good, actually. A close friend of mine did the interior design. It's absolutely amazing.'

Miriam laughed.

'Given the budget that Lionel didn't give me, I did my best. He's probably retrofitted a mirror on the ceiling in the bridal suite by now.'

'For his mistress, you mean?'

Miriam reflected.

'Hell, no. She got shagged in one of the staff bedrooms at the back, judging by the pictures. I doubt that Lionel would want to lose any bookings.'

'No, probably not. I'll see you at Menzies at one o'clock? How about that?'

'That's fine. Now I'll shortly receive a visit from this chap, Warren. A very strange story.'

'Yes. It was very odd really. He first came to us a while back to sort out his severance agreement, but rang me on Friday after he found out that you and I are friends. I gather he saw us together. That picture of us in the paper? He wanted me to effect an introduction. He seems a nice chap. Bit down on his luck. He lost his wife and his job in a single day. He said the matter he wanted to discuss concerned Lionel Pemrose and Janet Wells. I thought I'd let you know in case it's linked with Lionel's... other activities. I summarised the rest in my email.'

'Yes, you did. Well, to be honest, I've no idea what Lionel's up to. I decided to see Mr Warren here at the house as Lionel's away golfing. I'm not sure who I can trust in the office these days. Meldrum is here as well this afternoon, so I'm not on my own.'

'Mr Warren seems fine to me. Not weird or anything. Hope it proves useful. I'll see you tomorrow.'

Miriam replaced the telephone and picked up the envelope. She took a brief second glance at the pictures, and then locked them away.

'Oh, Lionel, how many more blind eyes can I turn?' she asked herself sadly.

She poured herself a coffee and went onto the terrace. There was another fine day in prospect. She looked down the garden, seeing Meldrum's bare-chested figure, tending the borders. She felt a pang of guilt. Was her fling any more respectable? How had their marriage got to this point?

The doorbell rang a few minutes later. She opened the door.

'Good morning, Mrs Pemrose, I'm Paul Warren.'

'Hello, Mr Warren. Come through to the terrace. Can I get you a coffee?'

She showed him out onto a large terrace in front of a huge, square lawn, closely mown. In the distance, he could see the sea. A gardener was tending the already immaculate borders, he noted.

Miriam arrived with a pot of coffee and sat down.

'You have a wonderful house, Mrs Pemrose. Quite a view, too,' said Warren, politely.

'Thank you, Mr Warren. It's taken a few years but it's very much as we like it now. You're not local, I understand?'

'No. Midlands born but all of my childhood holidays were here in Cromer.'

'I see. Has much changed? Except for the prices, of course?'

'Well, no, not really. That new hotel of yours looks very nice. Recently re-opened, I understand?'

'Yes. The Majestic. We bought it late last year. I did the interior design. I'm quite proud of it, actually. Bit of a rush job but it's worked out well.'

'Really? It certainly looks the part.'

'Thank you. Now, Julia said you wanted to see me. How may I help you?'

Julia was big on first impressions. For his age, Paul Warren was clearly pretty fit. He wore a short-sleeved polo shirt, which showed well-toned muscles. He seemed a cultured, intelligent man from Julia's comments, and wasn't like the caricature football manager.

'Well, thanks for agreeing to see me, Mrs Pemrose. It's quite a delicate matter, and you may think that it's none of my business.'

Miriam smiled matter-of-factly.

'If I think that, you will know quite quickly, Mr Warren. Julia and I go back a long way and thought it was worthy of a conversation. I gather that one of my husband's business activities is causing you concern?'

'Hopefully Julia explained the background?'

'Yes, I do know the background. A childhood romance rekindled. It is your motive that escapes me. To my understanding, you had your wicked way with a young girl, with no regard for the consequences. Sorry if I don't show much sympathy.'

Warren was bruised by her directness. She was clearly

someone who knew her own mind. She was also rather attractive. Her clothes, although quite simple, were obviously not from a chain store. Her watch was a Rolex and she wore a couple of diamond rings, which looked genuine enough. She'd had some cosmetic work done, but it wasn't as obvious as it can sometimes be. She had a healthy tan suggesting a recent holiday, a long way from the east coast of England.

He picked his words carefully.

'I can understand that point of view, Mrs Pemrose. But you need to consider the context. I've come back to a strange place that I haven't seen in years to discover that not only is my first love still here, but also a daughter. She is my only child. A child I've wanted for a long time.'

'So why is that of relevance to my husband?'

'Well, I know I'm being a bit emotional, but whatever you make of my previous behaviour, what is going on with the Pier Theatre now is wrong in my view, and I want to try to put a stop to it.'

Miriam knew nothing of the matter in question. Lionel had coveted the Pier Theatre for years, but had said nothing about it of late. Suspicious, she thought. She bluffed her way through.

'Why is it so wrong? Old Mr Wells was no paragon of virtue, let me assure you. He left a legacy of debt. Under the licence, Mrs Wells was supposed to redecorate the theatre every five years. That place hasn't seen a lick of paint of recent times. What are we to do? Let it go to rack and ruin?'

Warren shook his head. She was either oblivious to her

husband's motive or duplicitous. Either way, he had nothing to lose.

'But that isn't the motive and I think that you know it. It seems to me that your husband just wants the theatre so he has all of the toys in toy town. You've even squeezed out old Cyril, the Punch and Judy man.'

Miriam sensed that there was more to this matter than she understood, no longer being in day to day contact with the burgeoning Pemrose empire.

'Cyril Brown? I'm sorry, I don't follow.'

'Then check it out, if you will. I understand that you trebled his rent so he's moved on.'

Miriam was now shocked, but wasn't about to show it. Cyril was a mainstay in the town. A popular chap, by all accounts. Everybody liked Cyril. Except for Lionel, of course.

'Oh. Well, I agree that doesn't seem quite fair. I'll look into that. But as to the pier, well…'

'You'll just turn it into another bingo hall.'

Miriam now realised that Lionel had a plan of which she knew absolutely nothing. But she wasn't about to let Warren know that.

'Look, why should I get involved? It's just business, Mr Warren.'

'Because I think you know what is right and what is wrong. I think you know that your husband stitched it up so Janet had nowhere to go just before the licence deadline.'

Miriam was uncomfortable now. It sounded exactly like Lionel, and his banking friends were very close buddies indeed.

'So? It's business, Mr Warren. There's a recession on and from what I hear, the theatre is losing money. Banks are banks. They are making decisions like this all the time.'

Paul looked at her directly. There was suddenly emotion in his voice.

'If it's money you want, I can buy Janet some time, if nothing else.'

Miriam looked at him sharply. This was getting a little absurd.

'With no job and no home to go to, Mr Warren? Forgive me if I'm sceptical that you have much to offer financially.'

Paul was angry now. This lady and her fat cat husband were the sort of people who got what they had by treading on others.

'You're forgetting my payoff from United. I don't know the details, how much Janet owes and stuff, but if you just give me the amount you need, I'll sign the cheque here and now.'

'What? You're not serious?'

Warren returned her stare.

'I want to help Janet, Mrs Pemrose. And my Karen. Whatever it takes.'

Miriam found that the conversation was getting more bizarre by the moment. Warren was clearly becoming rather emotional, and she was getting very uncomfortable. She began to think this meeting a mistake. As she was wondering how to end this discussion, Warren continued.

'I don't care about the money. I've got plenty of offers of work. I've thought about it, and it's what I want to do.'

Miriam thought for a moment and shook her head.

'Then you need to talk to Janet, not me. This has nothing to do with Pemrose Entertainments, you must surely see that?'

'There is no chance that she will take money from me. She's just too proud.'

Miriam sat back for a moment, and smiled.

'Yes, knowing Janet Wells, you are very probably right.'

'Look, I can buy Janet time. I need you to help somehow.'

Miriam shook her head. She'd heard enough of this nonsense.

'Well it seems to me that you're on the ultimate guilt trip, Mr Warren. I'm sorry, but I can only advise you to keep out of things that aren't your concern. It seems to me that you've caused enough problems for Mrs Wells already, and have plenty of your own. Now if you'll excuse me, I do have an appointment I need to prepare for.'

She got up. She was quite angry but also rather embarrassed at his behaviour. Warren's frustration boiled over.

'Just hold on, Mrs Pemrose. I'm not proud of what I did, but I was young. I didn't take advantage of Janet and I didn't know she'd got pregnant. I can't turn the clock back, but I can help Janet and Karen now. That's why I'm here.'

Miriam showed him to the door in silence. He followed. As he left, she couldn't help but feel a little bit sorry for this incredibly naïve man.

'Look, Mr Warren, we can't take decisions based on nostalgia, sentiment or one man's guilt trip. I will think about what you have said, but don't kid yourself that a sticking plaster will solve the Pier Theatre's problems. I assure you that it won't.'

Warren extended his hand, and she shook it, albeit hesitantly. He spoke slowly but reasonably.

'Well, thank you for hearing me out, Mrs Pemrose. I'm sorry that you take that view. But if you change your mind, you know where I am.'

'No problem, Mr Warren. I think that Janet is rather lucky to have friends like you.'

# 19.

## Not Long Now

Les was pleased to learn that Lauren was back in rehearsals. Isobel confirmed that she'd arrived for a dance rehearsal that morning, and seemed fine. Isobel knew nothing of why Lauren had gone missing. Les said it was a family matter, and that was fine by her.

Frank Gilbert rang Janet Wells that morning to advise that, several days on, there had been no press contact. As the days went by, he hoped that they had escaped any press attention. That was a stroke of luck, and with the opening only days away, they needed some luck.

The cast members were posing for show pictures that day, and Les was grateful that the forecast sunshine had arrived. Lauren took Les to one side.

'Hi, Les.'

'Ah, my favourite Welsh dragon. How's Taff this morning?'

'Bloody pissed off, forgive my French.'

'So you're not looking forward to working your socks off to pay the bills then?'

'Don't make me laugh. If I have to live on what that guy says I must, I'll have to go on the game to get by.'

'Well, I doubt you'd be short of customers. You could sing to them afterwards perhaps? A shortened version of 'Money, Money, Money' maybe? You could offer them discounted show tickets, too.'

Lauren laughed. It was a grim laugh. Trust Les to make a joke out of it all.

'Thank you, Mr Westley. It wasn't very pleasant. Just saying.'

'It was never going to be. And?'

'Well, having fessed up, I do feel a lot better, at least. And he said that he'd seen worse, believe it or not. He's talked to all the people I owe money to. It looks like they'll do some sort of deal. It should be sorted this week.'

'Good. That's excellent.'

'That talking to you gave me really helped. It seems all my people wanted to do was bleed me dry.'

'You just need to be your own boss. You are blessed. Just keep hold of the dream… oh, and cut up the credit cards.'

'Goodbye, Hilton Hotel. Hello Bloomingdale's then. And goodbye, McCartney… hello, Matalan.'

'Alas, yes. And he told you to flog stuff?'

'Yes. All of my lovely shoes. Worth a small fortune, he reckons. It'll break my heart but it's got to be done.'

'Just how many does a woman need? I find two pairs quite sufficient.'

'That's a man talking and that's a fact. But the Jimmy Choos are going. They might be lush, but I've got to get straight financially. Whatever happens, I'm not going to let my dream drown in an ocean of debt, or an ocean of booze, for that matter. I'm not going to be a loser.'

\* \* \*

Carol drove out of Cromer and took the road towards Overstrand.

She had awoken quite late, and couldn't immediately recall where she was. She allowed herself to drift into wakefulness, realising that time didn't matter too much. She put on the annoying little kettle, but then spotted the posh coffee machine and decided that her head might feel better if she had a strong black coffee. She bathed again, just because she could, then it was time for breakfast.

She was shown to a little table looking out over the sea, and was swiftly presented with a fine china cup and teapot. Her freshly prepared breakfast arrived in suitably short order. What was that chap's name from last night? Pemrose. Yes, Lionel Pemrose.

The Majestic had obviously been recently refurbished, and everything seemed to gleam accordingly. But as a former waitress, she could see the signs of a well-drilled team, too. The staff were cheerful and personable, yet efficient. The detail stuff was there. Plates were cleared and tables re-laid in short order. The staff were very busy but coping well with the morning rush. Overall, she couldn't fault this place. This Pemrose chap ran rather a good hotel, she thought.

But this was not a holiday. She was here on business. Well,

sort of. She was in the business of saving her marriage. Because whatever the problems, whatever the faults on both sides, it was worth saving. She knew that she loved Paul Warren, and wanted him back.

But she had no idea how to approach their unscheduled meeting. She couldn't predict how Paul would react, or how she would react to his reaction. It was just such a bizarre and unreal situation. She parked outside the pretty bungalow with the back garden facing the sea.

His car was on the drive. It wasn't his car, of course. It belonged to the football club. Well, maybe he owned it now. She had no idea of what their financial position was. All she knew was that the mortgage and standing orders continued to be paid. There had been no unusual transactions on the joint bank account. It was as if nothing had happened.

It seemed that he had simply decided to run away and close the door on the past. Their past. At first, she could accept that, in the circumstances, but as the days and weeks went by, she found this approach to be simply heartless. He had every right to put his life on hold if he wished, but he had no right to put hers on hold by refusing to communicate.

As she walked up the path, her emotions went from one pole to the other. Angry at herself for her own stupidity, and angry at him for his refusal to talk. Then again, anger would get her nowhere, and if Paul became angry, this would all come to nothing. She rang the bell, but it didn't seem to ring, so she knocked. No answer.

She wondered what to do. Maybe he was hiding from

her? She thought about leaving but that was no solution. She decided to wait it out, but could hardly sit on the doorstep. She ventured down the side of the bungalow, feeling like a burglar as she did.

She emerged into a small but sunlit garden. There was a back gate, which opened onto a footpath, and with views of the sea beyond. She stood looking out over the sea, nodding a greeting to a couple of passers-by.

There was a patio with comfortable patio furniture. The sun was shining. This was not a cheap bolt hole, but something quite upmarket. She was surprised. Paul wouldn't normally splash the cash. He obviously wasn't too worried about money.

She sat down, deciding to wait it out. The sun was warm and she closed her eyes briefly. She checked her phone again as she did relentlessly, hoping that he'd call or email her. Nothing. She rearranged the cushions on the sofa, and settled back, and closed her eyes once again.

'What are you doing here?'

She awoke with a start, seeing her husband standing above her, the sun dazzling behind him. She had no idea if she'd been asleep for two minutes or two hours.

'Hello, Paul,' she said, sitting up quickly.

'Tea?' he said.

She mumbled a reply, and with that, he headed into the house.

She thought about following, but decided to wait and see.

He brought out some tea in two mugs, bearing some sort of nautical design, and set them down.

He sipped his tea and paused. He made no move to speak. He was rather sullen.

'So… nice place,' she said.

'Yes.'

'Lovely sea view.'

'I guess.'

He was dressed in a polo shirt, bearing the United crest, shorts and white trainers.

'Been for a run?' she said.

'Yep. Only a few miles. The pier and back.'

He sipped his tea. She tried again.

'I came down yesterday. Stayed at that Majestic place on the seafront. Lovely.'

'Yes. It only opened in the spring, I gather.'

She was running out of small talk.

'We need to talk, Paul.'

She sounded like a bad Hollywood movie, she decided. He didn't respond. His face was devoid of any emotion, but she continued.

'I've left countless voicemails, written tons of emails to you. No reply. I've said I'm sorry for what happened.'

'Maybe I've nothing to say to you,' he said, looking out towards the sea.

Carol knew at once that this was going nowhere. This was the monosyllabic Paul after the home defeat. Where was the laughing, smiling Paul from their Tuscany holiday? The Paul who twirled her around like a toy when she told him she was pregnant? She was angry now, but she knew that anger wasn't going to help. Keep calm and try again.

'Look Paul I know what I did was wrong and inexcusable. I'm so sorry that I've hurt you. I love you and I want to try to sort this out. I know you've needed time. I know you had an awful day that day. But sooner or later we need to talk this out.'

He looked away. He was not making any eye contact and barely acknowledged her presence.

'Not yet. I'm not ready yet. I'll be in touch when I am.'

It was like talking to a solicitor. It was as if they didn't know each other. She couldn't take this. She was desperately trying not to cry. He sat there motionless. She struggled to find the words.

'But… I can't take much more of this, Paul. I need to know where we stand… where I stand. It's just unbearable.'

He said nothing.

'There are practical things. There are things to sort out.'

He looked at her.

'I'm still paying the bills. Your housekeeping continues to be paid. You have nothing to be concerned about.'

'That's not the point, Paul. We need to talk about us. Please.'

'I'm not ready yet.'

She was crying now, her voice uneven.

'Then when, Paul? It's been weeks now. Weeks of worrying and waiting.'

'I don't know. When I'm ready, I'll be in touch.'

It was all so impersonal. Carol dug a tissue from her handbag and blew her nose.

'I need to sort things out. I'm living on hold. I can't stand this. It's been weeks.'

He stared at her.

'No need for that. Your bills are being paid. Shag who you like. It's none of my concern.'

He stood up and walked towards the fence, looking out to sea. Carol had had enough.

She stood and walked up to him. He turned. She smacked him on the face.

'You total bastard. I hurt you and I've said a million apologies for that. Now I want to try to rebuild things and you treat me like we've never met. You need to come back into this world from that football-obsessed bubble you've been in for the last two years. I love you and I want to fix things. But fixing things means talking about them, so if you won't talk, I'm done here. Thanks for the tea.'

She threw the cup on the patio where it smashed into half a dozen pieces, and she exited by the gate on the side of the house. Paul stood impassively looking out to sea, then started to cry.

*　　*　　*

Carol drove away at speed, nearly hitting a child who emerged from a side street on his bicycle. She parked up and sobbed for a few minutes. He'd been so cold and bitterly distant. She hadn't known what to expect, but thought that they would at least start talking. She'd even checked out of the hotel, thinking that she would stay with Paul while they talked things through.

Now she wondered what to do. Should she go home? It seemed that there was nothing to stay here for. But what was there to go home to? An empty house that used to be home.

She went back to the Majestic and parked in the car park. Unsure of what to do, she used the ladies loo and touched up her makeup to hide the signs of her tears. She sat on the terrace above the dining room and ordered tea.

There were children playing on the beach. If only, she thought bitterly. A harassed mother brought a buggy out onto the terrace bearing a little girl, fast asleep. As she went by a child's toy dropped out, and Carol recovered it. The lady smiled.

'Thanks. Where would she be without her Peppa Pig?'

Carol smiled back.

'How old is she?' she asked.

'Six months. She isn't usually as quiet as this, trust me. Good to get a few minutes' peace. Who would be a mother?'

I would, Carol thought to herself.

As all of the tables were all taken, she offered the lady a seat, and she gratefully accepted.

'I'm Chloe,' she said, sitting down.

'Carol.'

They shook hands and Chloe fussed with the baby while she ordered a cappuccino.

The child stirred but Peppa Pig placated her. Chloe sat back in her chair and relaxed.

'Are you here on holiday?' she asked.

Carol thought for a moment.

'Yes. Just a day or two. What about you?'

'Down here for the week with Grandma. She has a caravan at East Runton. How about you? Are you staying here?'

Good question, thought Carol.

'Yes.'

'Looks really posh. I wish I could stay at a place like this. Are the rooms lovely?'

Carol smiled.

'Yes, they're lovely. I love the view of the sea.'

They talked for a while. Idle chatter. It helped Carol to calm down and come back to normality.

The child awoke sleepily, and Carol held her while Chloe readied herself to feed. If only this beautiful little mite was hers.

She passed the baby over and Chloe fed her child. Seeing mother and baby together was touching, but every time she witnessed something like this, Carol found herself suppressing jealousy, which immediately made her feel guilty.

They finished up and said their goodbyes. Carol's mood wasn't helped by seeing a woman with a baby. She walked down to the pier and sat awhile. There were families playing on the beach, the children with buckets and spades, the parents joining in or grabbing some precious time for themselves, reading trashy novels or sunbathing.

She felt suddenly very lonely. She was trying to forget about this morning, but couldn't. She hadn't expected a total absence of emotion, his monosyllabic responses, his reluctance to engage and his intense bitterness and contempt.

She had expected dialogue and a gradual healing of the wounds that she had inflicted. That they could spend some time together here. It wasn't a place that she knew, but it was where Paul had run to, and she would learn why. Some shared healing time.

Instead, she was now contemplating for the first time that her marriage to Paul was broken beyond repair. She tried to work out what to do. On the one hand, staying here was pointless. On the other hand, going home wouldn't achieve so much either. She resolved to stay a few days.

She checked back in at the Majestic, and although she thought about staying only two nights, the clerk told her of an offer that was running. She booked for five nights, resolving in her mind that Paul would either be in touch by then, or she would return home and talk to a solicitor about filing for divorce.

She sat in her room and composed a long email to Paul, writing and rewriting it. When she was eventually satisfied, she pressed send, then decided to buy a swimsuit so she could use the indoor pool.

*    *    *

Paul went indoors as the afternoon clouded over. He tried to read the newspaper, but couldn't. His cheek was still stinging from her blow, and he had cleared up the broken cup from the patio. He had hurt her. He had hurt the woman as she had hurt him. An eye for an eye. She had it coming.

But although he tried to believe that he was in the right, he knew in his heart that he was not.

He remembered her tears. She hadn't cried very often in

their marriage. She cried when she lost the baby, of course. And as much as he told her that it wasn't her fault, she never seemed quite able to accept that.

He wondered where she had gone. Had she gone home? She'd been distraught when she left, and he found himself worrying whether she was OK. He'd been shocked to find her sitting there when he returned. He hadn't had any time to prepare. He'd said nothing because he didn't know what to say. He still didn't know how he felt. He knew that he'd sounded robotic and uncaring.

He walked down into the village, had a pint and ordered his tea. It started to rain as he walked back. The world seemed to be as depressed as he felt, and he suddenly felt very lonely. When he got back, he checked his emails.

He clicked on one from Carol.

*Hi Paul,*

*Sorry to have descended on you today. It must have come as a shock, but I couldn't allow the silence between us to continue. I'm sorry that I hit you. I was just so upset that you wouldn't talk to me.*

*I so want to repair the damage I've caused and I'll go on trying in the hope that you will feel able to forgive me, and work with me to heal our wounds.*

*I've decided to stay a few days at the Majestic, as home seems so lonely without you, and I can't bear to go back there. I will wait in the hope that you will feel able to meet me once again while I'm here, when you've had time to think things through.*

*I've made my apologies for what I did, without seeking to justify myself. I'm willing to engage in counselling with you to work things out. We must face our difficulties together, and we must both be willing to change. It will be tough, but I'm so sure that it will be worth it.*

*But I think you need to come to a decision soon, because I'm struggling with having my life on hold. If I've not heard from you by Friday morning then I'll return home. As little as I want to, I will be forced to contemplate a future without you, so please get in touch.*

*I love you.*

# 20.

## The Technical Rehearsal

The following day, it rained. It rained all the next day, too. For the cast of the show, it was, however, a big day. It was the technical rehearsal for show number one. Assuming it went well, the full dress rehearsal was set for later that week. Opening night was looming, and sales were buoyant. The Lauren Evans official fan club were due to come during the first week, guaranteeing that the show was sold out for the first couple of weeks at least.

Janet sat in the audience. Pride swelled in her chest as the show unfolded. They had rounded up a few locals to give it at least a bit of atmosphere. Peggy Bloomingdale and her family were in the audience, three generations sitting towards the front.

Les used his standard show one routine, but with Les, no two shows were the same, and given the nature of the audience, his gags were targeted accordingly. Lauren seemed relaxed, and delivered her dance steps like the pro she had become. Her confidence was back, and she looked stunning. The wardrobe mistress wore a tired smile as she took each of her stage costumes in yet again to reflect her further weight loss.

Lauren dedicated 'You'll Never Walk Alone' to the Bloomingdale family towards the end of the first half. It was a lovely gesture, which the family obviously appreciated. Peggy, in particular, understood the meaning.

Lech's hapless magician's act was hilarious, the cock-ups now rehearsed and slick. Les had written a sketch where he played the bad cop to Lech's incompetence, reflecting his growing rapport with the loveable Pole.

The dancers were as good as ever. Karen had demonstrated her leadership in taking Amy under her wing, and the youngster was obviously going to grow as a talent. Isobel had crafted some great routines and Janet was both relieved and delighted that Angela had vindicated her decision. She'd been alcohol-free since she had signed a letter in Janet's office to that effect.

There were a few problems, but that's what a technical rehearsal is about. Gerald's stunning arrangements of Lauren's new songs guaranteed strong publicity for the show, and Frank Gilbert was arranging for the release of 'Maybe' as a single.

Janet knew that the only problem ahead of the opening night was the deadline for signing the deal with Lionel. She'd bought all the time she could, but time was up. Her lawyer was checking the wording one more time, and she'd got more guarantees about her and Karen's future employment, but the reality was that Lionel brought the money and had her over a barrel. At times, she had wondered why he had allowed the extension, and why even now he was giving way on certain things. Maybe he did have a heart, after all?

But the size of the new theatre and the number of performances Lionel was suggesting meant that a summer show of the type that she had just seen was simply not going to be viable. A simpler and cheaper one might just work, but it meant that the show that she and her father before her had created was finished.

She'd explored every option, but saving the Summertime Special Show couldn't be sold to anyone, particularly in this financially stricken climate.

She went backstage and hugged each cast member a little tighter than usual. But at least the bookings were very good and might strengthen negotiations for next year with her new business partner.

She went into Lauren's dressing room and congratulated her.

Lauren was tearful.

'I'm so glad you enjoyed it, Mrs Wells. You've been so very kind. I feel like a new woman now.'

'You've made a fresh start, Lauren. You've learned such a lot in such a short time. Thank you for making the show so special.'

They hugged warmly.

Les and Karen joined her on stage as the cast drifted off into the rain.

'Well?' said Les.

'It's bloody marvellous, Les.'

She threw her arms around him, and then Karen.

'Well done to you both. It's been so difficult for you with the goings on.'

'Not a bad team effort, if I do say so myself,' said Les.

Karen couldn't resist.

'They'll be calling it the Lech and Les show with that double act.'

Les stared at her in mock annoyance.

'The Les and Lech show, please. I've taught that boy all he knows.'

'If you say so, Les,' said Janet.

They headed off up the pier together, but Janet stopped by at the office.

The new programmes had arrived. They incorporated the new slim line Lauren in her electric blue stage costume on the front cover.

Also, on her desk was the final contract from Lionel. She would have to sign it by the deadline or he could seize the theatre and lock out the cast. With opening night days away, she couldn't risk that.

She put the contract down and looked at a photograph of her father, which she had hung on the wall just after his death. His benign smile belied a dark side and a ruthlessness which few who met him were aware of. In some respects, Lionel had things in common with her father.

But as she looked at her father's picture and the contract sitting on her desk, she realised the extent of the betrayal that she was about to undertake. She looked at his picture.

'Sorry, Dad,' she murmured to herself.

She was meeting Paul Warren for dinner, so she switched off the light and headed out into the rain.

Paul had phoned her requesting that they have dinner, and she had conceded. She just didn't get out enough. Over the years, the theatre had become an all-consuming hobby and profession, and the impending change of ownership made her realise it.

She had no thoughts that she might rekindle her relationship with Paul Warren. She had thought that, at one point the other night, he was going to kiss her, and at the time in her vulnerable state, she had wished that he had. But on reflection, their love affair, if that's what it was, was so long ago. She did have a sense of unfinished business though.

Karen.

She'd brought up their child alone, and she didn't consider that Paul was Karen's father in anything but a biological sense. But Karen had asked questions from time to time, and she was owed a truthful answer.

Honestly, she was surprised that Karen had not demanded an answer before now, but she was not one to cause trouble. Karen was a team player and peacemaker, and when there was trouble in the show, it was Karen who saw it first and frequently sorted things out without her knowing. She seemed to take after her grandmother in that important respect.

When Paul first arrived back on the scene, Janet had decided that, whatever happened, there could be no reopening of past wounds. Under no circumstances would he have anything to do with Karen.

But she had changed her mind. She had a sense that, as she was facing the toughest week of her life, it was time to put the past behind her for good. So she set out that evening with an open mind on the matter.

Paul kissed her on the cheek as they met. They were more relaxed in each other's company than the previous time. The fact that initially they appeared to have had little in common actually helped, because they both found that their respective careers were quite fascinating in different ways.

Paul recalled her singing in the show all those years ago, and his recall of everything about the night was remarkable. His love of the theatre fed a long conversation, because it was clear that he had been to a number of shows with Carol in the intervening years.

They had reached the dessert course by the time she felt able to mention his wife.

'So, come on, Paul. Have you been in touch with Carol yet?'

There was silence as he looked away, and fiddled nervously with his napkin.

She apologised.

'I'm sorry, it's none of my business.'

He smiled and shook his head.

'She's staying at the Majestic. She came to see me. I blew it.'

He continued haltingly.

'Just couldn't talk to her. I didn't know what to say. She just showed up out of the blue… I didn't have time to think.'

Janet thought for a moment. What on earth was his problem?

'I should have thought that an expression of how you are feeling might have been a start.'

He shrugged. She had heard enough.

'So she came all this way, presumably to save your marriage, and you didn't know what to say?'

He nodded uncertainly.

She shook her head.

'Give me strength. Why do you men find it so impossible to express your feelings? What is it that makes you adopt the fake macho man persona?'

He laughed. He recalled that he had found her assured directness appealing when they first met. She had lost none of that.

'Because I'm the coward, I guess.'

'Yes. Probably you are. Look, I don't know the facts, but from the way you talk about her, it's obvious that you care for her a lot. What happened was probably a symptom, not a cause. She's at fault, of course, but you know the side of the story that I don't, which is why she did what she did.'

'Yes, I do.'

'Well I don't need to. But you need to deal with it, whatever it is.'

Paul thought for a moment, took a sip of wine and looked at her.

'She miscarried. A child we both wanted. She's much younger than me.'

Janet stared at him and put down her wine glass.

'My God. The poor girl.'

'And I wasn't there.'

'When it happened?'

'No, I wasn't there then, and looking at it, I wasn't there after either. For her, I mean. I thought she'd recovered. Just one of those things.'

Janet shook her head.

'Football. It's your job and your obsession. Just as mine is theatre. No time for anything and anybody else.'

'Yes. I just didn't see anything else going on.'

She smiled, and took his hand.

'You stupid, silly boy. You're just as bad as I am. You're totally obsessed with your job, and no thought for anyone else.'

'I guess.'

'But at least she's here in Cromer. So she still wants to sort it out. All you've got to do is forgive her for what she did, and I guess she'll forgive you, too.'

'But I can't.'

'But you surely can when you've told me it was your own fault.'

'It's not very easy.'

'Well, actually it is, Paul. When she arrived, you were still blaming her, but now you've accepted it was your fault, too. All you have to do is say that to her, and you start the journey back.'

'Perhaps.'

'But, of course, you're a bloke, so that's impossible.'

He thought for a moment. She was only telling him what he knew to be true.

'Well, OK, thanks. It's useful to talk to someone. I don't really have anyone to talk to at the moment.'

'No worries. From what you've said, you can't talk to your brothers either. Might be worth rebuilding some bridges there, too? Life is too short Paul.'

He nodded, and they sat quietly, sipping the wine and letting the matter rest. Eventually he spoke, rather hesitantly.

'Let's talk about another matter, if you will.'

'And what might that be?'

'Karen.'

'We've already discussed that.'

'Yes, and you are wrong. She has a right.'

Janet hesitated.

'Yes, she does.'

They talked around the subject for a while, and Janet agreed that she would give Karen the option of a conversation. She would pick the right moment to tell her, and let Paul know the outcome.

They came to the end of the dinner and shared the bill, as they had before, at Janet's insistence. As they hugged, he took out an envelope. It obviously contained a card of some sort. He handed it over.

'Here. It's a small token of our renewed friendship. It's a picture. Open it later.'

'Oh, Paul, you shouldn't have,' she said with some uncertainty in her voice.

She returned home and sat alone for a time, with a glass of whisky. Karen was at a show in Norwich, so would be late back.

Janet suddenly remembered the envelope and took it from her pocket.

Upon opening it, she found an enlarged copy of a photograph taken back in 1976. It showed Paul and her with their arms around each other. She remembered exactly when it was taken, that last sunny morning as they said their goodbyes. It was on the pier, and behind it was the Punch and Judy stand. The photographer was Cyril Brown.

But just then, something else dropped out of the envelope, too. A short note pinned to something else.

*Janet,*
*I was so in love with you, I didn't want to leave.*
*It's been lovely to be back in touch, in whatever circumstances.*
*I love this town, and the Pier Theatre. I hope that this donation will help.*
*If you can't accept it as a gift then call it a loan and repay it when you are able.*
*All my love,*
*Paul*

Attached was a cheque. A very big cheque.

# 21.

## The Dress Rehearsal

Les and Lauren sat out on the pier drinking coca cola at the end of the dress rehearsal. They were relaxed after another full-on session. The opening performance was imminent.

Les proposed a toast.

'To The Road to Cromer Pier.'

They clinked glasses, but Lauren was puzzled.

'I'm sorry? I don't quite follow.'

'That's what I call it. The Road to Cromer Pier. Sometimes it's the end of the journey, and for some it's a new beginning. We hope for the latter, but sadly, it isn't always.'

'I see. I guess that's the business we are in. Like ships passing this way and that in the night.'

'There are more reliable ways to make a living, Lauren.'

'It's a bit sad, really. For those who don't make it, I mean. This place is just so nice. Janet, Karen, even Lech. Especially Lech, I suppose. I've met some genuine people for once. Feet planted firmly on the ground. Some real professionals with real talent. Not fabricated by TV talent shows like I was.'

'Don't put yourself down, Lauren. You're going to leave here stronger than ever.'

'I might come back next year. If I'm wanted, that is. I might put down some roots at last.'

Les needed to stop her thinking this way. But she couldn't know the whole truth. Not now.

'My contract's up along with yours at the end of the season, Lauren. I think I'm moving on. It's time for something new.'

Lauren's face saddened visibly.

'That's a bit of a shock. I thought you were here forever?'

Les smiled, and put his arm around her shoulder.

'You can't think that way, Lauren. This business is about the next opportunity. Nothing is forever. Ask Frank Gilbert. By the end of this season, everyone will want Lauren Evans. We won't be able to afford you.'

She laughed.

'As if you won't. You are a real friend, Les. Following me down to Wales in my hour of need. And all these people here. I was so rude when I first came. I know that now and yet... well...'

'They forgive and forget? Yes, they do. We don't take anyone too seriously. My dad was a comic, too. He said that our job is to take people away from their reality and to a happier place for a while. We're in the dream business. It's just that sometimes we get carried away with our own ego.'

They stood for a moment. Lauren broke the awkward silence.

'A harsh reality sometimes, as I know only too well. I'm on The Road to Cromer Pier, too, then? Yes. I see what you mean. Anyhow, it's a long season, Les, and so much can change, can't it? I'd better get off. A girl's got to do her washing. There are certain things I don't want Peggy Bloomingdale to wash!'

She leant forward and kissed Les on the cheek. Les was suddenly hesitant and embarrassed. She moved to leave, but paused, sensing his discomfort.

'Look, Lauren. How about dinner? It might be the last opportunity we get before the season starts. My treat. Unless, of course, you have to wash your hair?'

Lauren smiled.

'In that en suite? You've got to be joking! You're on. I'll pick out a posh frock before I flog it.'

\*   \*   \*

Janet and Karen were relaxing, too, in the cubbyhole kitchen at the back of the stage, the rest of the cast having left.

Janet was waiting for a good time to talk, but this wasn't a good time. They were both high on adrenalin and she needed somewhere calmer, like at home.

Karen beat her to it.

'Look, I know that this is about the worst time, but something has been bugging me for a while.'

'Oh, yes. What?'

'Paul Warren. Your recent regular dining companion.'

Janet was caught out by the sudden reference.

'What about him?'

Karen took her mother's hand and looked directly into her eyes.

'He's my father, isn't he?'

Janet blushed and became tongue tied. She'd planned how she would tell Karen, but this was not the script she had in mind.

'Who told you that?'

Karen took that as her confirmation. She reflected before answering.

'Well, I suppose you did. That day you were with him at the box office. There was something, well, intangible. A tension. He's the guy in the picture on your dressing table, right?'

'That's not enough of an answer, Karen. Who told you? Did Paul? I told him to stay away.'

Karen railed at her mother's attitude. She'd done nothing wrong.

'Absolutely not. I haven't spoken to him at all.'

Janet shook her head

'Aunt Clara. It has to be.'

'Yes.'

'She agreed never to tell anyone.'

Karen had heard enough. Now it was her fault, apparently.

'Well, forgive me, but don't I have a right to know who my father is?'

Janet sat back, defeated. This was not how it was meant to happen.

'Yes, you do. Of course you do.'

Karen sat back, too, and closed her eyes. The silence was palpable.

Janet recovered, took out a tissue, and tried to explain herself.

'I've nearly told you so many times, but I couldn't summon up the guts. I'm a coward, Karen. I'm so sorry. I really am.'

They hugged each other.

'Oh, Mum, but why? We've told each other everything. We've had no secrets, ever… except this.'

'I was… I am ashamed, Karen.'

Karen wiped a tear from her mother's cheek.

'Why? Because you got pregnant? Forgive me but it's not exactly a capital crime is it?'

Janet relaxed a little. She was glad that the truth was out, however badly she had handled it.

'It certainly seemed it at the time. That was 1976. Last century. Things were pretty different. Sex before marriage was just about acceptable, although you'd never tell your parents. And as for living in sin, well…'

'So Paul got you pregnant and dumped you?'

'I thought so. I wrote to him several times. He didn't have a telephone. No reply.'

'My God, you were so alone. What a rat.'

'I thought so, too, until recently, that is.'

'How come? I played catch up with his story on the internet. I know who he is and what happened to him.'

Janet faced her daughter once again, and took her hands.

'He didn't know, Karen. That I got pregnant, I mean.'

Karen was sceptical.

'Oh, come on, Mum, you don't really believe that? If he'd loved you, he'd have contacted you come what may. Sounds to me like a typical holiday romance. When he realised what he'd done, he did a runner.'

'But he did try. I spoke to him once when he was on tour

in Munich. He rang me and said he loved me. But I didn't know I was pregnant then.'

'Even so.'

'I know it sounds incredible, but I believe him, I think. Oh, I don't know what to believe. Everything's falling to pieces. I've been so much in control for so many years, then my lies to you come back to haunt me. It's hard enough losing the theatre, but lying to you as well...'

Janet buried her face in her hands. Karen had never seen her this way before.

'Oh, don't cry. I don't think I've ever seen you... you are always so rock solid. Any time I had problems... when I bailed out in London... you are my rock.'

Janet rallied, choking away the tears.

'So I resolved there and then that I would bring you up alone and stuff them all, including my father and Paul bloody Warren.'

Karen was assembling the pieces now.

'So you watched Paul's whole football career unfold. He nearly made the England team, too. How on earth did you cope with that?'

'I've never been remotely interested in football. Then last year I saw him on the telly at Wembley. The years hadn't been too kind, but he was still Paul Warren.'

'I think I see what you mean. There's still something there you know. Between you and Paul. I sensed it when we met briefly.'

'Probably, possibly, I don't really know. He was suddenly just there, after all these years. It was just such a shock that day.'

'Did he come looking for you?'

'No. Well, sort of, I don't really know. He'd been through a tough time with his wife and ran away. I wasn't the motive.'

'How was he? When he found out I mean?'

'Shocked, I believe. We went to dinner one night, and he sent me some flowers the next morning. Very sorry about what happened. With a lovely letter.'

'But you went out again? Last night?'

'Well it was good to escape the theatre and its troubles for one night. But it depends on you now. I agreed that if you wanted to meet him, I'd arrange it. I meant to tell you today at the right time. I've been very selfish.'

Karen had calmed down now.

'Oh, Mum. No, you haven't. You did what was best as you saw it, and on top of everything else. This was all you needed.'

'I should have dealt with it long ago. It just never seemed the right time.'

'So why didn't you find someone else?'

'Well, for one thing at that time, I was damaged goods with a child in tow. And then what with the theatre, and you, I just didn't have the time or, as time went on, the inclination. What a pair of old maids we are! Your relationships haven't exactly hit the spot either.'

Karen smiled.

'Nope. A pretty fair assessment. We're both wedded to this bloody theatre I suppose. Now even that's divorcing us.'

'Yep, seems like it.'

There was a sense of relief to Janet that however

unintentional the spilling of the beans had been, she was so glad that it was out in the open. Karen was not one to dwell on things, and knowing that her mother was hurting saddened her deeply.

Karen got up and poured boiling water on a couple of tea bags in some mugs, added milk, and handed her mother one of the cups. She sat down once again and looked at her, with an impish smile on her face.

'So, go on then. Let's have a full confession. Where was I conceived?'

'Karen! No, I couldn't possibly.'

'Oh, come on, Mum. We don't have any other secrets, do we?'

'Well, no… but, you know… there are certain things.'

'Fess up, Mum. Bet it wasn't the Hotel De Paris.'

'Nothing as romantic, I'm afraid. I… we were fairly drunk.'

'Mother!'

'Well, if you must know, it was the beach.'

Karen thought for a moment and burst into a fit of the giggles.

'The beach! Sex on the beach. Wow. My mother had sex on the beach. That's dead romantic!'

'Shush! I don't want the whole pier to know. Look, I really don't think I want to discuss losing my virginity with my own daughter. It was not as romantic as you might think.'

'Oh, come on, Mum. My first time was with Phil the Plonker in the back of his Ford Mondeo, if it makes you feel any better.'

'Oh, no, not Phil. He was such a dickhead. What on earth possessed you?'

'He was, wasn't he? I must have been mad. Anyway, back to you.'

'There's not much to tell really. I'm certainly not going into details.'

'Spoil sport.'

'There is only one thing I recall.'

'Oh, yes. Do tell.'

'Well it was dark… very dark. I wouldn't recommend it. The sand gets everywhere.'

They were both giggling now.

'And afterwards, well, I couldn't find my bra anywhere. I looked all around, but I just couldn't find it. Not that we were in any state to look. So I went home without it.'

Karen feigned shock

'Oh my God! That is disgusting. So somewhere out on that beach is my mother's underwear cast aside in a fit of passion?'

'I rather doubt it, and what it would be like after 30-plus years doesn't bear thinking about.'

They set down their mugs and hugged for a long time.

Janet kissed Karen on the forehead.

'I'm sorry, Karen. I'm glad it's out in the open now.'

'So am I, Mum.'

'Would you like to meet him, then? Paul, I mean?'

Karen thought for a moment.

'Yes. I'd think I'd like that.'

Janet headed back to her office, relieved that one of many complications in her life had been sorted.

A couple of pink notes on her desk quickly brought her back to reality. She had to sign the deal; the deadline was nearly upon her, and Lionel was chasing. She hadn't told anyone about Paul's extraordinary cheque. Should she take the money? She couldn't. It was amazingly generous, but it was guilt money and she wasn't prepared to be beholden to him.

But it would buy her more time. It would give her an extended period of time to put in place new banking facilities. It could yet save this theatre from Mr Pemrose and his bingo hall.

It was a real dilemma. She was pondering this when the telephone rang. She picked it up. Betty had an outside call for her.

Janet heard the name and was immediately puzzled.

'Put her through, Betty,' she said.

\*   \*   \*

Carol had begun to wonder if he would contact her at all. She'd begun to think that he was just too stubborn to call her. She'd spent a couple of days trying to enjoy herself, yet all the time hoping that he would get in touch. He did not.

Then, as she was swimming in the pool after a lengthy session in the gym, he called, but the call went to voicemail. As she sat on the lounger, she noticed the missed call, and checked the message.

*'Hi Carol. I'm sorry I've taken some time, but think it's time we sat down. Could I come over at, say, three o'clock? If you feel comfortable with us meeting at the hotel then let me have your room number. I'd rather talk in private, if you're OK with that.'*

She was suddenly elated. At last, maybe they could progress things. She sent him a text back.

*Paul, Happy to talk of course. I'm in room 310. Looking forward to seeing you. Carol xxx*

She was just so relieved and delighted. She hadn't slept well since their previous meeting. She kept replaying that awful discussion at his holiday let, trying to find some crumb of comfort in the conversation, but there was none. She looked for an explanation, but the only one was unthinkable: that he had someone else.

She had a couple of hours to kill, so she went out for a walk. She walked to the church, and went inside. She was greeted by a retired volunteer, and decided to climb the tower. As she ascended, she realised that the gym session had utilised some muscles that had not been engaged for a week or two, and was winded by the time she reached the top.

She looked out towards Overstrand, and tried to make out where his bungalow was, but couldn't. It started to rain, a short shower, but enough for her to decide to descend once more.

She went towards the front of the beautiful Parish Church, and sat down quietly on a faded turquoise cushion in an oak pew. At one time, she was a church goer, but had lapsed some-time since. She took in the glorious stained glass windows and the soaring pillars. She saw a children's book forgotten in the Sunday school section, and thought about her lost child, and about Paul. She found herself praying silently, undisturbed by anyone.

She felt better somehow. The rain had stopped, and, thanking the volunteer, she headed out into the sunshine. She walked down to the pier and along to the end. She had a coffee, then decided to head back.

Reaching her room, she bathed and soothed her aching limbs. She got out and put on a dressing gown. She lay back on the bed, and in spite of telling herself not to, she fell into a deep sleep.

She was still asleep when the room bell rang. She awoke with a start.

'Oh, shit!' she exclaimed.

She opened the door, her hair a total mess.

'Paul. I'm so sorry, I fell asleep.'

Paul smiled.

'No worries. Do you need a few minutes? I can come back.'

She ushered him in.

'No, it's fine, I just did a long gym session this morning, then went up the church tower.'

He laughed.

'Ah, bit steep that climb. I've done it myself.'

'Yes, but you're a qualified coach. I'm just out of condition since…well, you know.'

He nodded and looked out to sea.

'A nice hotel, this. I had dinner one night. It's very good.'

'A bit pricey. Sorry. I got a good deal though.'

'No need to apologise.'

They sat down in two comfortable chairs next to a small coffee table. Carol made two cups of tea and set them down.

It seemed neither of them wanted to open up the discussion. Carol couldn't stomach another confrontational meeting like the last one, whereas Paul, although obviously in a better frame of mind, seemed to want to discuss anything but the topic that was most important.

They made small talk about Cromer, and how Carol had found the place. Paul knew the history of the town well, of course, and recounted childhood holidays. He didn't feel able to talk about Janet Wells. He doubted that Carol would be in any place to ponder over his previous love life, and especially over the child who, it was apparent, was his.

The conversation was one of those routine husband and wife chats that happened as they caught up on old news. Carol wanted to move the conversation onto the burning topic, but figured that Paul would get there in the end.

She poured more tea, and Paul set down his cup and looked at her – a look of hesitation and pain replacing the good humour.

'I'm sorry about the other day. I just wasn't prepared for you to show up.'

'It's OK, Paul, I get that.'

'I was rude and hurtful to you. I'm sorry about that.'

'I think I got what I deserved, Paul. I'm truly sorry. I was a fool. My mind was all over the place.'

'After you lost the baby, I wasn't there for you. Too obsessed with my job.'

'Yes, but it doesn't excuse what I did.'

'No it doesn't, Carol. But it does explain it.'

They sat in silence for a while, but then Paul continued.

'We rather lost the plot. We're both to blame. You can't live in a bubble, as I did. I guess they call it a work-life balance and I didn't have one.'

'And yet Tuscany was so relaxed, so together.'

'Calm before the storm. I'd told the Chairman which players I wanted, and trusted him to sign them while we were in Italy. He assured me things were in hand. I came back and two weeks later, he'd signed Enzo bloody Mariano.'

'Don't, Paul.'

'He'd been touted around various clubs, but he was damaged goods. He had a bad boy reputation both on and off the pitch. His present club wanted rid. He was a decent player in his day, but his legs were gone.'

'Please don't, Paul.'

'But there were allegations. Girls. Young girls. Only allegations but…'

'For God's sake, stop, Paul. Are you just trying to make me out to be the whore? A cheap slut? One of many?'

'Just saying.'

'Then don't bother. Don't you think I'm feeling used? Abused even? If you've just come to rub my nose in my own stupidity then please don't bother. I've done plenty of that in the last few weeks, thank you.'

Paul sat. Head down. He'd turned cold once again. Carol had seen enough.

'Don't you dare go silent on me again, Paul Warren. It won't solve anything.'

Paul looked up. She could see he was crying.

'No. I know it won't, Carol. I'm just… bleeding inside.'

She went across and held him in her arms and they both sobbed silently for a few minutes. He broke away finally, and they relaxed, with his arm around her shoulder. He gathered himself together and became human again.

'We're both bleeding, Carol. So much hurt. So much that we both either did or didn't do, which we should or shouldn't have done. But having lost everything I held dear in a blink of an eye, I think I'm now ready to just draw a line and start anew.'

Carol nodded, but Paul was having his say.

'Something just came unwired inside. I don't know what. Probably a shrink would say it's common in men of my age. Mid-life crisis. I don't know. I was just so desperate to succeed in the biggest league.'

She opened her mouth to respond, but he continued.

'I came here because I was desperate, but it was also where life was at its simplest. Just Mum, Dad and my brothers. My first love was here, too. 1976.'

She nodded, unsure of where this was heading.

'I need to make you aware that I only discovered recently that I have a child from that relationship. A daughter called

Karen. She's a dancer in the Cromer Pier Theatre, and Janet, my first love, runs it to this day.'

Carol looked up, and moved away. She looked out of the window at the pier in the distance. Please, no, she thought. She turned sharply to face him.

'You had a daughter and you never told me? Unbelievable.'

'No, I didn't know that Janet got pregnant. I only found out because I looked her up.'

'But why? Why would you do that? 30-odd years later?'

Paul thought for a moment.

'Idle curiosity, I guess. Nothing more, I can assure you. Janet and I had dinner a couple of times. Just old times stuff.'

'Did you sleep with her? Is that what you're going to tell me? Is that why you went missing for weeks?'

Paul shook his head.

'No, nothing happened. We're just old friends now. But I have a daughter, and I need to deal with that. I can't just leave it be.'

Carol thought for a while. This was more complicated than she imagined. She was still suspicious, but let it go.

'No, Paul. I guess not.'

'Yes, and I know that will hurt you because of what we lost last year.'

'Yes.'

'But I need to deal with it. And I didn't want any more secrets. Does that make sense?'

'Yes, I guess it does.'

Carol sat once again, opposite him this time. He took her hands in his, and looked at her, his sad eyes tearful but bright.

'I love you, Carol. And whatever it takes to repair the damage, we just need to do it. I just needed a long period to reflect and take stock. I'm sorry about that. I'm certain now that it's what I want, if it's what you want to do?'

She got up and moved across to him. He got up, too. She kissed him.

'Of course I do.'

He held her, and her dressing gown slipped apart. His hand slid inside, softly holding her left buttock.

She smiled and they kissed again.

# 22.

## Karen

It was late afternoon.

Paul dressed quickly, and left a note for the sleeping Carol.

He didn't want to leave. It seemed callous and unfeeling, but he had another appointment that he needed to keep.

He headed down to the Pier Theatre, and sat in the coffee shop as arranged.

He looked at the photographs and memorabilia in the foyer. There were pictures of people from the old casts, and he scanned through until he saw the one for 1976. There was Janet in her deep-crimson stage dress. She looked stunning, just as he remembered her.

Then, as he looked further across, there was a picture of another young woman. He checked the text under the picture. There she was, a young Karen Wells. He compared the two, and found any number of similarities, but then noticed that the shape of the forehead and eye line were very different.

She looked like him across the eyes, he thought, fascinated by this discovery, but then realising how logical it was that she did.

'Mr Warren?'

A voice came from behind him. He turned.

'Karen Wells.'

Paul took her extended hand as she smiled. A Bremner-like smile, he thought.

'Paul Warren.'

She was dressed in dance clothes, and her hair was bundled up. They sat in a corner. It was quiet at that time of day. He bought her a black coffee, and one for him. He sat down. He started to speak, unsure of where to start. She spoke, too, causing nervous laughter.

'You first,' he said.

'Well, I was going to ask if you were enjoying your holiday…'

She paused, her face betraying embarrassment as she continued.

'… If that's how you characterise it?'

Warren smiled.

'Well, it wasn't exactly planned, as you probably know.'

'No. I'm sorry, I… I read the reports.'

'This is a bit awkward, isn't it?'

'Yes. Just a little,' she conceded.

'Well, both of your parents tend to be plain spoken, so I guess you're the same most of the time.'

'Well, yes. But I'm more like my grandma and less like my granddad, they tell me. Look, Mr Warren–'

'Make it Paul. Dad doesn't feel quite right, does it?'

'Yes, Paul, whatever. Look, there's no easy way to start this conversation. After all these years of not knowing, I don't know what to say when the moment arrives. I prised the truth out of Mum, and I finally know what happened between you two.'

'So, what do you want to know? I really don't know how to do this conversation either. I've only been your Dad for a few moments, after all.'

He smiled at his feeble joke, and she smiled back. She seemed frustrated by her inability to communicate. She shrugged and continued.

'I don't know, why not just tell me about yourself? Tell me about the father I missed, I suppose. Might be a place to start? God, this is awkward.'

'Oh. Yes, OK then. Hell. Where do I start? I'm Paul Warren, the youngest of three brothers. My father was a machinist in a local car factory, my mother a housewife – both dead now. I was mad about football since childhood. I was a season ticket holder at City from seven years old. I sold programmes there from 14. Oh, I joined the youth set-up at 13. Our annual holidays were to Cromer every year. Because it was the nearest seaside we had.'

'I see. Where did you stay?'

'Mrs Bloomingdale's holiday flats in those days. It was odd to go back there. Funnily enough, I don't remember a single rainy day as a child. I don't remember any sunscreen. We used to get red raw, me and my brothers. Then my mum slapped on the calamine lotion. It was disgusting pink stuff, which stank and stuck to your clothes. We didn't even think of going abroad. That was for the rich middle classes, not us council house kids!'

'So how did you meet Mum?'

'On the beach. We were about five, I think. We were both naked, playing in the sand. Our mums just got talking. We came down each summer and we'd just bump into each other from time to time. We weren't friends, as such. Actually, thinking back, didn't your grandma run an ice cream stall at one time? That's how we kept in touch, I think.'

Karen smiled.

'Yes, I think she did for a while. So you knew my grandparents?'

'Well, not so much. Your grandma was lovely. She had time for us kids. Mum had so much to do with her boys. Your grandma just helped any which way she could, dusting off our sandy bottoms, getting sand out of our sandwiches.'

'I remember her. She was so kind and loving. She died too young. I was in my teens.'

'As did my parents, Karen. Smoking killed both of them.'

She nodded silently as he continued.

'By 16, Janet and I had fallen in love. She had become an attractive girl. I remember her wearing a blue halter-neck bikini. I probably came over as a total geek. I kissed her on the last night, when we went to this theatre to see her dad's show. Thinking about it, I kissed her in this very place.'

'So Mum was 16?'

'Yes, about that. I signed for City that year. The next summer, I met Janet again, and we became inseparable.'

'So an adolescent holiday romance then? It happens all the time, even in Cromer.'

He shook his head, his hand waving the thought away.

'It felt like so much more, Karen. How do I put it? Well, I suppose I was nerve-tinglingly, gut-wrenchingly, unable to sleep, head over heels in love. Every night, I watched Janet in the show. It was her debut season. She sang 'Over The Rainbow' and I cheered every night.'

'My God. No wonder that song is so special to her.'

'On my last night, we made love for the first and only time. I went home the next day and, shortly after, I left for a European tour with the youth team. I rang Janet a couple of times when I could, and sent cards from different places. When I got back, I rang. Her father said that she had taken up with a local boy, and that she wanted nothing more to do with me. I was stunned and bereft.'

'So, as far as you were concerned, it was over.'

'Well, yes, I moved on, as you do at that age. I was very upset at the time, but had no choice. My football career went well, and I'd made my first team debut earlier that year. Every girl wants a footballer, so I'll admit there were other girls. I never did forget Janet though.'

'I think we always remember our first love, don't we?'

'Well, yes. I'm sure that's true. A couple of seasons later, United bought me. I played for them for most of my career. Played for England under 23s, and was on the verge of a full cap when I picked up a knee injury, which put me out of action for 12 months. During that time, I met Carol, but it was a few years before we got married.'

'You don't have any other children?'

'No. Sadly, it didn't happen for us. It was just one of those things, I guess.'

'I'm so sorry.'

'My football career was good, but I never quite hit the high spots. I made an FA Cup semi-final appearance, but we lost in extra time. Then we got relegated. That was pretty awful. Then the newspapers began to talk of an England place again, but I broke my leg. Quit at 33 after another injury, and took a coaching badge.'

'So you were pretty unlucky then?'

'Well, no, I consider it a privilege to have earned my living playing the game I love.'

'That I can understand. I just love the theatre. I wouldn't have wanted anything else.'

'Of course you wouldn't! We are both so lucky in that respect...'

'Go on.'

'Well, I worked my way up to manager with different lower league clubs, with some success. My home life was happy, but we were childless. Carol is a beautiful, caring woman, so we considered adoption, but then I'd move clubs, so it just didn't happen. Last year, we got to Wembley and won the play off final. It was the greatest day of my career. Then the Chairman sold some of our best players. We struggled and got relegated, and the Chairman sacked me. The rest is in the papers. I ran away to Cromer. Why not? I had nowhere else to go. I just needed to run.'

'So you didn't come to find Mum?'

'No, not really. But then I found that she was still here. I went to find her, because I wanted to know why she dumped me, as I saw it. I was just curious to know what happened. So that's it I suppose. Your so-called dad has a marriage he has to rebuild and is currently unemployed! Not much of an addition to your life, I'm afraid.'

'I read the reports on the internet. What a dreadful time you had that day. What will you do next?'

Paul smiled, and put his hand on hers.

'Hold on, Karen, I just gave you my life story in five minutes, don't I get the same from the daughter I've always wanted but never had?'

She moved her hand away a little, but then put her other hand over his. She looked across nervously.

'Sorry, Paul. I suppose I haven't thought of it that way.'
She hesitated.

'Come on, Karen. It's not too hard if you start at the beginning?'

'Well, I suppose I led a very sheltered life. I just seemed to want to perform from an early age. In the blood, I suppose. The theatre just drew me in like a magnet. The pier at night, lit up with all the colours of the rainbow. The crowds, the music and the laughter. I just loved it, and couldn't wait to perform.'

'You sound like your mother. It's exactly how she felt. Probably still does.'

'Mum was in the show then. She has a fantastic voice. I made my debut at 14. I remember being scared to death. I threw up before I went on. Then I sang 'Over The Rainbow'.

No wonder Mum suggested it. It must have meant so much to her.'

'It's very special to me to this day.'

'I reached the high note at the end, and nailed it perfectly. I got to the end and the full house roared and cheered. It was the best feeling ever. Mum and Grandpa hugged me as I left the stage. Mum was in tears.'

'Let me assure you that your musical talent didn't come from me. I can't sing a note. And forgive me if I didn't have too many pleasant dealings with your grandfather.'

'Yes. Grandpa could be warm and charming, but he was a control freak and very status conscious, so a teenage pregnancy, well… He died a few years later. He had a heart attack. So Mum took the show on. She didn't have too much choice at the time.'

'I suppose that explains things.'

'Yes, it does, I suppose. But now things are so different. A child born to an unmarried woman. What's the big deal?'

Paul thought for a moment.

'Well, to be clear to you, if I'd known your mother was pregnant, I would have married her. There is no doubt in my mind about it. Things would have been very different for you, your mother, for us.'

'Well, Grandpa would have laid the law down, for sure. I was born and raised in Burnham, away from public view, I guess. Far away from the scandal.'

'How did Janet manage taking over the theatre then? She was so very young.'

'She wasn't well-equipped, for sure, at first. But she and Les took it on and made a go of it. I was in the show full-time by then. I learned to dance professionally. I was rather good at it.'

She paused briefly and then continued.

'Then one night, a man came backstage. He asked if I'd thought of auditioning in the West End. Of course, I hadn't. So I went to London, auditioned and got a decent part. Stewart became my agent, and eventually my lover. The leading lady left, and I got the part. Things looked good for a couple of years. Then he started doing cocaine, and eventually the show closed. I came home one day to find him in bed with two girls, all three of them high as kites. He suggested I joined them.'

He could see that she was becoming upset.

'What did you do?'

'I ran, too. I came back home to Cromer. I've been here ever since.'

'So a bit of déjà vu?'

'Oh, yes, Paul. It seems we have a bit in common.'

'High and lows? Yes, I've been the nearly man most of my life. Now I'm facing what you faced. I'm trying to make a fresh start. But let's remember that we've done things that lots of people have never done, or never could do.'

'Well, yes, Wembley must have been fantastic.'

'And playing the lead in the West End? It doesn't get much better than that.'

'I suppose not.'

'I heard you sing the other evening. You did an open mic night.'

'Ah, yes. We do that for fun once in a while. I'm the Dance Captain in the show now, so I don't sing solo very often.'

'It's a shame. You should have the lead in the show as you did in the West End.'

'Well, that's very kind, but I'm no Lauren Evans. I became Dance Captain because it's what Mum needed me to be at the time. But I'm over 30 now so my time as Dance Captain will end sometime, I suppose.'

'You should try again. You've done right by Janet. You need to look after your own career.'

Karen hesitated. Just how much did Warren know? Had Mum told him about the situation? Unlikely, she thought.

'You're very kind, and I'll admit I've thought of it, but in reality, I think my time has passed. I tried a few things 18 months ago, but it's a young person's business. I'm a bit too old now.'

'You're still very pretty though, if I'm allowed to say that these days.'

Karen smiled, and looked inside her handbag.

'Of course you are. Actually, I have something to show you.'

She handed over an old photograph. In faded colour. He looked at it closely.

'Oh, my, oh, my! Where on earth did you get this?'

'Mum's jewellery box.'

'It's both of us on the beach. 1976. It has to be. She looked great in that bikini.'

'You don't look so bad yourself. A well fit bloke.'

'I was in training then.'

They looked at each other. An onlooker would have seen just another father and daughter sharing a coffee. There was enough of a facial resemblance to make it very obvious.

'She didn't forget you, Paul. I wondered who the bloke in the picture was, but somehow I never dared ask.'

'That makes it worse somehow. Weren't there any other blokes then?'

'Well, one or two. But Mum had the theatre to run, and me to bring up. I suppose we were both a bit bruised.'

'I'm sorry, Karen.'

She shook her head as she sipped her coffee and set it down.

'Don't be, Paul. Mum and I are both happy doing what we love. She doesn't bear you any ill will. It was one of those things that happened. She was as much to blame after all.'

There was a brief silence. She gathered herself and took back the picture.

'So I was conceived under this pier then? Sex on the beach, so romantic.'

The impish sense of fun and naked directness was typical of her mother, he thought.

'Er, well, yes… but, no, not really.'

'Did you buy her dinner first then? Before you plied her with alcohol and had your wicked way?'

'What sort of question is that? Yes, I did. Of course.'

'Fine dining at the Hotel De Paris, let me guess?'

'Er, no, as it happens.'

'You're a cheapskate! It was fish and chips, wasn't it? Mum told me.'

'Well, yes, but…'

'My God. Fish and chips and bottled cider.'

He laughed, and decided to join in the banter.

'Come on, let's be fair. I didn't earn much in those days, and besides…'

'Yes?'

'Well, I did buy her mushy peas and extra scraps.'

'Last of the big spenders. Ha… I don't know.'

They talked a little more, but they had achieved what they both needed to, and Paul knew that he needed to get back. He fully intended to take his wife out that evening, and it wouldn't be for fish and chips. Neither did he intend to leave room 310 again before the morning.

Karen looked at her watch. She needed to go, too.

'Look, Paul, thanks for being so honest. This wasn't easy for me, or for you. I guess that I'm one more problem you don't need right now. But I just wanted – needed – to see who you are… where I came from.'

Paul smiled. He just saw so much of her mother in this lovely young woman. He thought carefully, trying to find the right words.

'I can completely understand that. And I'm here to be whatever you want me to be. Otherwise, I will leave you and your mother in peace, just as soon as I sort myself out.'

She looked up and nodded.

'Please see us before you go? Keep in touch?'

'Oh, Karen, of course I will. Whatever you want me to do. I'm here for you as much as you want, but I won't interfere.

I promised your mother. After all, as she said to me, 'your contribution was, in every respect, minimal."

'Just stay in touch, OK?'

They stood and Karen put her arms around him. He kissed a tear away from her cheek. He put his arm around her shoulder as they left, and she put her arm around his waist. As they got outside, she paused.

'Are you coming to opening night?'

'That's tomorrow, isn't it? Well, I hadn't thought.'

'You must. I want you to.'

'But I heard it was sold out.'

'Not for family. Please come.'

'Then I will. Could I bring Carol, too?'

'Of course. So you're back talking then?'

'Yes, work in progress.'

'Brilliant. I'll get you two tickets and see you backstage afterwards.'

*   *   *

Later on, after a lovely dinner at a pub in Cley, the Warrens returned to the Majestic Hotel.

Lauren and Les, meanwhile, had enjoyed each other's company at a rather down-market pizzeria. It was the pizzeria that Lauren had come to like, as they always managed to find her a table out of the way, where she wouldn't be recognised.

It was also what Lauren could afford on her new allowance, and she insisted on paying her half.

A glass or two of cheap Chianti later, with Les on mineral water, they were having a coffee to prolong the evening. They were pretty much the last people in the restaurant.

If this was a first date, they had both enjoyed it. He'd told her about the situation with the theatre. He thought that he had to tell her, but swore her to secrecy.

She'd declined a pudding.

'That was lovely, Les. I haven't had so much fun in ages.'

'It was. I don't do many dates. If that's what this is.'

'So what are you going to do? You obviously can't stay on and work for Pemrose.'

'I'm not sure. Go and find work, I guess. I haven't done that in a while.'

Lauren hesitated. There was something on her mind.

'Les, I have to be honest. I did a bit of research on the internet.'

Les looked away.

'So?'

'I know the story now. Your story, I mean.'

'So?'

'I know it was a bit sneaky but nobody would tell me. You included. I needed to find out.'

'So you know I did time. Prison.'

'Yes.'

'For hitting my wife, in front of my daughter.'

'Yes. Do you want to tell me what actually happened? I know by experience that newspapers don't tell the whole story.'

He paused, and blew out his cheeks.

'Come on, Les. It can't be as bad as they said. I know the papers.'

'Well, I came home drunk, as usual, about midnight, after a show. Mel and I had a row about it. I hit her. It was just once but quite hard. Lucy had come downstairs in the commotion. She was eight at the time. She saw it all.'

'Awful.'

'The Judge threw the book at me. I was a role model and celebrity. In fairness, there had been some cautions previously so it wasn't the first offence as such. He put me inside. They dried me out. But then I had to start again. I got divorced and came down here. Mel still won't speak to me. All conversation is via a solicitor.'

'Well, I suppose… from her point of view?'

Les nodded.

'She has a point, I know. I don't blame her at all. I wrote to her from prison, but I got no reply.'

'And Lucy? Your daughter?'

'She's at uni now. I managed to patch that up, at least. We keep in touch. So you see, we all have our secrets.'

Lauren looked at him intensely. His head was down. She put a finger under his chin, and made eye contact.

'Les, you paid your debt, you know. Don't beat yourself up too much.'

'I know.'

'Well, I'm glad we don't have any more secrets now.'

She leaned forward and kissed him.

He sat back. She shook her head.

'My God, you're slow. A girl could wait forever for a snog from you.'

He laughed.

'I think I forgot how, but practice makes perfect.'

He leaned forward and kissed her again. She spoke softly now.

'You're very special, you know. You've made me laugh more in these last few weeks than I have in years.'

'Well if I can't make people laugh, I'm not doing much of a job, am I?'

'I guess not. Should we get the bill?'

They got the bill and she picked out some cash to pay her half. The cards were all gone. They stood up, ready to leave.

'That's a lovely dress, Lauren.'

She looked up.

'If you want to buy it, it's on eBay tomorrow.'

He smiled as he held the door for her.

'I'll walk you back, Lauren. Thanks, I've had a fabulous time.'

She thought for a moment. He closed the door to the restaurant as she seemed to hesitate.

'Oh, I don't think so, Les. The bed squeaks too much and Mrs Bloomingdale wouldn't approve.'

Les was surprised. He put up his hands defensively.

'Look, I didn't mean to suggest…'

She looked at him, her arms at her waist, as if mocking him.

'Well, I did. Let's go to yours instead. I wasn't likely to sleep tonight anyway.'

# 23.

## Opening Night

This was the day that Les waited for every season. It was opening night tonight.

He got down to the theatre early. He had a ritual that he followed. Unlock the theatre, eat a bacon roll with a black coffee, and practice part of his set before the others arrived.

But this morning was a little different for two reasons. Firstly, he had every reason to stay in bed, grieving that he was leaving the delicious woman sleeping naked beside him. Secondly that Lech, desperate to get it right on the first night, wanted to run through their routine.

Les couldn't believe how much the hapless Polish magician had improved. He had natural comic timing and could produce some hilarious facial expressions. The set that Les had written for them seemed likely to be hugely successful, but relied critically on precise timing. Therefore, as Lech had requested one further run through, Les agreed to change his ritual.

He said a cheerful good morning to the girls on the restaurant counter, and went to the theatre doors. There were two stout chains with equally stout locks as usual. Les took out his keys, but then noticed that the lock wasn't the same. He tried his key, but it didn't work. The lock had been changed. He tried the other door. That lock was changed, too.

'You bastard,' he muttered, as he understood.

Lech was confused.

'Is there a problem, Mr Les?'

Les glared.

'Yes, Lech. The locks have been changed, and I suspect I know why.'

Lech smiled naively.

'That is no problem for Lech. I can open any lock! A special trick I learn! I try?'

Les laughed at the idea, but thought better of it.

'No, Lech. I think that would get us into serious trouble. Let's have breakfast. I'm sure that all will be revealed.'

He ordered bacon sandwiches, and the waitress confirmed that Lionel Pemrose had been in early and changed the locks.

Les smiled at her, and popped a five pound note in the tips box.

'Our little secret if you will, Debs.'

He sat down with Lech and they waited. The others arrived and were puzzled. Les just sat them down for breakfast, and waited for whatever theatrical episode Lionel had in mind to begin. Lionel could have communicated the message a different way, but this was payback time.

By the time Lionel strolled in, whistling a cheerful tune as he did, the cast had largely assembled along with the odd morning customer.

A minute or two later, Lauren came in, more than a little confused.

Les pondered for a minute. The obvious absentee was Karen. Janet often didn't come in until later, but Karen was Dance Captain. This was puzzling. Karen never missed a rehearsal.

Lionel spoke cheerfully to Debs behind the counter, and then called across to where Les was sitting, for maximum impact.

'Is there a problem, Mr Westley?'

Les got up, with Lech following behind him. Lauren began to work her way through the crowd.

'It seems that someone changed the locks, Mr Pemrose,' Les said with false geniality.

'That's because the licence fee hasn't been paid, Les, so as the landlord, I've taken lawful possession of the theatre. All legal and above board, I assure you.'

The cast looked at each other. The customers were puzzled. There was a low murmur of quiet chatter.

A Welsh voice chimed in.

'You can't do that. It's opening night. It's sold out and everything.'

As Lauren stepped forward, Lionel moved to greet her.

'I've always got time for talent. You're even prettier in the flesh than on TV. Forgive me darling, Pemrose. Lionel Pemrose.'

He offered his hand, and she went to shake it. Lionel took it kissed her hand lightly.

'It's a pleasure to meet you, Miss Evans.'

Lauren recoiled somewhat, but remained civil. Les was stony faced.

'Pleased to meet you, I'm sure,' she replied, with more than a little irony in her voice.

Lionel was enjoying the moment. His voice reached the whole room, but he addressed his remarks to Les alone.

'It seems that Janet has gone already, Les. That's such a shame. I offered her a deal, which would have saved some jobs, but I guess she was too proud. Like her father. Anyway, I may be able to help some of you. Lauren here is clearly very talented. I do love the Welsh. I love the hills and the valleys – particularly the hills.'

Les had heard enough.

'Sod off, Lionel. She'll eat a creep like you for breakfast.'

Lionel ignored the insult.

'As for some of your lot, they're a bunch of drunks, has-beens, wannabes and never-will-bes, in my opinion. That Polish fellow next to you, for example. Scraping the barrel, weren't you, Les? Doing shifts in my bingo hall in his spare time. Well, he was anyway, until I found out. Angela De Gray? One too many dwinkies last night, darling? She's seen better days, the old girl, hasn't she? Like you and the rest of your show, Les. Worn out and washed up.'

Les looked across contemptuously and took a small step towards him.

'Take that back, if you please, Lionel.'

'Are you still here, Les? Sorry, I don't have any jobs for ex-cons like you.'

'I said take that back, Lionel.'

'Or what, Les? Go on, make my day. That should get you put away for a while, what with your record. Go on. Have a drink. It's on me.'

He tossed some money at Les and laughed.

'Don't, Les,' said Lauren. Lech moved to pull Les back.

'It's OK, Lech. He's not worth the bother.'

Lionel's phone rang. 'Bunch of Coconuts' rang out eerily against the silence.

'My dear lady wife again. This is an honour. I'll call her later.'

He dismissed the call then looked at Les.

'Look, Les, the fat lady has well and truly sung, and I haven't had my money. As such, I need to officially inform you that Pemrose Entertainments Limited has taken possession of this theatre, since the license expired at midnight.'

Les decided to try reasoning with Lionel. Something had gone wrong. This needed sorting out.

'Look, Lionel, it's Janet Wells you should be talking to. She's not here yet. Can't you just let these guys inside so they can get ready? We have a show tonight. It's in nobody's interest for it not to go ahead. I'm sure Janet will sort things when she arrives.'

'She probably can't face you, Les. Let's be professional about this. Look, folks, I will, of course, help you to find new work where possible. Young Amy here already works for me. Could I suggest that you collect your personal belongings and go home? There's no show tonight.'

Nobody had seen Janet Wells walk in, with Karen behind her. But she now spoke slowly and deliberately.

'Ah, Mr Pemrose. Now why would they want to collect their things? They are preparing for a show tonight. If you'd like a ticket, I suggest you go to the box office. Sadly we're sold out for the first few weeks, but you can put down your name for returns.'

She walked into the centre of the room. Lionel smiled.

'Oh, nice one, Janet. I do like someone with chutzpah. But have we forgotten that the licence extension expired at midnight? And you didn't even have the courtesy to ring me about the final contract I gave you days ago! So I have here… a legal notice to quit.'

Karen spoke.

'Well, I'm a bit surprised Lionel, considering that my mother transferred the money yesterday.'

'And I also included the extension payment for a further five years, so I won't need this.'

Janet tore up the notice and threw it at Lionel's feet. The fake bonhomie had gone from his face now.

'Oh, yes? You're having a laugh. Where did you get the money?'

'She got it from me, dearest Lionel.'

Lionel turned and saw Miriam Pemrose leaning against the bar. She moved closer to him, a serene smile on her face.

'You see, Mrs Wells and I are in partnership together. If only you'd take my calls, I could have explained. We are married after all.'

Lionel's face turned crimson.

'You? What the hell is this?'

'I think they call it a stitch-up Lionel, a term with which you will be very familiar.'

'But why? What are you thinking of?'

'One step too far, Lionel. There are too many old scores being settled here. There are just too many casualties this time for my liking.'

'You just don't understand. Just leave the business to me, why don't you?'

'Well, I can tell you that the licence fee was paid in full last night. I could, of course, have told you in person, had you come home last night instead of shagging that Bimbo Lizzie in room 34 of the Seaview Hotel. You stingy bastard! You could have sprung for the bridal suite, or a sea view at least.'

The mixture of the general public and cast were beginning to murmur.

'That's my girl, Miriam!' said Debs behind the counter, who was heartily fed up of being groped.

Lionel was embarrassed, but recovered. He had another card to play.

'Well, I'm sorry, Mrs Wells, but you can't sign a deal with a third party in any event. The terms on the extension gave me exclusivity rights. I'll get an injunction.'

Janet laughed.

'No, Lionel, it doesn't. It gives the Pemrose Group and related family interests exclusivity. You insisted.'

'So?'

Miriam smiled.

'I'm family right? I've just become a shareholder in the

Cromer Pier Theatre Company Limited. I won't bore you with the details, darling.'

Lionel was struggling now.

'Look, Mimsy, love… we need to talk about this. I have great plans for this place. It's not for me. It's for the good of the town.'

Miriam shook her head.

'I'm sure your motives are as pure as the driven snow. I might have fallen for it but for what you did to Cyril Brown, you're an evil, vindictive piece of shit.'

Lionel had heard enough. He turned to leave, but Miriam had other ideas.

'Going somewhere, Lionel?'

He paused.

'I have some other papers for you. Divorce papers, Lionel. Don't worry, I'll settle for half of everything.'

'What? Look, now, hold your horses, Miriam. Let's have lunch, talk things over. You know Lizzie doesn't mean anything. We need a holiday. We'll work things out.'

Miriam shook her head. She held up a sheaf of papers.

'It's far too late, Lionel. How many affairs is it now? Do you think I'm blind or a total mug?'

Les couldn't resist it.

'Having a bad day, Lionel?'

Lionel went for Les, but Lech stepped in. Lech stood six foot, three inches to Lionel's five foot, eight inches.

'I don't think so, Mr Pemrose. I think it is time for you, as they say in England, to be slinging your hook.'

Lionel looked up at the towering Pole, stepped back and snarled at Janet.

'You think you're so clever, don't you? But I've got a long memory and plenty of friends. Have a nice day, folks.'

Lionel snatched the papers and turned to leave. Lech stood in his way, towering above him.

'I am thinking that you are forgetting the keys…'

Lionel pushed passed him and left. There was an embarrassing silence.

Lauren spoke up.

'So what's the score, Mrs Wells? Are we still on for tonight then?'

Janet smiled.

'That will be a yes, Lauren. The Pier Theatre lives on, thanks to Miriam. Thank you all for your understanding. It's over to you, Les.'

'The doors are still locked, mind,' said Lauren.

'This is not a problem. I will fix this with a little Polish magic trick,' said Lech.

With that, he produced a strange looking object from his pocket and picked the lock, the chain sliding to the floor.

\*   \*   \*

Miriam and Janet left the cast to it, and headed to Janet's office. Miriam's telephone call had resulted in a flurry of activity, and a hastily drafted legal agreement signed the previous evening. They sat down with a coffee in Pier Theatre mugs, and relaxed.

'I just couldn't take Paul's money. I so wanted to save the theatre but it wouldn't have been right. Not after all this time.'

'I know. It was a wonderful gesture from a really nice guy though. He must have been a bit fit at 17.'

'Yes, he was. Mind you, I could wear mini-skirts and hot pants then, too.'

Janet looked at the picture of her father.

'I'm sure he'd approve. It's all a bit sudden though, isn't it?'

'I guess, but who knows, Janet? Let's just take this one step at a time. To be honest, I took a leap of faith for once in my life.'

'Lionel probably has a point. After all, we're the only end-of-the-pier show left, and we don't even own the theatre. It's going to need sorting with Pemrose Entertainments, and frankly, I don't see how that will happen now.'

'Neither do I, at this moment. It will need a bit of time'

'Then why did you do it?'

'Because, like you, I'm stuck in a rut and I needed a challenge. The Pier Theatre is certainly that.'

'And Lionel?'

'Oh, our marriage has been dead for years. It was Paul Warren who showed me that when he visited me. He talked emotional clap trap about love and loyalty and fairness and respect. I suddenly realised that I hadn't really used my heart for a while. Paul wasn't being rational at all. It was completely ridiculous. I knew it and so did he, but he was lobbing the dice on the table and hoping for a double six.'

'We don't really have too much to offer a bank, do we? No real assets and Lionel's mates in charge locally?'

'Well, we won't make enough money from my WI jam stall. That's for sure. But with grants and donations from people, I know we can turn this place into the asset the town needs. Lionel may think he runs this town, but plenty of people out there despise him. I suspect that some will come on board. And when he calms down, I'll sort him out. He knows when he's beaten does Lionel, and he runs a good business most of the time.'

'And Paul's money? I don't need to cash his cheque?'

'I'll put enough money of my own in to shut Lionel up for now. I think that we can let Paul ride off into the sunset with his money. Unless, of course, you still fancy him?'

'Well, probably not after all this time. I think that boat sailed 30-odd years ago.'

'I think Lionel and I were holed below the waterline years ago as well.'

'I am sorry about that.'

'Let's face it, Janet, we've all had a reality check this week. Sometimes you've just got to face up to things and make some decisions.'

'Ha. The Road to Cromer Pier. The final stop in the journey.'

Miriam stood and looked at her watch.

'See you tonight, Janet. Break a leg, or whatever you people say.'

\* \* \*

Carol woke up and looked out. The sun was shining and she could feel the warmth of the sun as she opened the window. She could hear the seagulls and the chatter of the tourists heading for the beach.

She put the kettle on and slid back into bed. Paul was snoring more lightly than usual, but she still gave him a dig in the ribs, which had the desired effect.

He stirred, and instinctively slipped his hand to her backside. She moved his hand aside then whispered into his ear.

'Isn't it time you went out to find a job?'

He rolled onto his back sleepily.

'What time is it?'

'About 9:30. You'll miss breakfast at this rate.'

He went back to sleep again.

She made some tea and sat watching him. She was so glad that they were together. He never slept in. He was always up early for a morning run. She was never up first at home.

Perhaps it was the sex, she thought. But actually, she knew that he hadn't slept properly for months. He got up in the middle of the night too often. His brain had been ticking 24/7. Now his body was catching up, and she was glad about that, and let him sleep on.

They eventually headed downstairs at noon. He kissed her in the lift. It was like when they first met. There was an envelope for them as reception.

He opened it and smiled. There were two tickets inside, and a sticky note.

*See you tonight, Paul!*
*Karen xxxxx*

# 24.

## Showtime

It was an emotional opening night. It's always special in any theatre, from local Amdram to the West End.

'Ladies and gentlemen, his name is Lech Wojiek. Remember that name. Thanks, Lech… you'll be top of my poll any day. Well, ladies and gentlemen, that nearly brings us to the end of a very exciting opening night of the Summertime Special Show 2009, but we have an exclusive treat! A brand new song from our star, Lauren Evans. From her new forthcoming album, 'Maybe,' this is the title track. Watch out for the single coming out shortly. Ladies and gentlemen, give it up one more time for the sensational Lauren Evans!'

Lauren came on in her blue outfit, kissed Les on the cheek while furtively fondling his bottom, and sang the song that took her back to her broken relationship in her homeland in Wales. After the turbulent events of the last few weeks, she had so many emotions as she sang it to a live audience for the first time.

But she was in a much better place now. The days of posh dress shops had gone for the time being, giving way to simpler pleasures. For the first time in her life, she felt that she had someone in her life who was wise. Someone she could trust. She didn't care about the age gap. It was only years after all, and he just made her laugh so much.

There was a standing ovation, of course, after which they cut into the finale song. She was in floods of tears as the curtain closed for the final time that evening. The cast hugged each other and Les embraced Lauren. Many in the cast hadn't seen that coming.

Amy Raven hugged the giant Lech, and Les realised that they had created two new stars of the future, and resurrected another.

Angela and Karen had seen it all before. This was one performance with more than a hundred to go, and the matinees started the day after tomorrow. Two shows a day, five days a week.

As was tradition, the cast headed out to meet the audience, but Lauren was such a draw that the selfies were being taken long after the show had finished. The rest of the cast headed for the changing rooms and left her with Les out front.

Nevertheless, as they changed, Angela conceded that it was a special night.

'That Lauren is bloody marvellous, isn't she?'

Karen was cleaning off the stage makeup and was eager to meet Paul out front.

'Yep. It's a long season but if she keeps it all together…'

'She will. Les will see to that. He sorted me out. No more drink for me.'

'You've still got the talent, Angela. I only hope I can keep it together when I'm your age.'

'I'll be sore in the morning. Need a bit of physio. That one that works for Isobel has very good hands, I find.'

Janet and Miriam stood in the corner as the throng finally dissipated. Les finally spotted them and felt able to leave Lauren to her public.

'So, how was that for you, Mrs Wells and Mrs Pemrose?'

Janet hugged him. No words were needed.

Miriam shook Les's hand and clasped it with the other.

'I haven't seen this show in years. Terrific, Les. It was simply terrific.'

'I hope you think your investment worthwhile. Thanks for what you did. We are all in your debt.'

'Not at all, Les. This is just so worthwhile. I forgot what a good evening out feels like. There are just so many smiling faces.'

Carol and Paul Warren sat by the window and let the throng subside. Karen eventually appeared. She rushed across.

'Hi, Paul!'

He hugged her.

'Great show, Karen. Can I introduce my wife, Carol?'

Half an hour or so later, Karen sent Paul back stage. He walked through the empty theatre, and stood for a moment, taking in its deep red seats, walls and the now-closed safety curtain. Even the lighting rig was mounted on red oxide coated girders, clearly original, under a lattice of cast iron, holding the roof in place.

He went backstage and saw the cramped dressing rooms, makeup and various items of apparel covering every surface.

He eventually found a short tight staircase to the stage, hearing a familiar voice.

Janet was sweeping up on the stage alone. The cast had largely gone home now.

She was singing to herself, quietly getting on with her jobs, as always.

'Remember you, remember me…'

He remembered.

'That summer night… when it was meant to be.'

She looked up and smiled.

'We were so young, so wild, so free…'

They sang the last line together.

'We knew our love would never end.'

Paul held her close for a moment, and whispered to her.

'Now, tell me, where did that come from?'

Janet shrugged.

'We reworded it for the show. You remember the original?'

'Of course! You sang it on the pier that last night. You wrote it for us.'

'Yes. Not bad, was it?'

'It was a lovely thing to do, Janet. Getting Lauren to sing it with me in the audience.'

'Well, to be honest, Lauren wanted another track for her album so I got Karen to sing it to her. Les reworded it a bit, and Gerald did the arrangement so it's in show one for the season now. It's just one of those things.'

'She sang it beautifully. But it must have hurt you a lot, that song, over the years?'

Janet thought for a moment.

'Yes, it did. But, well… what a roller coaster. I sang it to Karen when she was small, with different words, and she always liked it. It just seemed appropriate this year.'

'What a night. The whole show was terrific. Your new partner must be pleased?'

'I think Miriam Pemrose is going to be a big asset. She's a ball of fire.'

'Yes, she's a formidable lady, to be sure. I'm puzzled though. I left Miriam convinced that she wouldn't get involved. The more I thought about what she said, the more ridiculous I felt.'

'Yes I can understand you thinking that. Miriam is a very sound business woman. But I think that she was re-assessing things in her own life when you showed up. A good dose of emotion was what she needed.'

'And Cyril Brown?'

'Ah, yes, that was your trump card but you couldn't possibly have known.'

'How so?'

'Well, the Browns are the oldest fishing family in the town. Some of Miriam's family were on the boats, too. This is still a fishing community at heart and those loyalties run very deep. When you told her what Lionel had done to Cyril, she realised that he had crossed a line.'

'So the show will go on? You're safe for this season?'

'Yes, the show will go on. We've a lot of work to do, mind. What about you and Carol?'

'We're starting to work things out. Some things are worth working for, aren't they? You told me that.'

'But you're still out of work?'

'Maybe not. The City chairman's talking about offering me the manager's job. That's why I'm heading off in the morning to meet him and hopefully sort my contract out.

'That's your boyhood team? That's great news.'

'You haven't seen the overdraft they've got, but yes, it's great. A fresh start for Carol and me.'

'I'm so pleased. Keep in touch, both of you.'

'I will. I'll treat Carol to a weekend at Mrs Bloomingdale's and a bag of chips.'

'No sex on the beach though.'

'The sand gets everywhere.'

'That night by the pier. It was all so special. We were both very young, I guess.'

'I'm just sorry, Janet. If only I'd have known.'

'Well, it's done now. I couldn't help but look back, but not now. Let's look to the future, both of us.'

# 25.

## Finale

Janet looked out from the theatre onto the beach. They were ready for the 2017 Summertime Special Show. The fortieth anniversary season of the only show of its kind in the world.

It was mid-afternoon, and she could see two young boys playing football on the beach near the pier. She could see Karen, too. Carol and Karen were sitting in deckchairs. An easterly breeze ensured that they were still wearing fleeces in mid-June.

Karen looked across to the boys playing happily with her father, and spoke to Carol, reading a book beside her.

'He seems happy enough,' said Karen. 'How old are the boys now?'

'Nine in September. It keeps him young,' said Carol.

'It's good to see. He seems so happy. You, too?'

'Yes, we are, Karen. He wanted to do this with them. Generations moving on in time. It's an old man thing, I think.'

'I might have preferred Tuscany?'

'So would I. But he loves this place. It's in his blood.'

'I'll need to be off soon. Lauren Evans is arriving shortly. I agreed to pick her up.'

'I'll bet she's not staying at Mrs Bloomingdale's this time?'

'No. Les secured the bridal suite at the Majestic. Mrs Pemrose insisted.'

'I bet she did. Lauren only performs in stadiums now, doesn't she?'

'Yes. She just wanted to do a one-night show here. All proceeds to the Cromer Pier Theatre Trust. It's a lovely gesture.'

'Well, we've bought our debenture. How are you enjoying life as the Director?' Carol asked.

'I think I've finally mastered it this year. I just couldn't keep dancing forever. It's a different sort of pressure mind.'

'And Amy Raven is one of the headliners this year, I understand.'

'Well, yes. Frankly, we've only managed to get her because we gave her the break and she's local.'

'And Janet?'

'Talks about retiring, then she does nothing,' Karen explained. 'She'll never retire. They'll wheel her down that pier in a box. Now, how is Paul behaving himself these days?'

'Not too bad. On Saturday, it's football as usual, but now he's coaching the boys' Sunday league team, too.'

'Nightmare.'

'Well, at least I get to watch them while I make the half-time Bovril.'

'Joy. It sounds delightful.'

'I wouldn't change a thing.'

--- The End ---